Dorey said, 'Well, there it is. Could be something, could be a hoax. I want you to handle it, Harry. Until I'm convinced she's got something or is just a nut, this remains unofficial.'

Harry rattled a cube of ice in his empty glass. Reluctantly Dorey called another round. 'I'll put one of my ops on it,' Harry said. 'It'll cost you thirty bucks.'

Dorey said sharply, 'It's not worth thirty bucks.' He hated parting with money, even when it was the CIA's. 'All he has to do is meet this woman and find out if she has something to sell.' She had. Violent death among other things.

WE'VE SAID IT BEFORE AND WE'LL SAY IT AGAIN – HADLEY CHASE IS THE MAESTRO OF THE THRILLER-WRITERS'
Manchester Evening News

James Hadley Chase

This Is For Real

Panther

Granada Publishing Limited
Published in 1968 by Panther Books Ltd
Frogmore, St Albans, Herts AL2 2NF
Reprinted 1969, 1973, 1975

First published in Great Britain by
Robert Hale Ltd 1965
Copyright © International Authors N.V. 1965
Made and printed in Great Britain by
Hunt Barnard Printing Ltd
Aylesbury, Bucks
Set in Intertype Plantin

This Is For Real

Chapter One

TWO AMERICANS sat at a corner table, well away from the group of newspaper men lounging up at the bar in the Paris Crillon Bar. One of them was an elderly, bird-like man, wearing rimless spectacles and a neatly pressed City suit. His name was John Dorey. He was believed to be something unimportant at the American Embassy.

His companion was Harry Rossland, a large, overweight man in his late forties. He wore a baggy Scotch tweed suit and dusty brogue shoes. Rossland had lived so long in Paris he had become part of the Parisian background. He appeared to make a modest living writing articles on Modern Art and was regarded as a harmless phoney.

The two men were talking in undertones. Rossland was drinking whisky on the rocks: Dorey a tomato juice.

No one, if they happened to be interested, could judge by their expressions, the importance or the triviality of the subject under discussion.

Dorey said, "Well, there it is. Could be something; could be a hoax. I want you to handle it, Harry. Until I am convinced she's either got something or is a nut, this remains unofficial."

Rossland rattled two cubes of ice in his empty glass. He said, "I don't handle any jobs personally. You know that by now, but I'll get one of the boys to do it if you like. He'll want thirty bucks for his trouble."

"It's not worth thirty dollars," Dorey said sharply. He hated parting with money. "All he has to do is to meet this woman and find out what she has to sell. If it becomes important, then of course, he'll get paid."

Rossland waved his empty glass at a waiter. He knew Dorey would pick up the check and he was thirsty. There was a pause while the waiter brought another whisky on the rocks. When he had returned to the bar, Rossland said, "It's thirty bucks or nothing. This could be some sort of trap. Have you thought of that? Warley might be getting fed up with the way you're interfering, Dorey. I'm not saying he is, but you're continually hand-ling things on your own when by rights they should be reported to him. This woman might be one of Warley's people. It's just possible he's setting a trap to get you sent home."

Dorey had already thought of this possibility, but he was sure Warley wouldn't do a thing like that. In a way, Dorey rather wished Warley would take enough interest in him to try to trap him.

"Well, all right. I'll run to thirty dollars," he said. "You don't have to worry about Warley. He's too busy being a new broom to bother about what I'm doing." He paused, then went on, "I want action, Harry. If this woman has something really worth selling – which I doubt – she might approach others."

Rossland grinned. He knew Dorey lived under the shadow of the Russian bogey.

"Give me the money and you'll get plenty of action."

Dorey studied the big fleshy face opposite him.

"I sometimes wonder, Harry, if you realise your responsibili-ties when you're working for me."

Rossland laughed.

"I've never let you down yet, have I?"

"There's always a first time."

"Cheer up. I'll get one of the boys to see this woman and I'll call you at your place as soon as he has seen her."

"Who will you send?" Dorey's pale eyes peered at Rossland from behind the shining lenses of his glasses.

"So long as he does the job, why should you care?" Rossland said and finished his drink.

Dorey shrugged, then he signalled to the barman and paid for the drinks. The two men got to their feet. As they stepped out into Rue Bossy d'Anglas, Dorey slid a crumpled roll of notes into Rossland's hand.

Rossland paused long enough to watch Dorey cross the street and head with brisk steps towards the American Embassy, then he turned right and walked along Rue Faubourg St. Honoré.

He hummed softly and from time to time, he fingered the roll of money in his pocket.

He paused at the intersection leading to Place Vendôme and waited impatiently for the traffic lights to turn red. There was a slight nip in the April wind, but fortified by two double whiskies, Rossland accepted the slight shiver of cold that ran down his fat spine.

As the traffic stopped, he strode across the road and continued on until he reached the side entrance to the bar of the Normandy Hotel. He entered and shook hands with the barman whom he had known for years. He ordered a double whisky on the rocks and then moved around the bar to the telephone booth. He shut himself in and dialled a Fontenoy number. Cradling the receiver between his ear and his shoulder, he took out a pack of cigarettes, shook out a cigarette and lit it.

A man's voice said over the line, "'Allo?"

"Girland? This is Harry."

"Oh. For God's sake! Look, Harry I'm busy right now. Suppose you call me back in a couple of hours?"

Rossland grinned. He knew just what was occupying Girland.

"You're way out of luck," he said. "Tell her to go home if she has a home. That horse we put our shirts on ran last."

Rossland heard Girland mutter, "Merde!" and he again grinned unsympathetically.

"Give me an hour for God's sake," Girland pleaded.

"See you in fifteen minutes. Entrance Odéon Métro," Rossland said firmly and hung up.

He moved out of the telephone booth to where his drink waited on the bar. As he reached for it, he looked around the well appointed bar. There were three or four couples drinking and talking. Rossland glanced briefly at them and then his eyes rested for a moment on a young man who was reading *France-Soir*, a full glass of Pernod and water on the table in front of him. Rossland looked immediately away, but he had registered every detail of the young man's appearance. He was around twenty years of age. He wore a shabby dark overcoat, belted like a dressing-gown. His closely cut hair was black and he wore a chin beard that made him look younger than he was. His eyes were dark ringed; his complexion sallow. He looked out of place in this bar and Rossland's mind became alert with suspicion.

He drank half his whisky, then leaning forward, he asked the barman, "That boy over there ... has he been here long?"

"Came in just after you, Mr. Rossland."

Rossland stubbed out his cigarette. Years of experience had taught him always to be suspicious of people who didn't fit into a background, and this young man didn't fit at all. He finished his drink and paid.

He shook hands with the barman, mentioned the cold wind and then walked into the hotel's lobby. He left by the main entrance, paused on the edge of the kerb to let three cars pass, then crossed the street, heading for the Palais Royal Métro. He again had to wait at the next crossing while the traffic fought its way into Rue de Rivoli. As he stood waiting, he took a small mirror from his pocket. He held this, half concealed in his large, hairy hand. The mirror picked up the young man who had been in the bar. He too waited for a lull in the traffic at the further crossing.

Rossland returned the mirror to his pocket. His expression was now thoughtful. Dorey had said this set-up might be a hoax. He had also said others might be approached. Maybe this bearded young man meant nothing, but Rossland was far too experienced to take chances. He crossed the street and walked down the steps of the Métro. He bought a ticket, then went slowly towards the Nation line. He would have to change at Châtelet for Odéon. There was a two minute wait before the train came in. Rossland got in, resisting the temptation to look along the platform. He remained by the doors. At Châtelet, he waited until the doors began to close, then he shoved them back with his immense strength and stepped onto the platform. The doors snapped to and the train moved out of the station.

He had a brief glimpse of the bearded young man staring at him from a third-class compartment, and Rossland saluted him with a cheerful wave of his hand.

Mark Girland dropped the telephone receiver back onto its cradle with an exclamation of disgust.

Tessa – she hadn't yet told him her other name – looked inquiringly at him. She was seated in a canvas deck chair, the nearest thing to comfort Girland aspired to.

Tessa was a well-built blonde, around twenty-four, with an oval-shaped face, large blue eyes, a good nose and mouth. She wore a green sweater across which was inscribed *New York Herald Tribune.* Her wool black trousers fitted her hips and long legs in a glove-like caress.

She had offered Girland the last of her newspapers on Boulevard Brune. He had been attracted by her long legs and her blue eyes and he had cast his charm before her. He had an easy, confident way with women. The fact they were both Americans broke down the usual barriers very quickly. They had a drink together. Girland found the girl amusing and sexually exciting. When he paid for the drinks, he said in his usual confident manner, "It seems a pity we should say goodbye. Would you like to come back to my place? We could spend the evening together." He paused and smiled at her. "Then if we find we like each other, as I think we will, we could spend the night together."

The girl had laughed. He was pleased she hadn't been shocked nor embarrassed.

"You're not shy, are you?" she said. "I'll come back to your place, but that's as far as it will go." She studied him, then added, "At least, that's what I think now."

He took her back to his sixth floor one room apartment in Rue de Suisses. He followed behind her as they climbed the stairs. He thought she had the prettiest shaped bottom he had seen on a woman for a long time. They paused, a little breathlessly while he unlocked the door to his apartment.

The room was large with two big windows overlooking the roofs, the chimneys and the television aerials of Paris. It contained only the bare essentials with no comfort. There was a double bed. Two benches stood either side of a worm-eaten refectory table. At the far end of the room, under the window, was a kitchen sink. There was a big radio and gramophone against another wall. Two canvas deck chairs substituted for armchairs. A wardrobe and a bookcase crammed with American and French paperbacks completed the furnishing.

The girl looked around while Girland closed the door and leaned against it.

"This is nice," she said. "I live in a closet. The space of it all! How lucky you are!"

Girland walked over to her and put his hands on her hip bones. They regarded each other, both smiling. He tightened his grip and pulled her against him. His mouth found hers. They remained like that, relaxed, for a brief moment, then she pushed him away and went over to sit in one of the deck chairs.

"Tell me about yourself," she said. "What do you do? But first give me a cigarette."

As Girland was searching his pockets, Rossland's telephone call came through.

When he hung up, he said, "I'm sorry, but I have to go out. This is one of those things. I don't know when I'll be back, but will you stay? Will you make yourself at home? There's the gramophone. There are books. You'll find food in the refrigerator. It'll be nice to think you are here, waiting for me."

"I don't think I'd better stay," she said, but she made no move

11

to get to her feet. She was looking at him, thinking he was handsome.

"You stay," he urged. "I won't be long. I want you to stay."

"Well, all right, then I will stay."

He nodded, then crossed the room and opened a door that led into a shower cabinet and toilet. He shut himself in. To the right of the shower was a ceiling high closet. He opened it, reached inside and found a cleverly hidden spring which he pressed. The back of the closet slide aside. He reached inside and took out a leather gun holster containing a small, flat ammonia gun. Taking off his jacket, he slipped the holster straps around his broad shoulders and put on his jacket again. He satisfied himself the gun showed no bulge, then he glanced at himself in the mirror above the toilet basin.

Girland was tall and dark. His face was thin, his eyes dark and deep-set, his mouth hard and his jaw aggressive. A few scattered white hairs either side of his temples made him look slightly older than his thirty-five years.

He ran a comb through his hair, then for the sake of appearance, he flushed the toilet and opened the door.

Tessa was kneeling before his bookcase, examining his books. She looked over her shoulder as he came to her and she smiled at him.

"Graham Greene, Chandler, Hemingway ... we share the same taste in reading."

He bent and kissed her.

"There'll be other things we'll share," he said and his hand moved down her long back and across her buttocks.

She remained motionless, but her eyes became hostile.

"You mustn't be too free with me. I don't like men who take me for granted," she said.

He stood away from her.

"I never take anything for granted," he said, "but I live under pressure. I feel life is always trying to escape me. I used to spend too much time manoeuvring with women. Now, I try the direct approach. Sometimes, more often than not, it succeeds."

She had nothing to say to this, but she asked, "Where are you going?"

He smiled. He looked young and guileless when he smiled.

"To see a man about a dog. Wait for me. If the telephone rings, don't answer it. Keep the door locked. You won't be disturbed. There's a beautiful steak in the refrigerator. It's all yours.

12

See you sometime tonight."

He left the apartment and began the long descent to the street.

Tessa remained on her knees, staring blankly at the books on the shelves. She listened to Girland's fading footfalls, then she got to her feet and walked silently to the door and opened it. She stepped out onto the dusty, dimly lit landing and leaned over the banister rail. Far below, she caught a glimpse of Girland as he pushed open the street door. Turning quickly, she re-entered the apartment and closed and locked the door.

Then with methodical patience, she began to search the room.

Girland walked quickly down Rue de Suisses to where he had parked his Fiat 600. The little car was on its last legs. He paused to inspect the blister on the front offside tyre. He decided the tyre might or might not survive another fifty kilometres. Climbing into the car, he coaxed the engine to start, then engaging gear, he edged the car into the continuous stream of traffic.

When eventually he arrived at the Odéon Métro, he found Rossland impatiently waiting for him. He pulled up by him.

Rossland came over, and with difficulty, squeezed himself into the passenger's seat.

"You're late, damn it!" he complained. "Let's go. Just keep driving." He shifted his bulk in the small seat as Girland started the Fiat moving again. "God! What a car! When are you getting rid of this horrible *poubelle*?"

"It gets me around," Girland said indifferently. "I'm no millionaire." He glanced at Rossland. "Not that you care, but you've ruined what could have been a very interesting evening."

"A woman again," Rossland said and snorted. "Why can't you leave women alone? You worry me, Mark. Seriously ... there are too many women."

"How's your sex life?" Girland asked and laughed. "Don't tell me you live like a monk."

"Never mind how I live. I manage, but I don't let women dictate my life ... that's the important thing. You think too much about women."

"Skip it," Girland said, suddenly impatient. "What's cooking?"

"A job ... it's a queer one. Could be something; could be a hoax."

"Is there any money in it? Right now I could do with some money."

13

"When can't you?" Rossland said sourly. "Women and money ... that's all you think about."

"What else is there to think about?" Girland was studying in his driving mirror a black Citroen car that had been sitting on his tail now for the past three minutes. The driver had his hat pulled down to hide his face and he sat hunched behind the driving wheel. Girland abruptly swung the Fiat into a narrow street, leaving the boulevard and accelerated. He watched the Citroen swing into the street after him. He interrupted what Rossland was about to say. "I think we're being tailed, Harry."

Rossland immediately became alert. He looked back over his shoulder at the cruising Citroen.

"Could be wrong. Let's see if we can lose him," Girland went on.

He turned right at the next intersection, drove down a one-way street, made narrow by parked cars, then turned right again where he was forced to stop at the traffic lights.

The black Citroen crawled to a stop some ten feet behind him.

"Don't look around," Girland said, peering into the driving mirror. "He's still with us." He drove on as the lights changed to green. "I'll stop and fix him."

"No! Let him alone. I want to talk to you," Rossland said sharply. "You keep driving. He can't hear what we're saying."

Girland shrugged. He drove in silence for a few minutes, then crossed Pont Sully and turned down Quai d'Anjou. When he had driven half way down the Quai, he saw the Citroen crawling after him. Ahead of him, a car pulled out from the line of tightly parked cars and went roaring down the Quai.

Girland swung the little car into the vacant space, stopped and turned off the engine.

"Now, let's see what he'll do."

The driver of the Citroen abruptly accelerated and swept past them without looking in their direction. At the end of the Quai, the car turned right and disappeared into the fast moving traffic crossing Port Marie.

"That's got rid of him for the moment," Girland said and lit a cigarette. "What's all this about? How did you get yourself tailed, Harry? He was after you; not me."

Rossland looked worried.

"I was tailed by a young punk with a beard. I lost him in the Métro. Looks like there were two tails."

Girland grimaced.

14

"You ought to know there are always two tails: one working in front, the other behind."

"You telling me this guy tailed me in the Métro in a goddamn Citroen?" Rossland demanded angrily.

"Another stooge was the front man. He saw you waiting for me. He telephoned this guy in the Citroen and he was ready for us when I arrived." Girland said with offensive patience. "But never mind. What's it all about?"

"This morning Dorey had a telephone call from a woman who calls herself Madame Foucher," Rossland said. "She claims to have something to sell. Dorey doesn't know if it is a hoax or not. She hinted she might approach others. He wants to be sure she isn't a nut. She wants to meet someone who'll discuss price and so on. Dorey has dropped this into my lap. I'm dropping it into yours. It's simple enough. She'll be at 'Allo, Paris' at eleven o'clock tonight. I want you to contact her and find out what she has to offer and what she wants for it."

"What's the rest of it?"

"That's all. You'll have to decide whether or not she does have anything worth buying. Don't commit us to anything. This first meeting is merely exploratory."

"But why bring me into it? Why don't you handle it yourself, Harry? It sounds right up your alley."

Rossland went through the routine of shaking out a cigarette from a crumpled pack and lighting it, before he said, "I always keep to the sidelines. That's why I'm useful to Dorey."

"You know something?" Girland said seriously. "You're now as useful to Dorey as a hole in the head. Why don't you grow up? This isn't a hoax, sonny boy: this is for real. She's already talked to others and they're watching their interests. They're on to you and they're now on to me, thanks to your dumbness. You've led them direct to me. All they have to do is to check the number of my car to know who I am and where I live. How smart can you get, Harry? What's happening to that white thing in your head you call a brain?"

Rossland shifted his bulk uncomfortably.

"Don't talk that way to me!" he blustered. "I don't like it!"

"You're not meant to like it," Girland said in a bored, flat voice. "You're beginning to show signs of being washed up in this racket. You're now too fat, too damned sleek, too sure of yourself. You've had a long, long run for your money and now you're over confident. You think this is a parlour game: giving

15

orders, raking in the money, waving your tiny wand and letting others do the dirty work. Two years ago, you wouldn't have let a front tail get onto you. This isn't a game, Harry. This is one of the most lethal rackets you can get into. Mugs like us who are crazy enough to work for drips like Dorey have to look out for trouble all the time. You've become so smug and stale you can't even recognise trouble when it actually sits in your fat lap."

"My God!" Rossland exclaimed, sweat breaking out on his forehead. "No cheap shyster like you can talk this way to me! You're not the only agent I have who can handle this and be glad to! I'm doing you a favour because I know you want the money. You stop picking on me or I'll..."

"No, you won't, Harry," Girland said and there was a bored note in his voice. "I happen to be the last of the suckers who are willing to do your dirty work and you know it. Jason's gone. Gray, Fauchet and Pierre ... they saw the red light as I'm seeing it now. I'm the last of your shabby little stable who you can rely on, so don't wave threats in my face."

Rossland breathed heavily. He wiped his forehead with his handkerchief and stared furiously through the dusty windshield of the car.

"What's it worth?" Girland asked finally. "I won't even consider it until I get some money."

Rossland hesitated, then groped in his hip pocket. He gave Girland two one hundred franc notes.

"Where's the rest of it?" Girland demanded.

"That's all for the moment. You know the way Dorey pays." Girland put the notes in his limp wallet.

"I need my head examined working for this kind of money," he said in disgust.

"I want action," Rossland said. "I'm going back to my place right now and I'll be waiting. Watch it they don't tail you."

"Very funny ... coming from you," Girland said.

Herman Radnitz sat in an alcove in the bar of the George V Hotel: a square, fat man with hooded eyes and a thick hooked nose. He wore an immaculate Savile Row suit, a dark red carnation in his button hole and Lobb brogue shoes. From time to time he drew on an expensive cigar which he held in his short, fat fingers.

16

He had been sitting in the bar for the past half hour, his ruthless face clouded with thought.

Radnitz was a well-known figure at the hotel. He was believed to be one of the richest men in the world. His financial machinations spread like the tentacles of an octopus over the whole globe.

A young man, wearing a chin beard and a shabby overcoat belted like a dressing-gown, came quietly into the bar. He paused, then at a sign from Radnitz, sat down in a vacant chair by Radnitz's side.

This young man whose name was Michel Thomas, said softly, "Dorey has had an interview with Rossland. They met at the Crillon Bar and talked for some time. As they were leaving, Dorey gave Rossland something ... could have been money. I wasn't close enough to see. Rossland then went to the bar at the Normandy Hotel and made a telephone call. Borg was with me. He followed Rossland from in front: I from behind. Rossland lost me in the Métro, but Borg stayed with him. Borg has just now telephoned that Rossland met an American in a Fiat car. We don't know who this American is, but we have his car number and Borg is making inquiries."

Radnitz stared down at his spade shaped finger nails. There was a long pause, then he said, "This must be handled quickly. Make Rossland tell you what he discussed with Dorey. I don't care what you do to him. He's expendable."

Thomas nodded and got to his feet.

"I'll be waiting here," Radnitz said. "Be quick about it." He reached for his drink as Thomas made his way quietly out of the bar.

On the Avenue, Thomas walked to where a black Citroen was parked. The driver, a short, heavily built man with a round fat face and cruel little eyes looked at Thomas inquiringly as he opened the car door and slid into the front seat.

There was another man sitting in the back of the car. He was tall and thin and dark. His lean hatchet shaped face was as expressionless as a mask. His very stillness gave him an extraordinary look of menace.

"The boss wants us to talk to Rossland," Thomas said. "He has an apartment on Rue Castiglione."

Borg, the driver, grunted, started the engine and pulled away from the kerb.

It took them ten minutes to reach Rossland's apartment block.

Thomas and the tall man, Schwartz, got out and Borg drove away in search of parking space.

"We can handle this without Borg," Thomas said.

"You mean I can," Schwartz said with a sneer.

Thomas looked sharply at him. He was getting worried by Schwartz's undisguised contempt, but he decided this wasn't the time for a showdown. They entered the lobby, moving quickly past the concierge's window and reached the lift. Pressed close together in the small cage, the two men were drawn up to the top floor.

They got out, closing the lift door silently.

Thomas pointed to the tiny spy-hole set in the panel of the front door which allowed anyone inside to have a view of the caller outside.

Schwartz nodded and stood aside. Thomas took from his overcoat pocket a .38 automatic. He screwed a small, but efficient silencer to the barrel, then he rang the front door bell as Schwartz put his hand over the spy hole.

There was a long pause, then they heard the sound of heavy footfalls.

Rossland was drunk enough to be careless. He didn't even bother to use the spy-hole. Unlocking the door, he jerked it open.

Thomas lifted the automatic and pointed it at Rossland's paunch.

"No fuss," he said quietly. "Walk backwards and keep your hands still."

As Schwartz appeared behind Thomas, Rossland's face sagged and turned grey. He walked slowly backwards into the living-room. Thomas followed him while Schwartz closed the front door and locked it.

Girland ran up the flights of stairs to his apartment. He had time to take the girl, waiting for him, to the little bistro across the way, he thought as he reached the top landing. After dinner, he would bring the girl back here, persuade her to wait for him again, and then see this woman at the 'Allo Paris' club. When he was through with her, and after calling Rossland, he would return to his apartment. The girl and he would have fun together for the rest of the night. It was typical of the confidence he had in himself that it never occurred to him that the girl might not be co-operative.

He unlocked the door to his apartment and stepped into the

lighted room, then he paused, frowning. There was no sign of the girl.

"Tessa?" he called, raising his voice.

Only silence greeted him.

He looked into the shower room, then satisfied that she had gone, he sat on the bed.

In disgust, he thought, well, she certainly had me for a sucker. She must have gone as soon as I. I really thought I was on to a sure thing. Then he frowned. But why? Why did she come back here and give me the treatment if she didn't intend to play? His eyes became alert and he got to his feet. He looked around the big room. Everything seemed to be just as he had left it.

He crossed the room to the big wardrobe and looked at the three drawers in the wardrobe. The lower drawer which he didn't use was his warning of alarm. He had gummed a hair across the opening to alert him if someone searched his room. He saw the hair was broken.

He went into the shower room, pressed the spring in the panel and looked inside. In the recess, he hid his professional equipment: an Exakta camera with its accessories, two microphones, a tape recorder, a set of burglar's tools, several guns and various other pieces of equipment he needed from time to time. The recess also contained an odd assortment of clothing for there were times when Girland had to change his appearance.

A tiny electric light in the ceiling glowed green. It told him the girl hadn't discovered the recess.

He snapped the panel shut and returned to the living-room. He stood for some seconds, thinking. He had criticised Rossland unjustly, he thought. Whoever these people were, they had known about him before he had met Rossland. He was angry with himself. The girl had been cleverly planted, and he had been stupid enough to have fallen for her.

He crossed the room to the telephone and dialled Rossland's number. He listened to the steady ring of the bell, and when he finally convinced himself there was going to be no answer, he replaced the receiver. He ran his hand thoughtfully up and down the nape of his neck.

Rossland had said he was returning to his apartment. He had said he would be waiting for Girland ... so why didn't he answer his telephone?

Girland went to the shower room and exchanged his ammonia gun for a .45 automatic. Leaving his apartment he descended the stairs and moved cautiously to where he had parked his car.

It took him twenty minutes to reach Rossland's apartment block. He parked the car around the corner and then walked back to the entrance to the block.

Leaving the lift at the fifth floor, he rang Rossland's bell. He didn't expect an answer, and after a minute wait, he opened the door with a piece of thick wire that he used expertly with any lock.

Gun in hand, he moved silently into the tiny hall, and then into the living-room.

He paused at the sight of Rossland, lying on the velvet covered settee. The muscles in Girland's face tightened at the sight of the fat man as he lay in painful death.

Rossland had been brutally strangled. The nails of his right hand had been torn off. Blood from his nail-less fingers made a small pool of dark blood on the carpet.

The mutilated hand told Girland all he needed to know. He knew Rossland hadn't the guts to withstand such torture. Whoever had killed him now knew that a woman calling herself Madame Foucher had a meeting with Girland at 'Allo Paris' club at eleven o'clock this night.

Girland touched Rossland's dead shoulder. He had worked for Rossland now for five years. He had watched Rossland grow fat and soft. The other men who had worked for Rossland had gradually deserted him. Girland had hung on because he had been too lax to look elsewhere. Rossland had provided him with just enough money to live the way he liked to live.

Girland looked down at the dead face with its bulging eyes, the tongue, a red ball, protruding between big yellow teeth, and he felt a sudden sorrow for what remained of Rossland. He had warned him. He had said, "This is for real." But Rossland had been too drunk and stupid to heed the warning.

Chapter Two

"I HAVE been able to identify the American in the Fiat car, sir," Thomas said. He was standing respectfully before Radnitz who was sitting in a lounging chair, looking up at Thomas. They were in the sitting-room of Radnitz's luxury suite. The hands of the gilt ornate clock on the overmantel pointed to twenty-five minutes to ten. "His name is Mark Girland, and he has a one-room apartment on Rue de Suisses. He calls himself a Freelance Journalist, but he doesn't appear to have any money. Under pressure, Rossland admitted this man is one of his agents. Girland does not deal direct with Dorey. Rossland has told him to meet this woman, Madame Foucher, at the 'Allo Paris' club at eleven o'clock tonight. Neither Rossland nor Dorey know what it is she has to sell. I am a little late, sir, because we went to Girland's place, but he had gone. I had hoped to get rid of him as we got rid of Rossland."

Radnitz drew on his cigar.

"You are doing very well, Thomas, but understand this: Girland is not to meet this woman. Make sure he doesn't get near the club. Have it completely sealed off. Get rid of him. Get hold of this woman. I must talk to her. Don't hurt her. Take her to Schwartz's place. I'll wait here until you telephone me. I repeat: Girland is not to talk to her. It is imperative I see and talk to her before anyone does. Is that understood?"

You are doing very well.

Such praise came seldom from Radnitz and Thomas flushed with pleasure. He was Radnitz's slave, admiring him with adulation bordering on fanaticism.

"Yes, sir," he said. "I will arrange everything."

Radnitz dismissed him with a wave of his hand. He thought Thomas ridiculous with his little beard and in his shabbiness, but he was content to use him as long as he served him efficiently.

Thomas left the hotel, walking on air. He returned to where the Citroen was parked. He and Borg discussed the instructions he had received. Schwartz sat motionless in the back seat. He

21

never took part in plan making. His job was to eliminate. Both Thomas and Borg regarded him as a savage and were secretly afraid of him.

Thomas said, "We will need more men. You wait here. I'll telephone. If we are to seal off the club, I must have at least another four men."

Borg watched him return to the hotel and he put a cigarette between his thin lips. He regarded Schwartz in the driving mirror. Schwartz was staring with brooding intensity before him. Borg grimaced uneasily. Thomas had told him what Schwartz had done to Rossland. There were times, Borg thought, when he wondered if the money Radnitz paid him was enough to compensate him for the way he was living.

A blonde girl, wearing a *New York Herald Tribune* sweater came up to the car and jerked the door open.

"Tribune?" she asked, offering the paper. Her blue eyes examined Borg, and they then shifted to Schwartz.

Borg grinned at her. He liked blondes especially when they had a shape like this girl had.

"Don't you peddle anything else besides newspapers, baby?" he asked and leered at her.

The girl stepped back and slammed the car door. He watched her walk away.

"I bet the guy who's lucky to have her has himself a good time," he said wistfully. "Selling newspapers! She must be crazy! With a tail like that, she could make a fortune."

Schwartz remained silent. Women meant nothing to him. Borg hated him for his superior disinterest.

A minute later, Thomas came out of the hotel. The blonde girl, her newspapers in her hand, was standing in the shadows. Thomas didn't notice her. As he got into the Citroen, the girl scribbled on the front page of the Tribune, the number of the car.

Thomas said as he slid into the passenger's seat, "Now Boul' Clichy. We'll have five of the boys there in half an hour. Hurry it up. We have to get there before Girland does."

Borg grunted and started the car's engine. He moved the Citroen out into the stream of traffic and headed towards L'Etoile.

Girland sat in a bistro at a table at the far end of the big noisy

22

room. He was eating a herb omelette without appetite, his mind busy.

In two hours' time he had to contact this woman. He was sure the men who had murdered Rossland would be waiting for him. If they were as efficient as they seemed to be, they would make sure he didn't get near the cellar club. They would by now have the place sewn up, and if he wasn't very careful, he could walk into lethal trouble.

He toyed with the idea of telephoning Dorey. He had never met Dorey. He had only heard of him through Rossland. He decided for the moment he would see this thing through by himself. The first move would be to get to this woman, Madame Foucher, and find out what she had to sell. Then he would decide whether to handle it himself or work with Dorey.

He pushed aside his plate and lit a cigarette.

He told himself he had two choices of action. He could either go to this cellar club and take the risk of walking into trouble or he could telephone the club and try to persuade the woman to meet him elsewhere.

After a moment's thought he realised that now the opposition knew the woman's name and where she was to be found, they would probably try to kidnap her. No woman would withstand the kind of torture Rossland had suffered. Once they had her, she would talk, and then he would be out of it.

He made up his mind to go to the club. He just couldn't operate from the sidelines.

He ordered a cup of coffee and continued to brood. He worried about the blonde girl, Tessa. Who was she? Where did she fit into all this? He thought of her lush, long-legged body. Okay, sucker, he thought, things never do work out right for you. Right now she and I could be rolling in the hay.

He finished his coffee, paid his bill and walked out onto the street. He hesitated for a moment, then decided to leave his car where he had parked it. He waited on the kerb patiently for ten minutes before an empty taxi cruised by. He told the driver to take him to St. Lazare station.

At the station, he paid off the taxi and began the long walk towards Boulevard de Clichy. He walked slowly, jostled by the crowd thronging the pavement, his eyes and senses alert.

The time now was ten minutes to ten. Girland used the back streets that ran parallel with the Boulevard. He wondered what they had arranged. They couldn't attempt to murder him in the

23

street. He was constantly surrounded by people. His hand moved inside his coat and his fingers closed around the butt of his .45. The feel of the cold butt gave him more confidence.

He suddenly experienced a prickle of excitement. Out of the corner of his eye, he noticed a thick-set man who was staring aimlessly into the lighted window of a photographic equipment shop. The man wore a wool-lined coat and a green Swiss hat decorated with a feather. He turned casually as Girland moved past him and began to walk behind him.

It was too casually done. Girland's mouth tightened. They had certainly spread a wide net. Well, all right, he would let them know they weren't dealing with an amateur. He walked on, aware of the soft footfalls of the man behind him, then abruptly, he turned into a doorway, leading to an apartment block. He walked into darkness, then into a courtyard, dimly lit by the pale moon. He moved back against the wall of the apartment block, becoming invisible in the shadows. He waited. Nothing happened. He listened to the scurrying footfalls of the crowd going home and to the grinding of gears as cars crawled in an impatient stream along the narrow road. He had plenty of time and patience.

He stood there for over ten minutes. This was something Girland could do without any tension to his nerves. Waiting had always been part of his professional equipment.

Then he saw a thick-set figure come cautiously down the dark alley that led to the courtyard. The man paused when he realised that he would have to cross the dimly lit courtyard. He seemed nervous. Girland waited.

Finally, the man made up his mind. Girland saw him take something from inside his coat that glittered for a brief moment. Girland thought: A knife man.

The thick-set figure came forward. He was within three yards of Girland before he saw him. He was a quick, competent killer, but not quite quick enough for Girland's reflexes.

The flat, stabbing knife flashed as Girland launched himself in a flying tackle at the thick-set man's knees. The two men thudded together on the concrete.

The thick-set man's hat fell off as he tried to drive the knife into Girland's throat. Girland gripped the man's stabbing wrist. They strained, each exerting their maximum strength. The knife came closer to Girland's throat, so close, he felt the scratch of its sharpness against his skin. Making an effort that set his heart racing, he shoved away the threatening knife and with his left hand, he struck a vicious Judo punch that sank into the thickset man's throat. The knife fell from the man's hand. He gave a gurgling sigh and went limp. Breathing heavily, Girland scrambled to his feet.

He didn't even bother to look at the prostrate body. Moving quickly, brushing himself down, he walked back to the lighted street, and again mingled with the jostling crowd.

He was very alert now. He was within two minutes' walk of the cellar club. He checked his watch. The time was half past ten.

There was a café-bar at the end of the street, crowded with young people: boys with crew cuts and chin beards; girls, wearing calf high boots, their hair matted in an imitation of the Bardot hair style.

He entered and walked through the noise of the juke box and the shrill chatter of the young people, down a short flight of stairs that led to the toilettes and to a telephone cabinet. He shut himself in the cabinet and dialled the number of 'Allo Paris.'

There was a long pause as he listened to the ringing tone. He leaned against the wall of the cabinet, his eyes searching the dimly lit lobby outside the security of the glass box.

A man said impatiently, "Yes?"

"Is Madame Foucher with you?" Girland asked in his fluent French.

He could hear the strident sound of distant dance music and the heavy thud of drums.

The man asked, "Who is that?"

"If Madame Foucher is there, she will be expecting me."

"Hold on."

Girland waited, listening to the rhythm of the drums. There was a long delay. He heard a girl in the bar above laugh hysterically and he grimaced sourly. "Women!" he said to himself. "Where there's a woman, there are always complications." He thought of the long-legged blonde. To have her lying across a bed would justify any complication. He remembered what Rossland, now a dead pathetic body, had said: "Why can't you leave women alone? Seriously, there are too many women."

Girland wiped the back of his neck with his handkerchief. It was hot in the cabinet. He shrugged. Rossland was dead. He was now only a voice from the grave. Maybe he was right, Girland thought, but I have always been a sucker for women. Again he thought of Tessa with *New York Herald Tribune* inscribed across her full breasts.

A man's voice over the telephone line said, "Madame Foucher is here. She is waiting for you."

Girland smiled mirthlessly. So were other much more lethal people waiting for him.

"I want to speak to her," he said. "Would you . . ." He broke off as he saw the shadow of a man moving across the opposite wall. He replaced the receiver and dropped onto his knees, hiding himself behind the wooden panel of the cabinet. His left hand reached for the door handle, his right for his gun.

He waited, motionless. He felt trapped. Whoever it was outside could jerk the cabinet door open and kill him before he could defend himself.

Then he realised the sound of a gun shot would bring the twenty or thirty beatniks in the bar crowding to the top of the narrow stairs. No gunman could get past such a barrier.

He heard a door slam shut and again silence. His fingers, gripping the gun butt, began to ache. He waited, then he heard a toilet flush, a door open and slam shut, and again silence.

He remained on his knees, listening. All he could hear was the strident voices of the beats upstairs. Very cautiously, he opened the door of the cabinet a crack, his gun ready. He looked into the empty, dimly lit lobby. He slowly stood up, feeling sweat on his face. He stepped out into the empty lobby and looked around. Then he drew in a long, slow breath.

You're getting as soft as Rossland, he thought in disgust. You've no more nerves than a spinster who thinks there's a man under her bed.

Then again he thought of Rossland and what they had done to him, and his lips drew off his teeth in a mirthless grin.

If I can avoid it, they won't do that to me, he thought.

He stood, hesitating, then seeing a door by the toilet, he crossed to it and opened it. He saw it gave access to a steep flight of stairs. There was a three minute time switch for the electric light which he pressed, then he ran up the stairs. When he had climbed four flights, he slowed his pace. He paused to look upwards. The narrow, steep spiral continued for another three flights. He began to climb again. On the fifth floor, the light went out. He cursed, and as he began to grope for the button, the light came on again and he heard someone coming down the stairs. His hand slid inside his coat and his fingers closed around his gun butt. A fat, middle-aged woman appeared at the top of the next landing. She had a heavy wool shawl around her shoulders and her greasy hair was protected by a hair net. He moved aside to give her room to pass him. She nodded, saying, "Bon soir, monsieur," and then she passed him and plodded on down and out of sight.

Girland continued to climb. On the seventh and top floor, a little breathless, he found himself on a long corridor. Four shabby doors lined the corridor, at the end of which was a bolted steel door.

He drew the bolt and opened the door to find himself staring up at the night sky. He moved forward onto a flat roof and closed the steel door behind him. The roof was guarded by a rail. Leaning over the rail, he looked down at the busy Boulevard far below him. He could see the bright canopy of lights from the Casino Theatre. Further to his right, he could see a flashing sign that spelt out: 'Allo, Paris'.

He examined the roofs ahead of him. Three of them were flat and easy, the fourth was pointed and could be tricky, the fifth that covered the building where the cellar club was, was half flat, half sloping. He decided it could be safer to gain access to the club by the way of the roofs.

It took him only a few seconds to reach the pointed roof. Here, he paused. After studying this obstacle, he reluctantly made up his mind to make the crossing by way of the gutter, leaning against the tiles, his feet in the gutter. He had no confidence in that gutter, knowing he dare not put his whole weight on the flimsy, soot-covered lead. He had ten yards to cross before he reached safety of the further flat roof.

He took his gun from its holster, slipped on the safety catch, then holding the gun by its barrel, he leaned forward and broke one of the tiles within reach. He removed the broken tile and let it slide into the gutter. Putting his fingers through the hole he had made, he gripped the wooden lathe that supported the tile. He rested one foot in the gutter very cautiously, supporting most of his weight by hanging onto the lathe. The gutter creaked, but held.

He leaned forward again and broke another tile. As he reached for the new hole, he had to transfer his whole weight onto the gutter that creaked ominously. He was now sweating, thinking of the long, lethal drop onto the Boulevard far below. He rested

27

for some moments before he again reached forward and made a third hole in the tiles. He put the gun back into its holster and reached for the hole he had made with his left hand while retaining his grip on the second lathe with his right hand. As he moved forward, the gutter gave way and his feet swung into sickening space. He held on desperately, grabbed at the third hole, missed, grabbed again and got a grip. He hung there, his arms outstretched, his feet scrabbling for a hold. One of his feet hooked into the next section of the gutter. He paused, then slowly began to transfer some of his weight from his hands to his foot. The gutter creaked, but held. Painfully and slowly, he dragged himself up and rested for a long moment, standing in the gutter, but holding on with both hands. Then he shifted forward, pulled out his gun and made a fourth and last hole in the roof. He returned the gun to its holster, his breath whistling between his clenched teeth. Then he cautiously advanced, put his hand into the hole, gripped and then swung himself onto the flat roof three feet below him.

He sank onto his hands and knees, his eyes searching the roof, but he saw nothing suspicious. Within a yard or so from him, he saw a skylight. Satisfied there was no one except himself up on the roof, he stood up and approached the skylight. He looked down through the dirty glass into darkness. It took him only a few minutes to lever up the glass frame, then taking a flashlight from his hip pocket, he shone the beam into the dark void. He saw a landing and stairs. He lowered himself through the opening, drawing the glass frame back into place, then dropped silently onto the landing floor.

Thomas said, "It's sealed off. He can't get near the place without us seeing him." He looked at his watch. "He could be here any moment now."

He and Borg were standing in a darkened shop doorway, opposite the cellar club. Borg was bored and beginning to feel chilly.

"So what do you do when you see him?" he asked. "This guy is a toughie. He's not like Rossland."

Thomas fingered the silencer on the gun concealed in his pocket.

"Shoot him. By the time anyone realises anything has happened, we'll be away."

"Make sure you kill him," Borg said. "Where's Marcel?"

"Down the road," Thomas said. "He knows Girland by sight. He'll alert us as Girland approaches the club."

Borg shifted restlessly.

"Well, okay, so long as you know what you're doing. You've got someone up on the roof?"

"The roof?" Thomas stared at him, his small eyes startled. "Why the roof?"

Borg shrugged.

"You said you got this place sealed off. This guy isn't stupid in the head. He could go in by the roof."

Thomas was shocked that a fool like Borg could have thought of such an idea when he should have thought of it himself. Although he was young, he had won Radnitz's approval because he used his brains. Sweat broke out on his narrow forehead as he thought that by such a slip-up he could have failed Radnitz.

"You go," he said urgently. "I should have thought of that. Go in there and take the lift to the top floor. Hurry!"

Borg scowled at him.

"Not me! You go if you want to. Why the hell should I stick my neck out?"

"You heard me!" Thomas said, his voice, vicious. "Go in there!"

Borg hesitated, then knowing that Thomas was Radnitz's pet and it would be dangerous to argue with him, he shrugged.

"Oh, anything you say."

Leaving the shelter of the doorway, Borg crossed the Boulevard and entered the building that housed the cellar club. As he walked into the lobby, he could hear the steady beat of the drums and the wild notes of saxophones coming up from the cellar.

Girland was about to descend the last flight of stairs when he saw Borg come in. He stopped moving and pressed himself against the wall. He watched Borg enter the lift and shut the doors. A moment later the lift began a slow crawl upwards.

As soon as the lift had reached the first floor, Girland continued on down the stairs to the lobby.

A neon sign in red with a down pointing arrow told him 'Allo Paris' was on the floor below. He walked into the light of the neon sign and looked closely at his suit.

The dark suit he was wearing only showed the dirt he had picked up from the roof climb in strong light, but his hands were grimed with soot and his shoes scuffed. He took from his wallet a fifty franc note. Folding it, he walked down the stairs to the gaudy club entrance.

The doorman in a red uniform, took one look at Girland, then blocked his entrance.

"Members only," he said in a flat, disapproving voice.

Girland grinned at him.

"That's okay, pal," he said in broad American. "Let's be buddies. I had a goddamn fall." He swayed on his feet, then thrust the folded note into the doorman's hand. "I'll get cleaned up and then we can all have a wonderful time."

The doorman looked at the note, then he grinned. He took Girland by his arm and led him into a brightly lit lounge and then into the Men's room.

"If there's anything you want, monsieur, you ask."

It took Girland some ten minutes to get rid of most of the soot and dirt he had collected during his climb, then he left the Men's room and paused at the entrance to the cellar club.

The noise, blaring at him from the dimly lit, smoke ladened room, set his teeth on edge. Saxophones wailed, drums hammered, people screamed at each other.

A small man, wearing a green smoking jacket with frogs, appeared before Girland.

"You have a reservation, monsieur?" he asked. "Without a reservation . . . I'm afraid . . ."

"Madame Foucher is expecting me," Girland said.

The fat man's face became alert. He studied Girland, then nodded.

"Come this way."

He led Girland around the side of the big room. On the stage a stripper was slowly taking off her clothes to the violent noise of the band. She was pretty and her movements were professionally tantalising. As Girland reached a door at the far end of the room, she slowly removed black lace panties. He paused to watch. When any woman took off her panties, Girland always watched. The girl turned her back to the disinterested audience and then went through the dull routine of 'bumps and grinds.' She had a large strip of adhesive plaster across her left buttock, concealing a painful boil.

Girland grimaced. Women were meant to be glamorous, he thought, but they were only so long as they didn't get boils, spots and the many other things they seemed cursed with.

The man in the green smoking jacket stood waiting, holding

30

open the door. Girland followed him. The door swung shut and the strident noise from the club room faded to a murmur.

They were now in a narrow corridor. Either side were doors. The man pointed to the far end of the corridor.

"Madame Foucher is in room six, monsieur," he said, then moving around Girland, he opened the door, letting in the violent sound of people clapping and the final roll from the drums. He shut the door behind him and the welcome hush made Girland sigh with relief.

He walked down the corridor to room number six. He eased the .45 automatic from its holster and tapped on the door.

No one told him to come in.

He tapped again. Still hearing nothing, he opened the door and looked into a square-shaped room. Facing him was a wide, ceiling high mirror. In the middle of the room stood a double divan bed. The room was well carpeted and comfortable, it was also empty.

Satisfied he was alone, he returned the gun to its holster.

A woman's voice said, "Sit down, please, on the bed and face the mirror." Her voice, with an accent that puzzled Girland, was slightly distorted. He quickly realised that she was talking through a microphone.

Then he got it and grinned. Madame Foucher had chosen their meeting place to her advantage. He was in one of those rooms where girls took drunken suckers to go through with them sexual manoeuvres while paying customers watched through this big trick mirror. The side Madame Foucher was on was like a window. The side he was on was a mirror.

He sat on the bed facing the mirror, thinking he wasn't as young looking as he imagined himself to be.

"Who are you?" the woman's voice asked and Girland had the feeling, although he couldn't see her, she was examining him with disturbing intensity.

"Do you have to be so mysterious?" he asked.

"Who are you?" she repeated.

Girland shrugged. This situation began to bore him.

"My name's Mark Girland. You called Dorey who called Rossland who I work for. Rossland has dropped this in my lap. I'm a sucker who does dirty work for dirty people. Is that the kind of information you want?"

There was a pause. Girland had the disconcerting feeling, as

31

he stared at his reflection in the mirror, he was talking to himself.

"Well, go on," the woman said, her voice impatient.

"Go on? What about? What's your proposition? I'm here to listen . . . not to talk. You started this thing."

"How do I know you are from Dorey?"

"Why else should I be here?" Girland said. "I was told you have something to sell. I was told to find out exactly what it is and how much you want for it. You take it from here."

"Who is this man Rossland you speak about?"

Girland rubbed the side of his jaw. He was getting used to examining his lean features in the mirror.

"You don't have to worry about him. He's dead. The last time I saw him, he was lying on his bed with the nails of his right hand torn off and he was very much strangled."

He caught the sound of a swift intake of breath over the microphone.

"Dead? You mean he's been murdered?" The woman's voice went a little shrill.

"He was strangled," Girland said. "So that makes it murder."

"Who – who did it?"

"Why should you care?" Girland leaned forward, resting his elbows on his knees and staring fixedly at his reflection, knowing he was staring at this woman hidden from his sight. "Rossland thought you were a joke. Dorey thinks you are a joke, but I didn't, so I'm alive at the moment. I think you've talked too much. We have competition. You should know who the competitors are. You must have talked to them. I'll tell you this in case you don't know: they play it very rough. They tortured and murdered Rossland. Knowing Rossland the way I do, he spilled everything he knew. He has told them we are meeting here. I came in by the roof. If they get their hands on you, they'll treat you as they treated Rossland. If they start pulling your nails out, I doubt if you will be any braver than Rossland. You'll talk, and then you'll have nothing to sell."

There was a long pause, then she said, "I don't understand any of this. I've only contacted Mr. Dorey."

Girland shrugged.

"Well, okay, if you say so, then someone else has talked. That makes the price less exclusive. So, suppose we get down to business? What is it you have to sell?"

Again a long pause, then the woman said, "I know where Robert Henry Carey is."

Girland cocked his head on one side, his eyes alert.

"You mean the American Agent who went over to the Russians four years ago?"

"That's who I mean."

"He's in Russia, isn't he?"

"He left Russia ten days ago."

"Where is he now then?"

"That's the information I have to sell."

Girland took out a cigarette and lit it. He remembered Robert Carey, a tall, blond man who Rossland had once said was the finest agent in the racket. Girland had met him with Rossland and the two men had liked each other. That had been five years ago, but Girland still remembered the man's pleasant, strong face and the straight blue eyes that gave his face its personality. There had been a hell of an uproar when Carey had defected. It was generally believed he was now being used as an instructor, coaching learner agents who would eventually work in the West. Now and then news filtered through from behind the Iron Curtain that hinted of a very efficient school for agents that had been recently formed, but no one knew nor could find out where the school was situated nor who was in charge, but it was thought to be Carey.

"You mean he's defected again?" Girland asked, leaning forward.

"Yes."

"Well, fine. Then why doesn't he just walk in and say so?"

"He knows too much. He wouldn't be allowed to get near the West." She paused, then went on. "He's ill. He hasn't long to live."

"So what happens?"

"I can tell you where to find him and you go to him. I want ten thousand dollars. He said you would give me that amount if I helped him."

"What do you mean . . . he knows too much?"

"He had access to certain files. He has them with him. He says they are important to the security of America," the woman said.

Girland got the idea that she was repeating a lesson carefully learned. Again he was puzzled by her French. She had an accent he hadn't heard before.

"My people aren't likely to part with any money on a claim like that," Girland said, alert and intrigued. "What else has he got?"

"During the years he was in Russia, he reorganised much of the Soviet spy system. He has all that information."

"That's a little better." Girland thought for a moment. "Well, I'll talk to Dorey. He might not be interested. Double Agents can be unreliable."

"I'm in a hurry," the woman said. There was an edge of panic in her voice. "I'll call Mr. Dorey tomorrow night. He must say either yes or no. There are other people who would be interested."

"Don't do that," Girland said hurriedly. "We now have competitors. If you haven't talked, then someone else has, so there could be a leak in Dorey's office. You telephone me. That'll be safer. I'll be waiting on Jasmin 00051 at seven o'clock tomorrow evening. Will you do that?"

"Will you have the money with you?"

"If Dorey wants to play, I'll have it."

"Then I will telephone you."

"Just a minute," Girland said. "Is Carey in Paris?"

"Good night," the woman said and he heard the sound of a door gently closing beyond the mirror.

Girland lit a cigarette. He wondered if he could persuade Dorey to let him handle this. He was pretty sure Dorey wouldn't. He was also pretty sure Dorey would be willing to pay much higher than ten thousand dollars to have Robert Henry Carey in his office and talking.

This wanted thinking about, Girland said to himself. There could be some nice money in it for him if he played it carefully. It was time he made some nice money out of the American Government.

He was still thinking, trying to find an angle when a faint sound behind him made him look up and into the big mirror.

Reflected in the mirror was Thomas, gun in hand, and behind him, mask-like, dark and tall was Schwartz.

Chapter Three

THE TWO men moved like shadows into the room and closed the door.

Girland's right hand itched to fly to his gun, but his position was hopeless. He had his back to these two and he saw the silencer screwed to Thomas's gun. He remained motionless, feeling a chill crawl up his spine as he realised these must be the two who had tortured and murdered Rossland.

"Where is she?" Thomas asked. His voice was husky, and looking at him in the mirror, Girland saw his sallow face was shining with sweat.

Thomas was so frightened he could scarcely keep his voice steady. He had failed! Radnitz had said that Girland must not talk to this woman. Through his own stupidity, somehow Girland had got into the club and had talked to her! This was the first time he had failed to carry out an order from Radnitz.

Girland thought quickly. He had a feeling he was within seconds of death.

"She's gone," he said, not moving. "She's been gone a good ten minutes."

Thomas turned his head for a brief moment to look at Schwartz.

"I'll kill him. See if you can stop her."

Girland said quickly, "Do you know what she looks like? I don't. We talked through that trick mirror. And why kill me? We could do a deal."

He was relieved to see Schwartz was still leaning against the door, showing no intention of moving.

"Find her!" Thomas snarled and raised the gun so the sight was aiming at Girland's head.

So this is it, Girland thought and suddenly he was afraid to die. Instinctively he lifted his shoulders and crouched forward in a hopeless attempt to evade the bullet. He stared into the mirror at the gun, then he saw Schwartz move forward with the speed of a striking snake and knock Thomas's gun arm down.

There was a faint plop as the gun went off and Girland saw a sudden small hole in the carpet at his feet.

If he hadn't been afraid to die, he thought afterwards, he could have spun around, got his gun out and have killed those two, but fear had paralysed him and in those necessary split seconds before he could recover, he saw Schwartz was covering them both with a gun. There was that cold professional look in Schwartz's eyes that warned him this man was far more dangerous than the bearded boy.

Thomas felt Schwartz's cold, damp hand clamp over his and wrench his gun away. He turned, panting, to stare at Schwartz who was looking at Girland.

There was a long pause. Girland was careful not to move. Thomas backed away from Schwartz.

"You'll be sorry for this!" he exclaimed shrilly. "I'll tell him! He said we were to get rid of Girland! You . . ."

"There's a phone over there," Schwartz interrupted. "Call him. Tell him what's happened."

"I don't have to! He's left this to me! I don't have to tell him anything!" Thomas said, trying to keep his voice down. "It'll be you who'll suffer! You fool! Don't you see we have made a mistake? If we kill him now, no one will know! Kill him!"

Girland listened to all this with cold sweat running down his ribs.

"You made the mistake," Schwartz said. "Your first mistake. Go on, tell him, or it'll be you who'll get killed."

Thomas backed against the wall, his face livid.

Girland watched in the mirror, aware that if he made the slightest move, this tall, dangerous looking man would shoot him.

"Go on!" Schwartz repeated. "Tell him his white-headed boy has made his first mistake."

There was a further pause, then Thomas moved to the telephone that stood on a table close to Girland. As he reached for the receiver, Girland said, "That's through the club switchboard. It's your business, but the girl is certain to listen in."

He was aware that Schwartz was staring at him. Thomas turned slowly and also stared at him.

"Do you have to act so tough?" Girland went on. "I'm ready to do a deal. Not with you two, but with your boss. This set-up could mean money to me. I need money. I can tell your boss how I got in here and I'll keep you both in the clear. Let's work together on this thing."

Thomas began to relax a little. He looked at Schwartz. Watching them, Girland saw he was nearly home, but not quite.

"You guys are in the same racket as I am," he said. "Okay, so let's work together. I'll go with you to where you can telephone. No fuss ... no trouble. All I want you to do is to call your boss and tell him I want to make a deal with him. I have a date with this woman tomorrow, but she won't meet anyone but me. Tell him that."

Still they remained motionless, staring at him.

"My gun's in a holster," Girland said. "Take it." That, at last, got some action. Thomas moved cautiously up to him. Girland sat as still as a stone man while Thomas found the gun and jerked it free from its holster. Then raising his hands and clasping them on top of his head, Girland slowly stood up. Thomas's hands ran over him, making sure he had no other weapon, then he stood away.

Thomas looked at Schwartz who nodded.

"Let's go then," Schwartz said. To Girland he went on, "This gun is silenced. You start something and you're dead."

"Don't be so unfriendly," Girland said, lowering his hands. "I tell you, I want to make a deal."

He walked to the door, opened it and stepped out into the corridor.

The two men, Schwartz in front, Thomas behind, followed him closely. Girland could almost feel the barrel of the concealed gun grinding into his spine.

Opening the end door, the blare of the dance band made him wince. He moved into the dimly lit, smoke laden cellar. The small stage was spot lit. There was a young redhead, naked, standing in a small bathtub with an enormous sponge in her hand. She was hiding parts of her body with the sponge while water from a shower trickled over her.

The tourists, crammed together at the tiny tables like well arranged sardines, were leering at her.

Even so close to death, Girland had to pause to look at the girl. A rough shove, just when he was thinking she had a nice shape, sent him forward and he walked on, out into the lobby.

The doorman grinned at him.

"I hope you enjoyed yourself, monsieur," he said.

Girland smiled crookedly.

"You bet," he said, then urged on by Schwartz, he left the club and climbed the stairs.

"Wait," Schwartz said when they reached the lobby.

Thomas moved around them and walked into the street. After a short delay, Schwartz urged Girland forward again. They moved into the crowded Boulevard to where the black Citroen was double parked. The drivers of cars behind the Citroen began to sound their horns. Girland quickly slid into the back seat. Schwartz joined him. Thomas was already in the front seat and a bewildered Borg sat behind the driving wheel.

Girland said, "There's an automatic telephone at the café at the far end of this street."

Schwartz turned swiftly and before Girland could avoid it, he received a crushing blow against his jaw. As he lurched forward, Schwartz hit him on the back of his neck with the barrel of his gun.

"All right," Schwartz said, "now back to my place. He won't make trouble."

"What the hell's all this about?" Borg demanded as he wrestled the Citroen into the heavy traffic.

"Shut your mouth!" Thomas snarled.

Borg gave him a startled glance, then concentrated on his driving.

Thomas, huddled in his seat, stared through the windshield. For a long time he had had an instinctive suspicion that Schwartz hated him: now it was out in the open. From now on, he would have to be very careful. He thought of Radnitz and his mouth turned dry. What would happen to him when Radnitz learned he had let Girland and this woman meet and talk?

Borg swung the Citroen down a narrow cul-de-sac. Schwartz had three rooms in the basement below a bread and cake shop. It was a convenient place. After eight o'clock the shop and the cul-de-sac were deserted.

He and Schwartz dragged Girland's unconscious body from the car and down the narrow stairs that led to Schwartz's rooms. They dropped him on the floor while Schwartz unlocked the door and turned on the light, then they dragged him into the big, sparsely furnished room. Thomas, following, closed and locked the door.

This was the first time Borg had been to Schwartz's place. He looked around curiously.

What a hole! he thought and wrinkled his fat nose. The walls had damp stains. There was one filthy, threadbare rug on the floor. Against one of the walls was a divan bed: the sheets and

38

pillow case were grey. There were four upright chairs covered in pale green, frayed velvet. A cigarette scarred table stood in the centre of the room. A naked electric light bulb hung from the ceiling, casting a harsh light over the room's sordidness.

Leaving Girland lying by the table, Schwartz crossed the room to the telephone that stood on a dusty shelf near the bed. He dialled a number, then waited while Thomas and Borg watched him.

"Mr. Radnitz," Schwartz said when he got his connection.

Thomas felt his stomach contract as Schwartz offered him the receiver.

"Go ahead and talk to him," Schwartz said.

Thomas took the receiver the way a snake-hater touches a snake.

There was a short wait, then Radnitz said, "Yes?"

"This is Thomas, sir. The operation did not go according to plan," Thomas said huskily. "We have him at Schwatz's place. He and she have talked."

He waited, feeling sick. Sweat beads ran down the fringe of his beard.

"You mean you have *her* there," Radnitz said in his cold, impersonal voice.

"No. She got away. Girland is here."

A long pause, then Radnitz said in a much sharper tone. "I see. Very well, I will come," and there was a click as he hung up.

Thomas replaced the receiver.

"He is coming," he said. In an attempt to regain his authority, he went on, "Get him on the divan."

Neither Schwartz nor Borg moved. Schwartz sat on one of the upright chairs. Borg took out a pack of cigarettes and began to smoke.

Thomas said shrilly. "I said get him on the divan!"

Schwartz sneered at him.

"You get him on the divan if you want him on the divan."

Girland moved, groaned and opened his eyes. He stared up at the damp stained ceiling. The three men watched him. As he began to struggle to sit up, Schwartz got to his feet and kicked him solidly in the ribs.

The sudden shock of the kick cleared Girland's brain. He rolled over, flung out his hand, grabbed Schwartz's trouser cuff and jerked. Schwartz sprawled on the floor. Girland groped for him but Borg reached him and catching him by his thick hair, dragged him away from Schwartz who was struggling to his feet.

Schwartz, his face white with rage, had his gun in his hand. Holding the gun by its barrel, he made to club Girland with the butt, but Thomas caught his arm and pulled him back.

"He wants to talk to him," Thomas said. "Cut it out!"

Borg moved away from Girland who sat up and peered at Schwartz.

"One of these days, Stone-face," Girland said, "we'll meet on more equal terms, then watch out."

Schwartz shoved Thomas away, sneered at Girland and went back to his chair.

Girland got unsteadily to his feet, holding the back of his neck. The three men watched him as he went over to the divan and sat on it.

Borg took a flat flask containing brandy from his hip pocket. He drank greedily, then offered the flask to Girland.

"Have a swig," he said. "You look like you need it."

Girland took the flask and let the cheap brandy trickle down his throat. He grimaced, then sighed as he screwed the cap on the flask. He handed the flask back to Borg who grinned at him.

"As you're giving things away," Girland said, "I could use a cigarette."

Borg tossed him a pack which Girland caught. He shook out a cigarette and lit it, then he made to toss the pack back but Borg said, "You keep it."

Thomas watched all this. He was now beginning to become frightened of Borg. Why should Borg treat this man this way unless he was now sure that he (Thomas) was finished?

Silence brooded over the sordid room while Girland smoked and slowly recovered from the blow on the back of his neck. From time to time, Borg took out the flask and drank. Schwartz remained motionless, his glittering eyes on Girland. Thomas got tired of leaning against the wall. He pulled a chair towards him, away from the other two and sat down.

Minutes dragged by, then they heard the sudden sound of a door shutting. Thomas got to his feet and went to the door. He opened it and stood back as Radnitz, cigar between his fat fingers, came in.

Radnitz wore a black cloak that hung from his square shoulders.

The cloak was scarlet-lined and looked impressive as well as theatrical. He came into the room like a man moving into a leper's hut.

Thomas said in a small, tight voice, "This is Girland, sir."

Radnitz glanced briefly at Girland, then waved his hand to the three men.

"Wait outside," he said curtly.

When they had gone and the door was closed, Radnitz took off his cloak and laid it carefully on a chair. He looked around the room, his face registering disgust, then he walked over to a green velvet covered chair and sat down.

As if speaking to himself, he said, "A pig would be unhappy in such a sty."

Girland watched him.

Radnitz went on looking around the room. Finally his small ice-cold eyes eventually came to rest on Girland.

"I am Herman Radnitz," he said. "You will have heard of me." As Girland said nothing, Radnitz went on, "I have heard something about you, Mr. Girland. You are a professional agent, working for the Americans. You undertake difficult work for very little money. It seems to me you are a very small man in a dangerous job. I believe you have certain talents and some courage which are being wasted. You have little to show for the years you have been working as an agent. I repeat, Mr. Girland, you seem to be a very small man in a dangerous job."

Girland grinned as he continued to rub his aching neck.

"Big trees from little acorns grow," he said. "I'm patient. Now, I'm beginning to become a big man."

Radnitz touched off the long ash from his cigar. He was indifferent that the ash fell on the filthy carpet, making a tiny grey puddle.

"You could become a big man, Mr. Girland, but on the other hand, you could become a dead man."

Girland took out Borg's pack of cigarettes and lit one.

"Could we talk business?" he said, letting smoke drift down his nostrils. "If you killed me, where would it get you? I don't bluff easily. You and I could make a deal."

"I hope we can, Mr. Girland," Radnitz said. "We either make a deal or you don't leave this room alive."

"So we make a deal," Girland said.

Radnitz shifted his bulk in the uncomfortable chair, then he asked abruptly, "You met Madame Foucher?"

"I met her."

41

"I told my men you were not to meet her."

"I was there long before they sealed off the club," Girland lied.

Radnitz stared at him and Girland stared back at him. Radnitz shrugged.

"She knows where Carey is?"

"Yes."

"Did she tell you?"

Girland shook his head and was immediately sorry. The stabbing pain that shot through him made sweat break out on his face.

He rubbed his neck, scowling before saying, "She wants to be paid for the information. I have a date with her tomorrow night."

"How much?"

Girland said without hesitation, "Fifteen thousand dollars in cash."

Radnitz studied him.

"I see, Mr. Girland, you are beginning to grow."

"Well, I warned you, didn't I?"

"So for fifteen thousand dollars, this woman will tell you where Robert Henry Carey is to be found. Am I correct?"

"That's it," Girland returned. "She is to call me at a certain telephone number tomorrow night. I have to convince her I have the money, then she'll tell me where he is."

"From whom will you get fifteen thousand dollars?" Radnitz asked and again touched off the ash from his cigar.

"From Dorey. I don't have to tell you about him, do I?"

"I know of Dorey." Radnitz's face was expressionless. "It seems to me, Mr. Girland, you are working for the wrong people. I want to find Carey. Fifteen thousand dollars, you said? What do you propose to make out of that?"

"I'll arrange something," Girland said, thinking that five thousand dollars profit would repay him for a bruised neck.

"It would be better, wouldn't it, if you put fifty thousand dollars in your pocket?"

Girland drew in a deep breath. This was the kind of money he had often dreamed about.

"It would be a lot better," he said cautiously.

"I would pay you that."

"I'll be talking to this woman tomorrow night. Give me fifteen thousand dollars and I'll be able to tell you where he is," Girland said. "I need the fifteen for her. We'll talk about my end when I've seen her."

Radnitz drew on his cigar. The end glowed red like a warning signal.

"If everything were as simple as that, Mr. Girland," he said, letting smoke drift out of his mouth as he talked, "life would have very few complications. It is not enough to know where he is. I want to make sure he is wiped out. I will certainly let you have fifteen thousand dollars, but before you earn your end, you will have to convince me that you can find Carey, that you are prepared to kill him when you find him and that you will bring back with you all the papers he took from Russia."

Girland again rubbed the back of his neck.

"Suppose I talk to this woman first, then we can develop this thing," he said finally.

Radnitz crossed one short, fat leg over the other. He regarded Girland.

"Mr. Girland, you have been an agent for the past five years," he said. "You have been content to pick up a hundred dollars here and there. You are now in a position where you can make a great deal of money, but I suspect your mind is so small, you don't really understand the meaning of fifty thousand dollars. You could be planning to cheat me. You could be planning to put this fifteen thousand dollars in your pocket and try to disappear from Paris. But I do assure you if you are thinking along those lines, it would be most unwise. You wouldn't survive for very long."

Girland stared steadily at Radnitz.

"I'll meet this woman, give her the money and tell you what she says," he said quietly. "It's up to you whether you trust me or not."

"I never trust anyone," Radnitz said. "But when I want something, I make arrangements to see I get it. I want to find Carey, I think you can find him for me. I think once you find him, you're the right man to kill him. I will pay you fifty thousand dollars to do this. Will you accept such an assignment?"

Girland thought of Robert Henry Carey. No one could ever offer him enough money, no matter how big the sum, to bribe him to take a life, least of all Carey's life. But Girland also thought of owning fifty thousand dollars. He had a lot of confidence in himself. This fat, squat man could be out-smarted.

43

He decided he would go along with him. After all, he had time and the room in which to manoeuvre.

"It's a deal," he said. "There's not much I wouldn't do for money like that."

Radnitz looked around the room as if thinking, then he asked, "You are quite sure about this, Mr. Girland?"

Girland caught the note of menace in Radnitz's voice.

"I'm sure," he said.

"You must be careful not to allow your previous small-minded methods to tempt you into cheating," Radnitz said with deceptive mildness. "I know quite a lot about you, Mr. Girland. Once you commit yourself to me, you stay committed."

"I said it was a deal, and it is a deal," Girland said.

Radnitz nodded and got to his feet.

"The money will be delivered to you at your apartment to-morrow afternoon. You will contact this woman and find out where Carey is hiding. You will then come to the George V Hotel and tell me where he is. We will then decide the best method of getting rid of him."

"I'll do that," Girland said.

Radnitz swung his cloak over his shoulders and walked to the door.

"Then sometime tomorrow evening, Mr. Girland, at the George V Hotel. You are committed." He paused to stare at Girland. "I do assure you that you won't live very long if you have a change of mind."

He left the room. Propelled by a sudden draught, the door gently swung shut.

John Dorey walked down the steps leading from the American Embassy, slightly hunching his shoulders against the cool wind. He nodded to the guard at the gates who saluted him, then he crossed to where his Peugeot 404 was parked, again nodding to the gendarme who was patrolling around the block of parked cars and who, on recognising him, also saluted.

Dorey unlocked the car door, slid under the driving wheel and put on the side lights. He looked at his modest silver Omega he had bought some years ago in Geneva. The time was twenty minutes to ten.

It was his habit to work late. While he had been working he had eaten a sandwich and drunk a glass of milk, brought to him by one of the messengers. It was also his habit to eat this kind of supper before returning to his apartment. He lived alone. It was so long since he had divorced his wife, he never even thought of her. He preferred living alone.

John Dorey had worked in the American Embassy in Paris for thirty-eight years. He had had a variety of jobs and had finally ended up as Head of the French Division of the Central Intelligence Agency. He had become engrossed in this particular work, and for some years he had run the division successfully. But now, at the back of his mind, was the constant and dreaded thought that he would be retired in another three years' time. It had come as a considerable shock when Washington had sent Thorton Warley to Paris to take over the division two months ago. They had said that Dorey was to carry on with his own agents and with his own contacts, but that Warley was to supervise and reorganise the division.

Although Dorey would admit it to no one but himself, he was convinced that Washington had become dissatisfied with his work and had put Warley over him to find some excuse to get rid of him before his three years were up. Dorey had told himself often enough that it would be through no fault of his own if Warley succeeded.

It was true what Rossland had said. Anything that looked promising that arrived through the mail or over the telephone, Dorey kept to himself. He was now living in hopes that he would pull off something so big that Washington would relent and not only remove Warley but extend his three years to even five.

Thinking about Warley, Dorey drove across Pont de la Concorde, edged his way into the rush of traffic that roared along the Quai d'Orsay and finally reached Avenue Bosquet. In one of the small side streets off the avenue, he had his apartment. He spent five or six minutes of irritating frustration, trying to find parking space for his car. Finally, he had to leave the car at the far end of the road and then walk back. Although this happened every night, it never failed to anger him.

As he entered the lobby of the building, the concierge who he tipped regularly and well, nodded and smiled at him through her window. He nodded back and got in the lift that took him to the fourth floor.

He entered his apartment and closed the door. Taking off his light overcoat, he hung it in the hall closet, then walked into his large, well furnished living-room, clicking on the lights as he did so.

45

He crossed to the desk and sat down, took keys from his pocket and unlocked a drawer. Just as he was about to take from the drawer a thick file of papers, the telephone bell rang.

He frowned, hesitated, then lifted the receiver.

"John?" A woman's voice.

"Yes."

"Janine. I wanted to be sure you were back. I am coming over in half an hour."

"Certainly," Dorey said and hung up.

He sat for some minutes staring down at the snowy white blotter on his desk, then he closed and locked the desk drawer. He got up and walked over to one of the big easy chairs. His thin bird-like face was thoughtful. His eyes, behind the glittering lenses of his spectacles were a little uneasy. He picked up a copy of the *New Yorker* that was lying on an occasional table and began to flick through it. He was flicking through it for the fourth time without having registered any of its contents when the front doorbell rang.

He looked carefully through the spy-hole before opening the door.

Janine Daulnay moved quickly past him into the hall. Dorey closed the door as she turned, pulling off her gloves, to give him a faint impersonal smile. She was a woman between thirty and thirty-five years of age: trim, medium height, dark and wearing an expensive mink coat. She had big, dark eyes: their mocking expression gave her a sophistication that most men found irresistible, but not Dorey. Long ago, he had decided that women were not only dangerous, but a nuisance. He disliked dealing with them, although he accepted the fact they were necessary.

"Come in and sit down," he said, leading the way into the living-room. "I have still a lot of work to do. I'm afraid you can't stay long. What is it?"

She took off her coat, dropped it on a chair, then followed him into the living-room. As she sat down, she gave the hem of her Dior dress a little tug to hide her beautiful knees.

"Have you given Harry Rossland a job?" she asked.

This unexpected question so startled Dorey that for a split second his usual poker face expression slipped.

Janine noted the slip as she noted every change in any man's expression.

"Why do you ask?" Dorey said carefully.

"Look, John. I either work with you or I don't," Janine said

46

quietly. "I'm asking you a simple question: is Rossland working for you tonight?"

Dorey regarded this immaculate, cold-faced woman and he remembered various things she had done for him in the past. He wished now he had consulted her before he had talked to Rossland.

"He is working for me tonight," he said.

"Something important?"

"Could be. I don't know yet."

She opened an expensive handbag, took out a gold cigarette case, removed a cigarette and lit it with a gold lighter.

"Do you want to tell me about it, John?"

Dorey hesitated.

"What is all this? It is really nothing to do with you, Janine."

She let smoke drift down her small nostrils and she smiled.

"All right. If that's the way you want to play it." She smoothed down her skirt. "Then I'll go and let you get on with your work."

As she made no move, Dorey said, "You know I rely on you, Janine. You know something, don't you? What is it?"

She sighed and flicked ash onto the Persian carpet.

"All right. It was mere chance. I saw Harry Rossland tonight. He was being followed by a youngish man with a beard. Ahead of him was another man. Harry caught on to the bearded man, but not to the front tail. He lost the bearded man in the Métro. I didn't think it was all that important so I let him go. Then I remembered seeing the bearded man before." She paused, then went on, "He works for Herman Radnitz."

Dorey sat forward.

"You're sure?"

She made an impatient gesture.

"You should know by now, John: I'm always sure."

"Well?"

"I wondered, knowing Rossland worked for you. I had a date, but I passed it up. I went to the George V Hotel. Radnitz was in the bar, waiting. The bearded young man appeared, talked with Radnitz, then left. He returned after five minutes and made a telephone call. I was, by then curious, so I called Harry's apartment. There's no answer. So I called you and here I am."

Dorey took off his glasses and began to polish them with his handkerchief. He looked disturbed. For a long moment he frowned in thought while Janine watched him.

"This happened in a hurry," he said finally. "I should have talked to you, but there wasn't time. I didn't take it very seriously at first. I thought Rossland could handle it."

"People get into a rut," Janine said. "They get too sure of themselves. I think you're getting too sure of yourself, John. You won't accept the fact that Rossland is finished. I told you that before, but you are so used to him, you continue to employ him. Well, never mind . . . just what is all this about?"

"This morning I had a telephone call from a woman who called herself Madame Foucher. She said she had information to sell," Dorey said, shifting in his chair. "We get quite a lot of nuts offering information. I thought she could be another of them. She said she couldn't give me details over the telephone but would I meet her? She said she would be at a third rate cellar club tonight. She then said that her business was to do with the security of America and she hung up. So I decided to send Rossland to meet her."

Janine stubbed out her cigarette in the ash tray by her side.

"What has he to report?"

"I'm waiting. He's not seeing the woman himself. He has given the job to one of his men."

"Why?"

"You know Rossland. He keeps to the sidelines."

"Then who is seeing this woman?"

"I told you . . . one of his men."

"You don't know who he is?"

Dorey took off his glasses and began to polish them again. "No."

"When do you expect to hear?"

"They don't meet until eleven."

She glanced at her watch. The time now was quarter to eleven.

"I don't think you should wait," she said. "If Radnitz is in this, it could be dangerous."

Dorey was thinking the same thing. He went over to the telephone and dialled Rossland's number. After a long pause, he replaced the receiver.

"He's not there."

They looked at each other.

"He could be there," Janine said and got to her feet. "I think we should go. This is bothering me."

Dorey nodded. He went to his desk, unlocked a drawer and took from it a .38 automatic. He checked it with the hand of an

48

expert, then put it in his hip pocket. He went to the closet for his coat.

Twenty minutes later, they were riding up in the lift to Rossland's apartment.

As Dorey was about to ring the bell, he saw the door stood ajar. He took out his gun and transferred it to the pocket of his overcoat, then he gently pushed open the door and moved into the hall. Janine followed him. The lights were on in the sitting-room. Moving like a ghost, Dorey edged the door and looked into the room. He gave a convulsive grunt when he saw Rossland.

"Shut the door," he said softly. "He's in there ... he's dead." Her face expressionless, Janine closed the front door. She then entered the sitting-room and came close to Dorey who was looking down at Rossland. She gave the murdered man one horrified glance, then turned away.

"Look at his hand," she said unsteadily.

Again Dorey grunted. Grimacing, he joined her as she looked around the room.

"Doesn't look as if they searched here," she said. "They were in a hurry. They persuaded him to talk, killed him and cleared out."

"We'd better leave, Janine," Dorey said, moving to the door. "We don't want to be caught here."

They left the apartment as quietly as they had come in.

Once in Dorey's car Janine said, "This is something big, John. You shouldn't have given it to Rossland. You should have seen this woman yourself."

"How was I to know?" Dorey said defensively. "I tell you I'm always getting cranks calling me on the telephone."

"Where is this cellar club?"

"Boul' Clichy."

"We'll go there."

Dorey glanced at her.

"It'll be too late. It's half past eleven."

"We'll go there," Janine repeated, "and hurry." As Dorey started the car and edged out into the traffic, she went on, "This is Radnitz's work. I'm sure of it! If this isn't something really big, he wouldn't have had Rossland killed. Haven't you any idea who Rossland sent to meet this woman? Don't you know any of his men?"

"No. Rossland would never tell me the names of his agents. He was scared I might take them away from him."

"This isn't going to look very good to Warley, is it, John?" she said quietly. "You get the tip-off. Instead of reporting to Warley, you turn Rossland on to it ... Rossland of all people. He turned an unknown onto it and Radnitz moves in. By now Radnitz will have caught Rossland's man and he'll know what the woman has to sell ... something important to the security of America. Not brilliant, is it?"

Dorey felt his hands turn clammy. There were times when he found himself uneasy about Janine. Not for the first time, he wished he had made her his mistress. There was a time when she would have been willing. As his mistress, he might have had a firmer hold on her.

"We all make mistakes," he said. "I don't see how I can be blamed."

She lit a cigarette.

He glanced at her uneasily, then decided it would be better not to make further excuses.

They reached the cellar club at a few minutes to midnight. By then Dorey had recovered from the shock of Rossland's death and his nimble brain was working efficiently again.

"You had better wait in the car," he said. "I'll handle this." She nodded and he entered the club.

The fat man in the green smoking jacket whose name was Husson, greeted him.

"I want to talk to you," Dorey said curtly and showed his Embassy pass. "This could be police business."

Husson looked started. Dorey's air of authority impressed him. If the police came here and found that trick mirror, he thought, there would be a lot of tiresome unpleasantness.

He led Dorey to a small office behind the bar.

"Now, monsieur, what can I do for you?" he asked, waving Dorey to a chair and sitting behind the desk.

"A woman who calls herself Madame Foucher has been here I understand," Dorey said.

He saw Husson hesitate, then nod.

"That is right, monsieur."

"Is she here now?"

"She left some time ago."

"She met someone?"

"An American came to see her."

"What can you tell me about Madame Foucher?"

Husson lifted his shoulders.

"She came here yesterday, asked for a private room where she could meet a friend tonight at eleven. She paid well. I saw no reason why I shouldn't oblige her, monsieur."

"Can you describe her?"

"She was coloured: unusually tall, handsome, young and well-dressed."

"Coloured?" Dorey said, leaning forward to stare at Husson.

"West African ... Senegalese I should imagine."

Dorey then remembered the woman's odd accent when she had spoken to him on the telephone. He should have known she was Senegalese and he was irriated with himself for not knowing.

"The man kept the appointment?"

"Yes, monsieur. He has only just left with two other men. He hasn't been gone more than ten minutes."

"Who were these other two men?"

"I don't know. They came into the club, had a drink, then the next time I noticed them, they were leaving with this American who had the rendezvous with Madame Foucher."

"Can you describe them?"

Husson thought for a moment. "I didn't particularly notice them, monsieur. It isn't easy to see people in the club. I think the smaller man had a beard. I didn't notice the other man."

"And the American?"

Husson gave him a fairly accurate description of Girland which meant nothing to Dorey.

"You have never seen Madame Foucher before?"

"No."

"Did she have a car?"

"I wouldn't know. She arrived and I took her to the room."

"She didn't tell you the name of this man who visited her?"

"No, monsieur."

Dorey gave up. At least he had found out something, but he couldn't see for the moment if it were going to be of any use to him. Rossland's man had met the woman. She had gone, then Radnitz's men had taken this man away.

He stood up.

"Thank you. I think you have given me all the information I need," he said.

Husson looked sharply at him.

"There will be no trouble?"

"No, there will be no trouble," Dorey returned and leaving the club, he joined Janine in the car.

Quickly, he told her what he had learned.

She said, "Don't you think you should now report the whole thing to Warley, John?"

"Certainly not!" Dorey said without hesitation. "I can handle this. I'm going to find this Senegalese woman. I'll have a check made at the airports. She might have arrived only within the last few days. It shouldn't be too difficult. I have a good description of her. Someone at the airports might remember her."

"By now they are persuading Rossland's man to talk," Janine said. "In a little while, they will know who this woman is and where to find her. I think you're going to be too late, John."

"I must chance that. If I'm too late, then Warley will also be too late. He can't do better than I can."

With an obstinate expression in his eyes, Dorey drove fast in the direction of his apartment.

Chapter Four

SECONDS AFTER Radnitz had driven away, Thomas came into the room and looked anxiously at Girland.

"Did he say anything about me?" Thomas demanded.

Girland rubbed the back of his aching neck while he looked at Thomas's white, frightened face.

"I told him I was in the club an hour before you sealed it off," he said. "It seemed to make him happy: should make you happy too."

Borg and Schwartz came into the room. Borg grinned at Girland.

"You're pretty smart," he said. "I was getting ready to dig a hole for you."

"I'm smart all right." Girland looked at Thomas. "It's getting past my bedtime. I'll have my gun."

Thomas hurriedly gave him the .45 which Girland pushed into his holster.

"This could be the beginning of a beautiful friendship," Girland said and moved to the door. He paused and looked directly at Schwartz, "Business before pleasure, Stone-face. I'll even the score when we have wrapped up this little job."

He went out of the room to the sound of Borg's explosive laugh.

The time now was a little after one o'clock, but Girland had something to do before he went to bed. With some difficulty he found a taxi and told the driver to take him to *Le Figaro* building on Champs Elysée.

When the taxi pulled up before the arched entrance leading to the offices of the newspaper, Girland paid, got out and walked to the busy reception desk.

"Mr. Verney in?" he asked the elderly woman who looked at him with tired eyes.

"He's in his office. Who shall I say?"

Girland spelt out his name.

The woman spoke on the telephone, then beckoned to a girl in a blue overall who came over. She told her to take Girland to Verney's office. The girl had a nice figure, but it was a pity, Girland thought that her nose was too sharp and her mouth bad-tempered. He followed her into the small lift, reached the third floor, then followed her swaying hips down a long corridor to a tiny office where Jacques Verney was sitting behind a desk, talking on the telephone.

Verney was a leg man for the paper's gossip columnist. He was thin and dark with close cut hair, a chin beard and a taste for loud sports clothes that set Girland's teeth on edge.

He waved to a chair when he saw Girland, completed his conversation and then hung up.

"Hello, Mark," he said. "What's it this time?"

He and Girland had known each other for a long time. Verney had his suspicions that Girland was some kind of agent, but there had been a time, some three years ago when Girland had given him money to help him out of a very tight jam. Verney had known that Girland couldn't afford to part with the money, but he had parted with it. This was something Verney hadn't forgotten. He was happy to give Girland any information he could supply without asking questions.

Girland sat down and offered Borg's pack of cigarettes. When the two men were smoking, he said, "What do you know about Herman Radnitz, staying at the George V Hotel?"

Verney squinted at Girland through the cigarette smoke.

"Radnitz? Why, surely, everyone knows about him."

"I don't," Girland said, a slight edge to his voice. "I wouldn't be here if I did."

"Sorry, Mark," Verney said. "I just assumed everyone did know about him."

"Who is he and what is he?"

"Well, suppose you want to build a dam in Hong Kong. Suppose you want to put up a power plant in Bombay. Suppose you want to launch a car ferry service between England and Denmark. Before you start even to think about it, you'd consult Radnitz who would fix the financial end. Radnitz handles anything big that costs big money." Verney tapped ash off his cigarette. "He's in practically everything: ships, oil, building construction, aircraft. You ask who he is. He's Mr. Big Business."

Girland frowned. His neck was aching again.

"Then why the hell haven't I heard of him if he's that big?"

Verney smiled.

"He hates publicity. He knows all the newspaper bosses. He helps them, so they lay off him. He's the Rasputin of finance: probably the most powerful magnate in the world."

"Any idea what he's worth?"

"None at all. I'll bet he could lay ten million pounds sterling on the table without disturbing his financial balance. He's big. Mark: really Mr. Big."

Girland shifted on the hard seat of his chair.

"Does he live permanently at George V?"

"He doesn't live permanently anywhere. He has a château in the Loire district. He has his own place in Paris. He has places all over the world, but he seldom lives in them. He prefers a good hotel. He lost his wife a couple of years ago, so why should he worry about a permanent home? He moves around all the time. He's just back from Moscow. It wouldn't surprise me if he hadn't put in a bid for the Kremlin as a week-end place. He's that kind of a man."

Girland became alert.

"What was he doing in Moscow?"

"I wouldn't know," Verney said and shrugged. "More big business." He looked thoughtfully at Girland. "You come in from time to time and ask all kinds of questions, but this is the oddest. I wouldn't have thought you would have interested yourself in Radnitz."

"It's for my scrapbook," Girland said and got to his feet. "Well, thanks, Jacques. I'll leave you to get on with your work. Don't pine for me. You'll see me before long."

"I don't ask questions," Verney said, his face serious, "but as you are my friend, I have to warn you to have nothing to do with Radnitz. He's dangerous."

"Thanks." Girland smiled. "When I have saved up enough money, I'll buy you a beautiful dinner."

He waved his hand and left the office. After he had taken the lift to the ground floor, he walked out into the chilly wind that blew up the Champs Elysées.

He found a taxi to take him back to his apartment. He climbed the stairs slowly, thinking, so this is how it feels like to be old. It had been quite a night, he thought, but now, at last, I'm free of Rossland, and I'm heading for the big money.

In his apartment, he stripped off his clothes and took a hot shower, then he put on pyjama trousers and flopped into bed.

In the darkness, he thought about this mysterious woman,

Radnitz and Robert Henry Carey. He thought too of Rossland, lying alone in his room, his finger nails torn off, his face congested and very dead.

His final thought before he fell asleep was of Tessa, with her long legs, her blonde hair and her compactly built, beautiful body.

Sleep closed over him and washed even her out of his mind.

The telephone bell brought Dorey out of a light doze. He was sitting at his desk, his head in his hands. He stiffened to attention, glanced at his desk clock and saw it was twenty minutes after three.

Janine, lying on the settee, started out of an uneasy sleep and half sat up.

Dorey lifted the receiver.

"Hello, yes? Dorey here."

"This is O'Halloran. I'm calling from Orly airport," a tough cop voice said. Captain Tim O'Halloran was one of the best officers of the American Security Branch. "Drawn blank down here. We've checked thoroughly. During the past week, around a hundred or so Senegalese have passed through the barriers. She might have been amongst them, but I doubt it. We've gone through all the embarkation cards. Most of the women were with men and those on their own were old. Do you think he was travelling with a man, Mr. Dorey?"

"I don't know. I don't see why not."

"Well, okay, I'll get some of the boys to check all the married couples. It'll be a job, but it can be done. She might have come in by boat. S.S. *Ancerville* berthed a couple of days go. I've alerted the police at Marseilles to check. There was also a cargo boat from Dakar, berthing at Dunkirk. She could have been on that."

"How long will all this take?" Dorey demanded.

"For a complete check at least five days. Best we can do."

"She could have left the country by then," Dorey said.

"I don't think so, Mr. Dorey. We're now ready for her. She can't get out. We've sewn up the airports, the trains, and the ships. We may take time to find her, but if she tries to leave, we'll have her."

Dorey thought bitterly, She'll probably be dead by then. "Okay, Captain, do your best. This is urgent."

"We'll keep working on it," O'Halloran said and hung up.

Janine looked inquiringly at Dorey who shrugged.

"You're right: we're too late. They can't hope to trace her within five days." He rubbed his hand across his forehead. "What has a woman from Senegal got to sell that's important enough for Radnitz to have a man killed?"

"Why don't you send one of your men to Rossland's place and search it? He might have kept records of his men," Janine said. "We should have looked ourselves."

"If someone had walked in on us, we would have been in a hell of a mess," Dorey said. He thought for a moment, then reached for the telephone. "Jack Kerman could do it." He dialled, then waited. A sleepy voice demanded who was calling. Dorey quickly explained what he wanted done. "This is top priority, Kerman. I must have a list of Rossland's operators. Go over there and take the place to pieces."

The man at the other end of the line was alert now.

"Can do . . . will do," and he hung up.

Dorey nodded to Janine.

"He might find something."

"We're late starters," Janine said. "This man of Rossland's could be dead by now."

Dorey said, "I'll put two men to watch Radnitz's hotel. If they spot this youth with a beard, we'll pick him up and we'll talk to him the way they talked to Rossland."

Janine got stiffly to her feet.

"Now you're getting into gear, John. I'm going home. I need my beauty sleep."

Dorey hesitated, then he waved to a door.

"You can use my spare room. Go ahead. Save yourself a journey."

Janine smiled as she shook her head.

"I like sleeping in my own bed: even if I don't always sleep in it alone. I like my own night clothes and my own toothbrush. Good night."

"If I have any news, I'll call you," Dorey said, not getting up. He was reaching for the telephone.

"But not before ten unless it is urgent," Janine returned and put on her mink coat.

"I won't call you at all unless it's urgent," Dorey said and dialling, he began to talk into the mouthpiece.

Janine let herself out of the apartment and rode down in the lift to where her car was parked.

A little after eleven o'clock the following morning, Girland was frying eggs and bacon and grimacing with pain every time he moved his head when someone rapped on his front door.

He cursed under his breath, lowered the flame of the gas, then patting his hip pocket to make sure he was carrying his gun, he walked softly over to the door and peered through the spy hole.

Borg, wearing a leather hat and a leather coat, stood just by the head of the stairs, waiting.

Girland opened the door.

"There you are, palsy," Borg said, his thick lips moving into a friendly grin. "How's the neck?"

"Like hell," Girland said, moving aside to let Borg come in. He noted Borg was carrying a black leather briefcase.

"I'll fix that," Borg said, sniffed and lifted his scanty eyebrows. "Hmm . . . smells good!"

"Want some? There's plenty," Girland said, shutting the door.

"Not for me. I've had mine." Borg slapped his paunch. "I gotta watch this: like twins: grows all the time, but don't let me stop you."

"You won't," Girland said and going back to the stove, he expertly dished up the bacon and eggs and carried the meal over to the table.

Borg looked around.

"Nice nest you have here: except for those goddamn stairs."

"Coffee?" Girland asked, pouring a cup for himself.

"Always ready for coffee," Borg took off his hat and coat and sat down opposite Girland. He helped himself to black coffee without sugar, lit a cigarette and watched Girland as he began to wolf down his meal.

Neither of the men said anything until Girland had finished. Then with a sigh of satisfaction, Girland carried the plate to the sink. He lit a cigarette and came back to the table and sat down.

"You remember Kid Hogan?" Borg asked. "The best lightweight for years? I bet you do. At one time I used to be his trainer. He went on the skids after he lost the world title. That put me on the skids too. What I mean is if that neck of yours is bothering you, I can fix it."

"Go ahead and fix it," Girland said and finished his coffee.

Borg took a small white pot from his pocket.

"Get on the bed. This is bear's grease. Stinks a bit, but it fixes anything."

Ten minutes later, Girland sat up, moved his head cautiously, then more violently and jumped to his feet.

"You've fixed it!"

Borg grinned happily and went over to the toilet basin to wash his hands.

"I told you: it fixes anything." Then he looked over at the briefcase lying on the bed. "Got the money for you," he went on. "The boss gave it to me for you this morning."

Girland crossed over to the briefcase, but Borg, still grinning, blocked him off.

"Hold it, palsy," he said. "There are strings to this dough. There are seven thousand bucks in there. You have to be sure she knows where this guy Carey is before you give her the rest. Understand?"

Girland thought about this. It was fair, he decided. This woman could be leading them on.

"That's okay," he said, opened the briefcase and counted the money. Satisfied it was in order, he put it back in the case and snapped the fastening shut.

"I'm glad you have joined our mob," Borg said, helping himself to more coffee. "It's been run too long by that spineless wonder, Thomas. Okay, he's smart, and he's done a couple of jobs that made an impression, but if there's one thing that drives me nuts it's being bossed around by a kid."

"Stone-face seems a little dangerous," Girland said, also pouring more coffee. "Has he been with your outfit long?"

"Too long," Borg grimaced. "He's an animal, but he serves his purpose. We have to have one toughie and he's just that. The things that guy has done makes me puke to think about. Radnitz pays well, but look at the way that guy lives ... worse than a hog."

"What does Radnitz want men like you for?" Girland asked casually. "Just what do you do for him?"

"Oh, jobs," Borg said vaguely, finished his coffee and stood up. "I have to run along. I have a date with a blonde who works nights and sleeps days. Don't lose that money. So long," and he was gone.

Girland locked the door after him, then went back to the briefcase, opened it and spread the money out onto his bed. He had never seen so much money in one lot, but beside what fifty thousand dollars would look like, this was chick-feed.

He stared at the money for some time, then once more counted it. He put aside five thousand dollars and put two thousand in the briefcase. He decided he would give Madame Foucher two thousand dollars and put the rest in his bank. When she had told him where Carey was, he would get the rest of the money from Radnitz and give it to her: this way, he would be sure of keeping his own profit.

He lit a cigarette and considered the situation.

He had a slight feeling of guilt. Rossland had given him an assignment and had paid him to do it. Girland knew the money had come from Dorey. If Radnitz hadn't appeared on the scene with his offer of fifty thousand dollars, Girland would have, by now, contacted Dorey.

He moved uneasily. Then he thought of how he had nearly lost his life crossing the roofs to the cellar club, how Schwartz had nearly broken his neck and he thought of Dorey's mean payment.

Radnitz is right, he thought. I'm a small man in a badly paid job. This is my big chance. I'd be a dope not to go along with Radnitz. Somehow I have to get fifty thousand dollars out of him and still let Carey live and keep alive myself. Now, how do I do that? Then he remembered what Madame Foucher had said about Carey being ill and wouldn't live long. It would be lucky for me if Carey conveniently dies after I've talked to him. Then I would be in a sweet position. But why is Radnitz so anxious to get rid of Carey? He frowned, then shrugged. That's not my affair. I've worked for Dorey for years for peanuts. Now, I'm heading for the big money.

He discovered to his irritation that he had still a feeling of guilt. Until now, he hadn't realised what a grip Rossland had had on his life. He knew he should contact Dorey, but he also knew he wasn't going to.

While Girland was eating his breakfast, watched by Borg. Dorey sat at his desk in the Embassy, talking on the telephone to Jack Kerman.

"No luck," Kerman said. "I really took that apartment to pieces, but he didn't keep his records there . . . if he kept any records at all."

Dorey made an exasperated movement with his hand.

"All right, Jack, thanks. Forget it."

"Look, Mr. Dorey, Rossland is getting a little high. Shouldn't we do something about it?"

"Yes, of course. Call the nearest police station from a café and report a dead man in Rossland's apartment. Get away quickly."

"I'll do that, Mr. Dorey," Kerman said and hung up.

Dorey rubbed his tired eyes, then looked distastefully at the pile of files in his In tray. He kept asking himself what this Senegalese woman had to sell that was big enough for Rossland to be murdered. As he reached for a file, the telephone bell rang.

It was Captain O'Halloran calling.

"Could be we have a little luck, Mr. Dorey," he said, his cop voice bouncing against Dorey's ear-drum. "A Senegalese woman answering the description you gave me was on board a cargo Motor Vessel that berthed at Antwerp three days ago. I've talked to the ship's captain. He knows nothing about her. She remained in her cabin for the length of the trip. According to him, she was a bad sailor and they certainly hit bad seas. I've sent a telex to Dakar and our man there checked the address on her Embarkation card. No such place exists. She could have rented a car and driven to Paris. I'm checking."

Dorey was very alert now.

"Check the Belgium and French frontier police to see if they remember her," he said. "You instructed Dakar really to dig for information about her? If her passport is in order . . ."

O'Halloran said, a slightly bored note in his voice, "All that's being looked after. She could have been travelling on a faked passport. I have the French police working on this: they're checking the Paris hotels. This can't be wrapped up in five hours, Mr. Dorey. I said five days. Anyway, at least we are making progress. I'll be willing to bet this Rosa Arbeau is the woman you want."

"Good work, Captain," Dorey said. "Keep at it," and he hung up.

He sat for some minutes thinking, then glanced at his watch. The time was twenty to twelve. He called Janine. After a little delay, she answered and her voice sounded cross.

When she learned it was Dorey calling, she said, "I was in my bath, John. What is it now?"

"Have lunch with me at one o'clock," Dorey said. "We seem to be making a little progress. Shall we say Lasserre?"

"All right," Janine said and broke the connection.

At ten minutes to seven, Girland, carrying the briefcase under his arm, walked into a noisy café off Avenue Mozart. He went up to the bar and shook hands with the barman.

"I'm expecting a telephone call at seven, Jean," he said. "I'll be over there in a corner."

Jean, grey-haired, big, his face cheerful, winked.

"A woman, of course."

Girland grinned.

"What else? A monkey?" He ordered a Scotch on the rocks then carried his drink to a corner table and sat down.

He glanced at his watch, a movement that revealed his impatience, then drank some of the whisky.

At exactly seven o'clock, he saw Jean waving to him. He hadn't heard the telephone bell above the uproar of voices in the café.

He went quickly to the end of the bar and picked up the receiver.

"This is Girland," he said.

"Is it yes or no?" He recognised Madame Foucher's voice.

"The answer is yes."

He heard her draw in a quick, sharp breath.

"You have the money with you?"

"I have some of it."

"What do you mean?"

"You'll get the rest when you've shown me where he is."

"How much are you giving me now?"

"Two thousand."

There was a long pause and Girland wondered, suddenly uneasy, if he had been too generous to himself.

"Very well," she said finally. "I will be in the first-class waiting-room, St. Lazare station at half past eight." And she hung up.

Girland replaced the receiver, waved to the barman, then went through to the restaurant. He ordered an Entrecôte with fried potatoes, a green salad and a carafe of Beaujolais.

Just after eight o'clock, he settled his bill and went out into the crowded street. He had some trouble in finding a taxi, and when the taxi finally pulled up outside the station, the time was one minute after eight-thirty.

He walked briskly to the first-class waiting-room and paused for a moment to peer through the glass doors.

A woman and a small child were sitting on one of the benches: further along, an elderly man, nursing an untidy brown paper parcel, was dozing. On the opposite side of the room, sitting in a corner, was a handsome coloured woman, dressed in a black coat and skirt. Her long slim legs were crossed and her hands were folded in her lap. She had the stillness and the unreality of an ebony statue.

Girland pushed open the door and walked into the room. A train crawled to a halt at the platform beyond the waiting-room. The woman with the child took the child's hand and hurried out.

Girland hesitated, then as he was about to sit down, the coloured woman gave him a slight nod and signed for him to sit by her side.

Girland was startled. The last person he was expecting to deal with was an African. He went over and sat down.

"Madame Foucher?" he asked, aware of the sensual attractiveness of the woman.

"Yes." He saw her large liquid black eyes look intently at the briefcase he was carrying. "You have the money?"

"Two thousand dollars in cash."

"May I see?"

Girland glanced across the room at the old man who was still dozing, then he unzipped the case and handed it to her. She peered at the contents.

"You are sure there are two thousand dollars in there?"

"Yes."

"I must have more."

"You will, later."

She hesitated, then zipped up the case and put it on the bench on her far side.

"Well? Where is he?" Girland asked.

"Diourbel, some miles from Dakar."

Girland stared at her.

"You mean he's not in Paris?"

"I never said he was in Paris. He's in the bush outside Diourbel, where no one can possibly find him."

Girland's mouth hardened.

"Suppose he's not there? Suppose this is a gag to pick up some easy money?"

"I will take you to him."

Girland rubbed the side of his jaw, frowning.

"Well, all right. Now about you. Who are you and how did you get mixed up in this?"

"I work in a nightclub in Dakar. I . . ."

"Don't rush it. What's the name of the nightclub?"

"The Florida. It is the best nightclub there."

"Well, go on."

"A client of mine . . . he often comes to the club . . . asked me if I would like to make ten thousand dollars."

"What is his name?"

"I don't know. I call him Enrico. He is a Portuguese."

"What's he look like?"

"He is heavily built with a moustache. He wears a very large gold signet ring on his left little finger. He dresses well and he pays very well."

"Go on."

"He said I was to go to Paris and I was to telephone Mr. Dorey about a certain man. He said Mr. Dorey would give me ten thousand dollars."

"So you haven't actually seen Robert Henry Carey?"

"Yes, I have seen him. When Enrico said he would pay all my expenses, I didn't see what I had to lose. So I said I would go. He took me out into the bush where I met this man." She opened her handbag and took from it a quarter plate sized photograph which she offered to Girland.

He studied the photograph. It was a close-up shot of Carey and Madame Foucher. He recognised Carey although he looked much older and thinner than when Girland had last seen him. It was unmistakably Carey. The photograph had been taken from a low view point and only the sky showed as the background.

"May I keep this?"

"Yes."

Girland put the photo in his wallet. At least, he thought, that should convince Radnitz.

"You talked to Carey?"

"Yes. He told me what I told you last night."

"Last night, you said he was ill."

"Yes, he is ill."

"What's the matter with him?"

She lifted her shoulders.

"I don't know . . . something bad. I have seen men look like that before. I don't think he will live very long."

"Enrico was there when you two met?"

"Of course. He took the photograph because he said it would be convincing proof that I had met Carey."

"Did he and Carey seem friendly?"

"I suppose so. We didn't stay long. Enrico said I was to go by ship. He booked a cabin on a cargo vessel for me and I left three days after meeting Carey. I want to fly back tomorrow. If you will come with me, I will take you to Carey."

"I can't come tomorrow," Girland said. "I have to get a visa. As soon as I get it I will contact you and then we'll go."

"I must go tomorrow," she repeated.

"What time does the plane leave?"

"Twenty-one fifty."

"I'll see what I can do. Where can I contact you if I can't make it?"

She gave him an Odéon number and got to her feet. He was startled to see she was as tall as himself.

"I will expect to see you on the plane," she said. "There is one thing more. I must have three thousand more dollars before I will go with you. You must give it to me at the airport."

"I'll do that," Girland said, hoping he would be able to persuade Radnitz to part with more money.

She moved to the door which Girland opened for her. Without looking back, she went away, walking quickly towards the entrance to the Métro.

Girland watched her go. This could be the last time he set eyes on her, he told himself. If the money had belonged to him, watching her walk away with it so quietly and calmly would have given him a sleepless night. But the money belonged to Radnitz and Girland had five thousand of it already stashed away in his bank. He could afford to take a chance. If this finally turned out to be a hoax, he at least had been paid for his trouble.

He walked over to the taxi rank and told the driver to take him to George V Hotel.

The hotel bar was crowded as Girland paused in the doorway, then seeing an empty table for two near the door, he went over and sat down. A waiter appeared and Girland ordered a whisky on the rocks. He looked around the room and quickly spotted Radnitz sitting with two other men at a corner table across the room. Both his companions were elderly: one of them held an expensive looking briefcase on his knees. Radnitz was talking, making stabbing emphases with his thick finger. Girland lit a cigarette and sipped his drink. The millionaire showed no signs of recognising him. Finally, the three men got to their feet and moved out of the bar, still talking. As Radnitz passed Girland, he looked blankly at him, then passed on. Girland finished his drink. From where he sat he could see the three men talking in the lobby. They all shook hands, then the two men left and Radnitz went over to the desk and spoke to the clerk. Then he crossed to the lift and was whisked out of sight.

Two minutes later a page came up to Girland.

"Will you please go up to Suite 127, sir?" he said. "Mr. Radnitz is waiting for you."

Girland nodded, got to his feet, paid for his drink and then sauntered out into the lobby. He ignored the lift and walked up the stairs to the first floor. After making sure he had the long corridor to himself, he walked quickly past the numbered doors until he reached room number 127. He paused, looked to right and left, then knocked.

The door was immediately opened by a young Japanese servant, wearing a white coat and black silk trousers. Girland moved past him into a small hall. The Japanese opened a door and bowed him into a large, elegantly furnished room where Radnitz stood by the big window, looking down at the tightly packed, crawling traffic, struggling towards the Champs Elysées.

The Japanese closed the door behind Girland who waited.

Radnitz turned.

"Ah, Mr. Girland, come in and sit down. Will you have a drink?"

"No, thank you." Girland selected a comfortable armchair and sank into it.

"A cigar?"

"No, thank you."

Radnitz selected a cigar and took from his pocket a gold cigar cutter.

"What news?" he asked, coming over to another chair near Girland's and sitting down. He cut the cigar, examined it, then glanced at Girland. "You have met Madame Foucher?"

"I've met her," Girland said and briefly described the meeting.

Radnitz listened. When Girland gave him the photograph of Carey and Madame Foucher, he took it and stared at it for a long moment.

"Yes, that is Carey," he said finally and put the photograph on the table beside him. "You have done well, Mr. Girland. I am pleased with you."

Girland didn't say anything.

"You will of course go with this woman tomorrow night."

Radnitz paused to release a stream of expensive smelling smoke from between his thin lips. "I will arrange about your visa." He paused again, then went on, "Well now, Mr. Girland, here is where you begin to earn the fifty thousand dollars I promised you. You must not forget that Carey will believe you are representing Dorey. You must give him no reason to suspect otherwise. When you meet him find out what he has to offer. I think he has got hold of something of considerable importance. Whatever it is, it is to come to me and not Dorey. Is that understood?"

"Yes."

"When you are satisfied Carey has nothing more to tell you," Radnitz went on, "and that he has given you whatever it is he has taken from Russia, you will kill him." He got to his feet and walked over to a desk, opened a drawer and took from it a small box. He picked out a heavy gold signet ring. "See if this fits your finger, Mr. Girland," he said, handing the ring to Girland.

Girland found the ring fitted the third finger of his right hand well enough. Watching him, Radnitz nodded with approval and then stretched out his hand for the return of the ring. Girland gave it to him.

"This ring, Mr. Girland, has its uses. If you will come here, I will show you how it works."

Girland got to his feet and stood over Radnitz.

"This tiny plate bearing the initials slides off," Radnitz explained. "Like this." He pushed against the side of the ring and the flat top slid away without any trouble. In the tiny hollow, covered by the plate, was something that looked like a stiff hair that projected above the level of the plate. "When you say goodbye to Carey, you will naturally shake hands with him," Radnitz said. "You will be wearing this ring in the reversed position: that is, the seal will be turned inwards. This little bristle you see projecting from the ring will come into contact with Carey's fingers as you shake hands. That is all that is necessary. Within an hour after your handshake, Mr. Girland, Carey will be dead. As he is already ill, I doubt if much attention will be paid to his death. Even if there should be a post-mortem, the poison on the bristle is so rare, no doctor would be able to identify it. So you see, I am making things absurdly easy for you." He replaced the plate on the ring and then tossed the ring to Girland who caught it, stared at it, then slipped it on his finger. "How expert are you, Mr. Girland, in changing your appearance?" Radnitz asked as Girland sat down.

"Not bad ... why?"

"We mustn't underrate Dorey. No doubt he has been to that cellar club and from the doorman and the staff, he now has a good description of you and of Madame Foucher. There is nothing we can do about Madame Foucher. If they are watching the airport, then I think it is likely they will pick her up. It is a chance we must take. What is important, they must not pick you up." Radnitz touched ash off his cigar. "I have had the passengers' list examined. There are five American business men travelling on their own on the plane. You will be the sixth. Tomorrow morning, Borg will come to you with a new passport. You will be travelling under the name of John Gilchrist. The object of your visit to Dakar is to explore the possibilities of opening a factory in competition with Schweppes factory already installed outside Dakar. You must not overlook the fact that the Russians are also hunting for Carey. Their agents are almost certain to be in Dakar. They will be suspicious of you when you arrive as they will be of the other five business men. You will stay at the N'Gor Hotel for two days before trying to contact Carey. Leave the papers I will suppy you with in your hotel room so that their curiosity will be satisfied. Then after two days, and not before, you will contact Carey. Is all that understood?"

"But suppose Madame Foucher gets picked up at the airport?"

Radnitz lifted his heavy shoulders in a shrug.

"That is not your concern. You will get on the plane without her. It may take a little longer to find Carey without her, but you have two important leads. The Florida Club and this Portuguese. He must know where Carey is. If Madame Foucher can't help you, then you must rely on this man to do so."

"But if Madame Foucher is arrested and once she realises I'm not working for Dorey, she will talk," Girland said.

"Again that is no concern of yours. All that will be taken care of." Radnitz got to his feet. "There is every possibility that she won't be arrested. You are not to return to your apartment. It is possible that Dorey knows now who you are. I have booked a room for you in the name of John Gilchrist at the California Hotel. I often put American business men up there. They will not ask you to fill in a police card. You will go there now and you will remain in your room until Borg comes to you at ten o'clock tomorrow. He will bring everything necessary for the journey."

"Madame Foucher wants another three thousand dollars," Girland said. "She was emphatic about this."

Radnitz studied him.

"Still growing, Mr. Girland?"

"I'm not asking for anything for myself," Girland said. "It's for her."

"Very well. I will see the money is available," Radnitz said. "Good luck, Mr. Girland. When next we meet I hope you will be able to tell me Carey is dead."

Girland said good night, stared for a moment at Radnitz, then turning, he went out of the room.

Radnitz remained motionless, smoking his cigar until the Japanese servant came in and told him Girland had left the hotel.

"I want to talk to Schwartz," Radnitz said. "Find him."

The Japanese bowed and left the room.

Chapter Five

CAPTAIN O'HALLORAN was a tall, solidly built man of around thirty-eight years of age. He had a red fleshy face, the shapeless nose of a boxer and the eyes and mouth of a shrewd, ruthless cop.

He came into Dorey's office a few minutes after eight o'clock, closed the door, took off his peak cap and paused for an invitation to sit down.

Dorey pushed aside a file he was working on.

"Hello, Captain. Come in and sit down. Any news?"

"We nearly caught up with her half an hour ago," O'Halloran said, sinking into the big leather chair that faced Dorey's desk.

"She booked in at the Astor Hotel three days ago as Madame Foucher, Dakar. She checked out at six this evening. I'm pretty sure it's the same woman from the description. She is on her own, so that's something learned. She's probably moved to another hotel. The check is still going on and all the hotels are alerted to look out for her."

"No sign of this young fellow with the chin beard?"

"He hasn't been near the George V Hotel. I have a couple of boys staked out, waiting for him. So far, he's keeping clear of the place."

"Radnitz have any interesting visitors?"

O'Halloran shrugged.

"A stream of them. Some we know: some we don't."

Dorey moved his letter opener from the left side of his blotter to his right.

"I'm trying to trace an American," he said finally. "This man could be connected with this business, Captain. I have a description of him here." He took a sheet of paper from his desk drawer and handed it to O'Halloran. "Have you any suggestions as to how I find him?"

O'Halloran read the description, then looked at Dorey, a quizzing expression in his light blue eyes.

"Why do you imagine this man could help?"

Dorey rubbed the end of his beaky nose and avoided O'Halloran's cop stare. Until he had talked to this Senegalese woman, it would be dangerous to tell O'Halloran too many details.

"I can't tell you that, Captain: not just yet, anyway. But it is important that we find this man."

"Who gave you this description?"

"A man called Husson. He runs the 'Allo, Paris' club."

O'Hallorn looked interested.

"I know the joint. It's out of bounds to service men. We have had trouble with Husson in the past. Do you want me to go along and talk to him?"

"We want to find this man, Captain."

"Is he a resident in Paris?"

"Yes."

"Every American in Paris is registered with the Prefecture of Police," O'Halloran said. "They hold their dossiers and their photographs. Do you want me to take Husson along there and see if he can spot your man?"

Dorey felt a rush of blood to his face so angry was he with himself for not thinking of this simple solution as soon as Husson had given him Girland's description.

"I would be most grateful, Captain. When could you arrange to do it?"

"What's the matter with now?" O'Halloran asked. He looked at his watch. "No, the club doesn't open 'til ten. I'll send a couple of boys down there at ten, collect Husson, run him down to the Prefecture and we'll know who your man is in a couple of hours or less."

"And in the meantime, you will continue to search for this woman?"

"We'll keep hunting for her until we find her."

"If you find out who this American is," Dorey said, "call me at my apartment no matter how late it is."

"I'll do that," O'Halloran returned, and nodding, he left the office.

Dorey sat for some minutes, thinking, then he reached for the telephone and called Janine.

"The net's closing," he told her when she came on the line. "O'Halloran almost caught up with her this evening. He's now working on the identity of Rossland's man. I think by midnight we'll know who he is."

"Or who he was," Janine said. "Look, John, I'm in a rush. I'm catching the 21.50 plane to Dakar tomorrow night, and I have a lot to clear up."

Dorey stiffened.

"You're ... what?"

"I'm going to Dakar."

"I haven't authorised you to do that. You can't go rushing off without my say-so. It is a costly journey and I see no reason why you should go."

"I'm going, and I'm paying for myself," Janine said firmly. "I'll be more use there than I am here. I think Rossland's man is dead by now. You might telephone the American Embassy at Dakar and alert them that I am coming. I may need help."

Dorey thought for a moment. Now he was sure this wasn't going to cost the division anything, he began to see it was an excellent idea to have Janine out on the spot.

"Very well then," he said. "You may have some luck. You'll need a visa."

"I've seen to that," she said crisply. "If I find out anything important, I'll telephone you. Goodbye, John," and the line went dead.

Dorey returned to his apartment a little after ten o'clock. He sat down at his desk and began to work on papers he had brought with him from the Embassy. Around midnight, he cleared his desk, locked up his papers and went over to sit in one of the big easy chairs. He kept looking at his watch. He sat there, waiting, and when the telephone bell finally rang at ten minutes to one, he got hastily to his feet and snatched up the receiver.

"We've identified your man," O'Halloran told him. "His name is Mark Girland. He has a top floor studio apartment on Rue de Suisses. He describes himself as a free-lance journalist. The reason why I am calling you so late is because I went around to his place with a couple of the boys and gave it a going over. There's no doubt he's an agent. He has all the tools of the trade. He's not there, of course. The Concierge told me he left the apartment building around half past six, so he could still return. You want me to bring him down to H.Q. if we catch him?"

"Yes," Dorey said. "I want to talk to him. I don't want anyone else to question him. This could be a tricky one and the responsibility must be mine."

"If he shows I'll call you," O'Halloran said.

"He may be planning to go to Dakar with this woman," Dorey said. "You'll keep a watch at the airport for him?"

"We're already doing that," O'Halloran said, and hung up.

A little after ten o'clock the following morning, a tap came on Girland's hotel bedroom door.

He had just finished a substantial breakfast and was reading the *New York Herald Tribune*. He got silently to his feet and reached for his .45 automatic that lay on the table.

"Who is it?" he called.

"Me and a boy friend."

As soon as Girland recognised Borg's voice, he put the gun under the newspaper, crossed the room and unlocked the door.

Borg came in, followed by a thin, elderly man with a mop of white hair. Girland closed and locked the door as Borg and his companion took off their overcoats.

"This is Charlie," Borg said, jerking his thumb at the elderly man. "He's going to fix your face." He grinned. "A goddam marvel is Charlie. Your own mother won't recognise you by the time he's through with you."

Charlie had opened a suitcase he had brought with him, and humming under his breath, began to get out various boxes, bottles, a pair of scissors, a comb and a barber's towel.

"Now, sir," he said to Girland, "if you would just sit here."

Girland sat down and was enveloped in the towel. Borg took the only armchair, lit a cigarette and crossed one fat leg over the other.

"You get that bag I left at the hotel last night?"

"I got it," Girland said.

He had been surprised to find an expensive piece of air luggage in the room when the porter had shown him in. As soon as the porter had gone, Girland had opened the bag to find three expensive tropical suits, shirts, pyjamas, handkerchiefs, sports clothes, a dressing-gown, slippers, a selection of good ties, toilet accessories, a light-weight raincoat, sun glasses and a worn, but expensive looking wallet with the initial J.G. in gold and which was stuffed with Senegalese money. Once again, he had to admire Radnitz's thoroughness.

"It's a trick bag," Borg said. "There's a false bottom to it. Inside, you'll find everything you want for trouble. I'll show you how it works when Charlie is through with you."

73

Charlie at this moment was busily cutting Girland's thick hair to a crew cut. He then led Girland into the bathroom where he gave him a strong peroxide rinse. Girland lost count of time. Every so often, Borg would stare at him, mutter 'Sweet Pete!' and then return to reading the *Tribune*. Two and a half hours later, Charlie drew back and announced himself satisfied.

From the suitcase he now produced a heavy well cut suit, a white shirt with J.G. embroidered on the pocket, a pair of expensive looking brogue shoes and invited Girland to change.

Five minutes later, changed, Girland accepted a gold cigarette case, also bearing the initials J.G., a gold cigarette lighter, a monogrammed handkerchief, some small change in French currency, all of which he put in his various pockets. The nicest touch of all was a Diner Club ticket made out in the name of John Gilchrist which Borg handed to him with an expansive grin.

"Well, now, Mr. Gilchrist, take a look at yourself," Borg said and waved to the big mirror at the far end of the room.

Girland approached the mirror, paused and stared. He found himself looking at a tall, blond man with a typical American crew cut, whose startled eyes regarded him with interest. Even the lines of his lean face had been altered by the use of small rubber suction pads inside his mouth. A pencil line moustache, put on hair by hair, gave him a rakish man of the world appearance and his complexion, instead of being sallow from constant late nights was now heavily sun tanned. Charlie hadn't neglected his hands either and these matched his face. The transformation was so astonishing that Girland couldn't believe he was looking at himself and it was only when he lifted his arms and moved about before the mirror that he was convinced.

Charlie quickly packed away his things, nodded approvingly at Girland, then let himself out of the room.

"Knock out, isn't he?" Borg said. "I told you, didn't I? Your own mother wouldn't know you."

"I damn well don't know myself," Girland said, turning away from the mirror. "But will it all last? I mean this moustache? My hair will grow dark again."

"It'll last long enough," Borg said. "You can always touch up your hair if you have to. The moustache is waterproof. You can grow your own later. That sun tan will be replaced by your own tan as soon as you get into the African sun."

"I guess you're right." Girland put the wallet he had left on the table in his pocket.

Borg went over to the bag and showed Girland how the false bottom operated. In the recess was a .38 automatic, a flick knife, a small bottle containing a number of tablets which Borg explained were tasteless knock-out drops. "You can even drop one of these in water: they dissolve immediately and the drinker is put away for at least six hours," a lethal looking cosh and a box containing a hundred rounds of ammunition for the gun.

"Well, that's it," Borg said. "If there's anything else you can think of you'll want, just say so and I'll fix it. I was told to give you the V.I.P. treatment."

Girland shook his head.

"That's as complete an outfit as anyone would want," he said.

Borg picked up a bulky briefcase he had brought with him.

"You'd better spend the rest of the day, going through these papers. You are representing the Orangeolo Corporation of Florida. Here's all the dope. You're visiting Dakar to see if it is worth while setting up a factory there. You want to know by heart the names of the directors, the sales manager and the complete background of the Corporation. It's one of Radnitz's babies and if anyone takes the trouble to check, they'll back you." He looked at his watch. "Time for lunch. I'll pay your hotel check and take your bag to the air terminal. You'd better clear off now. Walk down the stairs. No one will recognise you. Take the briefcase ... there's five grand in big bills in there ... and go somewhere where you can work through all the dope." He grinned cheerfully at Girland. "Well, so long and good luck."

Girland nodded, picked up the heavy briefcase and after shaking hands with Borg, he let himself out of the hotel bedroom and walked quickly down the stairs.

Away from the hotel, he went to a café and called the number Madame Foucher had given him. When he got her on the line, he told her would be on the aircraft that night.

"I have your money," he went on. "I don't know what you are going to do with it. You'd better not take it through the Customs."

"I am at the Palace Hotel," she told him. "Will you bring the money to the hotel and leave it with the hall porter for me?"

"I'll be around in half an hour," Girland said. "Once again, don't try to walk it through the Customs control."

"I'll manage," she said impatiently. "Just bring it to my hotel."

At 20.30 hours, Girland arrived at the Air terminal in a taxi. He walked briskly to where the bus to the airport stood waiting.

He spotted Borg, sitting on a bench, Girland's suitcase at his feet. He slowed his pace as Borg stood up and walked away. Without stopping, Girland picked up the suitcase and went on to the bus.

At the airport, he checked in the suitcase, got his boarding ticket, and then joined the small queue passing through the Police control. Just ahead of him was a smartly dressed woman, and as she handed her French passport: Janine Daulnay. He admired her small waist and her long, slim legs, then as she passed through the barrier, it was his turn to hand in his faked passport. He became aware of a large, bulky man standing behind the control officer. By the cut of his hair and by the steady movement of his jaws as he chewed gum, Girland recognised him as an American. He guessed he would be one of Dorey's security officers.

Both the control officer and the American stared intently at Girland who looked back at them with an indifferent expression. The control officer examined his passport, then handed it to the American who also examined it.

"What is your reason for going to Dakar, monsieur?" the control officer asked as the American handed back the passport.

"Business purposes," Girland said.

"What business?"

Girland zipped open the bulky briefcase, took from it a printed card and a letter. Both the control officer and the American examined the card and read the letter that came from Orangeolo Corporation of Florida, instructing John Gilchrist to investigate the possibilities of finding a site in Dakar for a branch factory.

The control officer looked over his shoulder at the American who was scribbling down the address of the Corporation in a notebook. The American nodded and the control officer stamped Girland's passport and waved him through.

Girland walked into the enclosure where Customs officers were checking the baggage. He glanced back over his shoulder. At the end of the queue, Madame Foucher had suddenly appeared. She was carrying a large handbag and under her arm, the briefcase that Girland had given her.

Girland winced. Surely she wasn't crazy enough to attempt to pass through the Customs with all that money under her arm, he thought. Before she was within ten yards of the Passport control window, three men, one a French police inspector, the other two obviously American policemen in plain clothes, cut her out of the queue and surrounded her.

Girland, his hands clammy, watched. He saw Madame Foucher protesting. People began to stare. Then quickly the three men moved away with her, heading for the Security Police office.

No one noticed Schwartz as he sat on a bench by himself, his hand in his trench coat pocket, a cigarette hanging from his thin lips.

Radnitz had given him his orders the previous night.

"If this woman is arrested at the airport, she is not to talk. Is that understood?" Radnitz had said. "Take any risk. She's not to talk."

Madame Foucher and the three policemen were coming towards him. One of the Americans walked behind, the French Inspector and the other American walked either side of her. Her big black eyes rolled with terror and her lips were trembling.

Schwartz's finger closed around the trigger of the hidden gun. He was confident the silencer on the gun, together with the noise of the jet aircraft warming up would conceal the sound of the shot.

He lifted the gun inside his pocket. It was a difficult shot as it had to be lethal, but Schwartz was no stranger to difficult shots. He squeezed the trigger and felt the gun recoil in his hand. He heard a faint 'plop' as the gases from the firing gun were trapped in the silencer. He saw Madame Foucher stagger, then fall forward as the French Inspector made a futile grab at her.

Casually, Schwartz withdrew his hand from his pocket and flicked open a newspaper he had on his lap. As he began to open it, he seemed to become aware that something had happened. Already a crowd of people surrounded the three policemen and the fallen body of the Senegalese woman.

Girland saw what had happened through the glass partition, then the Customs officer arrived and asked him if he had anything to declare.

"No . . . nothing," Girland said, an empty cold feeling in the pit of his stomach.

"Would you please open your bag, sir?"

Girland opened the bag.

Quickly, but thoroughly, the official went through the contents of the bag. While he was doing this, Girland again looked through the partition. He caught sight of Schwartz who was standing on the fringe of the crowd peering over their heads, and Girland knew at once what had happened. He had no doubt that Schwartz had killed the woman on Radnitz's orders.

"Thank you, sir," the Customs officer said and chalked Girland's bag. "Straight through to your right."

Picking up his bag, Girland walked towards the embarkation bay where some thirty people were already waiting.

As a number of police officers began to break up the crowd, Schwartz turned aside and walked out of the airport and across to where Borg was waiting in the black Citroen. He got in, and Borg, sweat showing on his fat face, drove carefully and without hurrying towards the Autoroute.

The police quickly carried Madame Foucher's body into the Police Security office and shut the door on the gaping crowd. One of the American officers put a call through to Captain O'Halloran while the other examined the body. He stood away and cursed.

"Dead and shot," he said. Turning to the French Inspector, he went on, "The killer's out there somewhere. Get your men and check." He knew it was a useless order. By now the killer would have vanished.

John Dorey was thinking about going to bed when his front doorbell rang. He glanced at his watch and saw the time was twenty to twelve. Frowning, he went to the door and peered through the spy-hole. Seeing Captain O'Halloran waiting outside, he unlocked and opened the door.

"Come in, Captain," he said, standing aside. He saw by the grim expression on O'Halloran's face that he had bad news.

It wasn't until O'Halloran had sunk into one of the big comfortable chairs and lit a cigarette that he said, "The Senegalese woman you wanted to talk to, Mr. Dorey, is dead. She was shot when we arrested her."

Dorey stood staring at him. His face seemed to become thinner, his eyes behind the thick lenses of his glasses turned a shade darker.

He walked slowly to his desk and sat down.

"Who shot her?" he asked finally.

"I don't know. We spotted her as she was about to pass through the police control. Two of my men with Inspector Delrieu approached her and he asked her to go with them to the Security

78

office. She became terrified, but she went with them. It was only a short walk, but suddenly she dropped, and at first, my men thought she had fainted. They carried her into the office and as soon as they examined her they found she had been shot and was dead. The gun was obviously silenced. There was a jet aircraft warming up. No one heard the shot or saw the killer."

Dorey rubbed his temples with the tips of his fingers.

O'Halloran opened a briefcase he had brought with him.

"This belonged to her. It contains seven thousand dollars and a passport made out in the name of Rosa Arbeau. I'm having the passport checked with the Dakar police."

Dorey took the briefcase and examined the dollar bills.

"Any hope of tracing these?"

"No."

"Any news of Girland?"

"Not yet. He certainly wasn't on the plane that left for Dakar tonight. We checked everyone. My men will continue to wait there and we have alerted all shipping to Dakar."

Dorey wasn't surprised. He was now firmly convinced that Girland had suffered the same fate as Rossland.

"We don't seem to have any luck, do we, Captain?" he said. "Well, all right, let's leave it for tonight. I'll keep this," he waved to the briefcase. "No sign of this boy with the beard? He seems to be our only hope now."

"No sign of him. My men are still watching the hotel. He could show, of course, any time and if he does, we'll have him."

When he had gone, Dorey sat for some minutes, thinking. He was thankful now that Janine had had the sense to leave for Dakar. He would have to send her a coded cable to tell her the Senegalese woman was dead. The scene of activity now seemed to Dorey to be shifting to Senegal. Abruptly, he decided to send Jack Kerman to Dakar in case Janine needed help. Kerman was a good man. Dorey now regretted he hadn't sent Kerman to meet Madame Foucher instead of leaving her to Rossland to deal with.

He reached for the telephone and in a few moments he was talking to Kerman.

"I want you around here, Kerman," he said. "It's urgent."

Kerman said, "Can do . . . will do," and hung up.

Twenty minutes later he was sitting in the chair recently occupied by O'Halloran and listening to Dorey talk.

Kerman was a small, wiry man, around thirty-three, with

brown hair cut in a crew cut, alert eyes and a humorous, pleasing appearance. He made a reasonable living as partner in a garage which left him time to work for Dorey when Dorey needed him.

Dorey gave him the picture of what had been happening, omitting no details.

"This has now got a little out of hand," he concluded. "Frankly, Kerman, I should have given O'Halloran's report to Warley. It is obvious this woman had vital information to sell which Radnitz is determined should not be known. You know how I feel about Radnitz. It has always been my ambition to nail him. From the very beginning, I should have reported to Warley. I know that, but Warley being what he is and I being what I am, I didn't do it. Now I am sure Radnitz is mixed up in this, I am even less inclined to bring Warley into it. If I can pull the rug from under Radnitz's feet, I'll have achieved something no one else has achieved in spite of trying their damnedest. You see that, don't you?"

Kerman nodded.

"I'll go along with you, Mr. Dorey. You tell me what you want done and I'll do it."

"Janine Daulnay is already on her way to Dakar. She's no fool and she may be able to pick up the trail out there, I want you to catch tomorrow's plane and join her. Working together, you could find out what this woman had to sell and why Radnitz is involved."

Kerman bit his thumb as he stared at Dorey.

"All this is going to cost money," he pointed out. "If it is to remain unofficial, where's the money coming from?"

Dorey picked up the briefcase on his desk.

"There's seven thousand dollars in here, Kerman. The Foucher woman had it with her. It's my bet the money came from Radnitz. It would be poetic justice if we used Radnitz's money to bring him down. Take it. I'll arrange the visa for you. Come to my office at nine tomorrow morning with your passport and photographs. I'll have everything fixed for you by then."

"Well, okay," Kerman said. "You're still sure you shouldn't bring Warley into it?"

"Never mind Warley," Dorey said sharply. "You do what I tell you."

"This guy Girland. I've heard of him although I've never met him. Do you think he'll try to get to Dakar?"

"I think he's dead. The last I heard of him, he was in the

hands of Radnitz's men. They are almost certain to have treated him as they treated Rossland."

Kerman looked down at his hands.

"Radnitz might have bought him, Mr. Dorey. Thought of that?"

Dorey looked startled.

"What do you men . . . bought him?"

"Let's face facts," Kerman said. "You don't pay all that well, Mr. Dorey. Don't think I'm complaining, I'm not, but Radnitz has all the money in the world. He could have made it worth while for Girland to change sides."

Dorey thought about this, then shook his head.

"Radnitz has his own organisation. Why should he waste money on a man like Girland? It would be much simpler to get rid of him. Girland's dead. I'm sure of it."

Kerman got to his feet.

"Well, okay, then tomorrow at your office at nine."

Borg drove the Citroen back from the Airport to his apartment on Rue Louise-Michel. Neither he nor Schwartz had exchanged a word during the drive. Borg pulled up outside his apartment block and the two men took the lift to the fourth floor. Borg unlocked the door and entered a big, sunny room with lounging chairs, a table, a big mirror over the fireplace and on the walls, framed reproductions of naked girls he had picked up at a tourist *boutique* on the left bank.

Thomas was sitting in one of the chairs, nervously flicking through a copy of *Lui*. He had been staying with Borg for the past two days, and he had been instructed by Radnitz to keep off the streets.

"Well?" he asked, staring at Schwartz.

Schwartz sneered at him and pointed to a small hole in his rainproof pocket.

"Is she dead?"

"I don't make mistakes, white-headed boy," Schwartz said and sat down.

Borg went into the kitchen and took from the refrigerator two cans of beer. He poured the beer into glasses and gave Schwartz one and drank from the other himself.

Thomas looked at the two men uneasily, then went back to his aimless fidgeting with the magazine.

Schwartz lit a cigarette and leaning back in his chair, closed his eyes. Borg refilled his glass and went over to the window to stare out into the street below.

Ten minutes later, the front doorbell rang. Borg opened the door.

Radnitz entered and stood looking at the three men. Thomas and Schwartz got to their feet.

"So you had to kill her," Radnitz said to Schwartz.

"They were on to her. When she reached the barrier, they jumped her. She looked ready to spill her guts so I shot her."

Radnitz moved around the room, his heavy face dark and scowling.

"If Girland doesn't produce something in three days, you and Borg are to go to Dakar," he said, pausing to look at Schwartz. "You are to work with him. I don't entirely trust him. Understand?"

Schwartz nodded.

"But what about me, sir?" Thomas asked. "Don't I go?"

"You are going to London," Radnitz snapped. "Get rid of that ridiculous beard. Dorey's men are looking for you. For the time being you are of no use to me. Report to my London office. They might find something for you to do."

Thomas turned red, then white. "Yes, sir."

"And be careful how you leave Paris." Radnitz took a roll of money from his pocket and tossed it on the table. "Split this amongst you. You, Schwartz are to have fifty per cent of it. You have done well," then ignoring Thomas, he left the apartment.

As Schwartz crossed the room to the money on the table, he said with a sneer, "He doesn't seem to love our little pal any more, does he?"

Girland gave the air hostess his embarkation ticket, then mounted the steps behind the slowly moving line of passengers making their way into the tourist section of the aircraft.

He moved down the aisle, saw an outside vacant seat just ahead of him, slid into it and sat down. He became aware that he was sitting next to Janine Daulnay, the smartly dressed woman whose name he had read on her passport. She was occupying herself with fastening her safety belt and with a quick, approving glance at her, Girland also fastened his belt. He then put his briefcase on the floor and settled himself comfortably in his seat.

It was now Janine's turn to look at him. Their eyes met and she said, "Did you see what happened to that coloured woman?

They were arresting her, weren't they? I saw you watching. From where I was I couldn't see much. I thought she fainted. Is that right?"

Girland looked into her large wordly eyes. He thought she was one of the most attractive women he had seen for a long time.

"Well, she certainly fell down," he said. "I wouldn't know what happened. It's my guess she was trying to smuggle something through and they got on to her. That's just my guess for what it's worth."

The jet engines started up with a roar, silencing any further conversation. Girland lay back and closed his eyes. Janine looked at him. She thought: Hmmmm . . . quite a man. Speaks French fluently, but he's an American. I like the line of his jaw and his hands: strong but gentle. Yes . . . quite a man.

Girland was worried. His only lead now to Carey was through this Portuguese known as Enrico. If he couldn't find him, he wouldn't find Carey.

The aircraft began to race along the runway and in a few seconds was airborne. Girland released his safety belt and took out his cigarette case. He offered it to Janine who took a cigarette. When they were smoking, he said, "My name's John Gilchrist. Is this your first trip to Dakar?"

"I'm Janine Daulnay. Yes, it is my first trip," Janine replied. "I'm only going for a couple of weeks: just to get some sun."

"Madame Daulnay?" Girland asked, smiling at her.

She laughed.

"No. I find life more amusing being single. Are you married?"

Girland shook his head.

"For the same reason."

They both laughed, then she said, "You speak French very well, but you are an American, aren't you?"

"My mother was French. They tell me it's pretty hot in Dakar right now, but the N'Gor Hotel beach is something special."

"They told me that too. Are you on vacation?"

"No, worse luck. I'm on business."

Janine lowered the back of her seat slightly, then stubbed out her cigarette.

"We get in around three o'clock, don't we?"

"That's right."

"Well, then, if you'll excuse me, I'm going to catch up with my beauty sleep."

"It's an idea," Girland said. "Me too."

Janine closed her eyes, and after a while she seemed to be sleeping. Girland finished his cigarette, then he too closed his eyes, but his mind remained active for an hour or so. He thought of Madame Foucher. The ruthlessness of Radnitz angered him. Maybe there would come a time when he would level the scores and revenge both her death and Rossland's death. Later, he relaxed and drifted into a heavy sleep. He was aroused by the air hostess.

"Please fasten your safety belt, sir," she said. "We will be landing in three minutes."

Girland sat up, yawned and fumbled with his belt.

Janine was touching up her face.

"It seemed to take no time at all," she said. "I slept. Did you?"

"I guess," Girland said.

She looked through the window at the lights of the airport as the plane circled to come in.

"Africa! It's exciting, isn't it!"

When the aircraft had landed and the exit doors were opened, a blast of hot humid air surged into the aircraft.

"Phew!" Girland said as he got to his feet. "This is hot!"

He walked with Janine across the tarmac and into the airport building. They passed through the various control points with little delay and found the N'Gor Hotel bus waiting.

A tall, coloured porter, wearing a red uniform, took their bags and put them in the bus. Three American business men also got into the bus with them for the short drive by the sea road to the hotel.

There was a slight delay as they checked in at the hotel and Girland noticed that this woman who interested him had a room next to his.

"Why, you're my neighbour," he said. "This is a coincidence. I hope we'll see more of each other."

"But you're going to be busy, aren't you?"

They entered the lift.

"Oh, sure," Girland said airily, "but not all that busy. I'll have time to try out the beach."

"Good . . . then we'll meet."

The lift took them to the seventh floor and they followed the porter down a long corridor, down a short flight of stairs and into a tiny lobby. To the right and left of the lobby was a door.

The porter unlocked one of the doors and carried Janine's luggage into a big, airy room.

"Well, good night again," she said, offering her hand.

Girland held it a shade longer than necessary and when she lifted her eyebrows, he released it.

"Good night," he said. "I look forward to seeing you tomorrow," and he followed the porter into his room.

Chapter Six

AT HALF past nine the following morning, Girland ordered breakfast. He then spoke on the telephone to the Hall Porter, telling him he wanted to hire a car for three days. The Hall Porter said a car would be outside the hotel within an hour.

After breakfast, Girland unpacked his suitcase, dressed in a tropical suit and locked the suitcase in one of the closets. He left his bulky briefcase on a chair, and went down to the reception hall.

The Hall Porter told him the car had arrived, and after tipping him, Girland walked down the long flight of steps to where a D.S. Citroen stood parked in the shade.

He drove along the wide Autoroute to Dakar. Parking the car in Place de l'Independence, he set off on foot to explore the town. The streets, crowded with gaily dressed Africans, had much to offer and for the first hour, he was content to wander around and get the feel of the town. He visited a bookshop and bought maps of the town, the surrounding district and a guide book. As the girl wrapped his purchase, he asked her where the Florida nightclub was to be found.

"At the far end of rue Carnot," she told him. "Second on the left past Place de l'Independence."

Girland returned to his car and drove down rue Carnot until he located the nightclub. He parked a few yards past the club, then walked back to it. From the outside it looked dingy. There was a rusty iron grille drawn across the entrance. A shabby, painted sign told him the club opened at 21.15 hrs.

The time now was just after midday and the shops were closing. Girland decided there was nothing further he could do, so he drove back to the hotel.

A few minutes after he had set out for Dakar, Janine had been awakened by the telephone bell. Sleepily, she picked up the receiver.

"A cable for you, Madame," the clerk said. "Shall I send it up?"

"Yes, please and let me have coffee and orange juice," she said and replaced the receiver. She got out of bed, slipped on a wrap and went into the bathroom.

Some minutes later, a waiter, his white teeth gleaming against the blackness of his skin, put down a tray and handed her the cable.

When he had gone, Janine opened the cable and saw at a glance that it was from Dorey and would have to be decoded. She drank the orange juice, lit a cigarette, poured coffee and then taking a pencil from her bag, set to work to decode the cable which read:

Woman murdered at airport. Sending Kerman, arriving on 15.50 plane to work with you. Relying on you. Dorey.

She set fire to the cable with her cigarette lighter and dropped the ash on the tiled floor, then carrying her cup of coffee out onto the balcony, she sat in one of the reclining chairs, her mind busy.

A little after eleven o'clock, she put on a swim-suit and slipping on a beach wrap, she went down to the beach.

There were already a number of people on the beach, either swimming or lying under sun umbrellas. An African set up an umbrella for her and laid out a Li-lo mattress.

Opening her beach bag, she took out the last novel by Françoise Sagan and stretching out on the mattress, she began aimlessly to turn the pages of the book.

But her mind was too occupied for reading and she laid down the novel and reached for a cigarette. As she began to hunt for her lighter, a shadow fell across her and looking up sharply, she saw a tall man, wearing only brief swimming trunks, had come up silently and was now offering her a light from a gas lighter.

She had seldom seen such a powerfully built giant of a man. His muscular body was burned to a golden brown by the sun. He was so blond, his hair, cut short, was the colour of silver. His square shaped face, with its high cheek bones, its powerful, aggressive jaw, its short blunt nose told her he was of Slav extraction. He would be twenty-eight or nine: a splendid looking athlete until she looked into his flat green eyes that were windows revealing a ruthlessness combined with something so evil that Janine recoiled from him.

Staring intently at her, he bent, thrusting the flame of his lighter towards her cigarette. Recovering, Janine lit her cigarette.

She forced a smile of thanks.

"Four and two and six are twelve," he said in guttural French. "I'm Malik."

She stiffened, staring at him, her violet coloured eyes opening wide.

"A car will be outside the hotel at 15.00 hrs.," he said. "Be ready," and turning, he walked with long, swinging strides across the hot sand and into the sea.

Janine watched the movements of his muscles as he walked and watched as he dived into the sea. He began swimming away from the beach with the power and ease of a professional.

She inhaled a lungful of smoke, then settled down on the mattress again.

Malik! She had heard of him. So this was Malik. She had once heard someone say of him: "The only difference between Malik and a Black Mamba is that Malik can walk and the snake only crawl."

She was still thinking about him when Girland, wearing swimming trunks, came across the sand and paused at her side.

"Hello," he said, his eyes moving with inquisitive frankness over her body. "Have you been in yet?"

She sat up.

"No." She suddenly wondered now Malik had appeared on the scene if it was wise to get friendly with this handsome American.

"Let's go in and then have lunch, shall we?" Girland offered his hand.

She grasped it and let him pull her to her feet, then together, they ran down to the water. She saw that he, like Malik, was a powerful, expert swimmer.

They swam for ten minutes, then came in. Slipping into beach wraps, they walked to the thatched roofed open air restaurant that was only a few yards from the beach.

"That was fine," Girland said as they sat down at a table for two. "Let's have a drink."

An African waiter approached.

Janine asked for a vodka martini and Girland a double gin and tonic. He then studied the menu.

"How about king sized prawns, cold chicken and green salad with a bottle of very cold Chablis?" he asked, looking at her.

"Perfect for me." When he had given the order, she asked, "Did you have a successful morning?"

"I've been exploring Dakar. I'm supposed to find a site for

my Company," Girland said glibly. "What are you doing this afternoon? I have hired a car. Will you come for a drive with me? I thought I'd go inland and see what the country looks like."

The waiter brought their drinks.

"I can't this afternoon. I have a friend to see."

Girland glanced at her.

"You have friends here?"

"Just a girl friend."

They drank, sighed and smiled at each other.

"This is a lot better than Paris," Girland said.

"You don't live in Paris, do you?"

"No. Florida." He paused and a quizzing expression came into his eyes. Janine followed his glance and she saw Malik coming towards the restaurant.

"Wow!" Girland said softly. "Now there's a real hunk of gorgeous male."

Malik went up the bar and ordered a coke.

Janine studied his long, muscular back and nodded.

"You're right. Perfectly cast to play Samson."

"A Russian," Girland's expression was thoughtful. "I wonder what he's doing here?"

He didn't notice Janine's slight start nor the quick hard look she threw at him.

"He's probably thinking the same about you," she said.

At this moment the waiter came with their order and Malik, finishing his drink, turned and walked with his long, swinging strides towards the hotel.

Girland watched him go. He remembered Radnitz's warning about the Russians who were also hunting for Carey. Was this blond giant one of them?

"You've become very thoughtful all of a sudden," Janine said as she peeled an enormous prawn. "What are you thinking about?"

"Don't insist or you'll be embarrassed."

"About me?"

"Well, of course."

She laughed.

"Oh, I can guess. I have lived long enough in the company of men to know what they often think when they are with me."

"You have only your beauty to blame for that."

She deliberately changed the subject, asking him to tell her about Florida. It was some years since Girland had been to Great

Miami, but he managed to give an interesting account of the City. They were still chatting idly when he paid the bill.

"I must run," she said, getting to her feet, "or I'll be late."

"I'm coming up too. You're sure I can't give you a lift in my car?"

"No, a car's being sent for me, thank you."

They rode up together in the lift and parted at their doors.

Girland took a shower, dressed, and then moved to the window that looked down on the entrance to the hotel. He was in time to see Janine, wearing a sleeveless emerald green frock, get into a black Cadillac, driven by an African, wearing a red fez, and he watched the car drive rapidly towards the Autoroute.

Janine had no idea where she was being driven. She stared at the back of the chauffeur's black neck and wondered if she should ask him, but decided not to.

The chauffeur slowed the big car and turned to the left and she saw a signpost that read: *Rufisque*. That meant nothing to her. She found the heat of the afternoon sun stronger than she had imagined it would be, but she didn't dislike it.

After driving for some miles, the car left the main road and slowing, began to bump along a sandy road, throwing up a cloud of fine sand either side of the car. An avenue of trees made a welcome shade, and finally, the car turned into a concealed drive and pulled up outside a large, bungalow type house, each window covered with green sun shutters.

The chauffeur got out and opened the car door for her. Janine stepped into the violent sunshine, and then followed the chauffeur onto the terrace and to the front door of the bungalow. He opened the door and waved her to go on ahead.

She moved into a cool, dimly lit lobby and the driver went away.

Malik appeared from a room off the lobby. He was wearing white shorts, a white sports shirt and sandals.

He stood aside, motioning her to enter the room which she found to be large and cool, sparsely furnished and pinned on one of the walls, a big map of Senegal.

Malik waved her to one of the chairs and sat down at the table.

"The reason why we told you to come here," he said, staring at her, "is that we want to know exactly what has been going on in Paris and how much Dorey knows or guesses. The situation here is complicated."

Without omitting any details, Janine told him what had been happening since Madame Foucher had first telephoned Dorey.

Malik listened intently. When she had finished, he said, "So the fool has no idea what she had to sell?"

"He has no idea."

The evil green eyes examined her.

"And you have no idea?"

"No."

"So the only other people who know are Radnitz and this man Girland."

Janine didn't say anything.

"Dorey thinks Girland is dead?"

"Yes."

"He isn't dead. He's here," Malik said.

Janine looked sharply at him.

"What makes you think that? Dorey told me if he happened to be alive, it would be impossible for him to leave Paris."

"Dorey is a fool. Girland is here. You lunched with him this afternoon."

Janine lost colour.

"The man I had lunch with is an American business man. I have a description of Girland. These two men are utterly unlike. I think you have made a mistake."

Malik's thin lips tightened.

"I don't make mistakes. I searched his room when you were lunching. He had a trick suitcase with him. Why should a business man carry with him a gun, a knife, a cosh and drug pills? He is also representing a certain company in Florida and this company is owned by Radnitz. It's Girland all right. A clever make up. Obviously he is no longer working for Dorey. Radnitz has bought him."

"Do you think he knows about me?" Janine asked, her hands in tight fists, her knuckles showing white.

"Why should he? Girland is a womaniser," Malik said. He paused for a moment, then went on, "When I heard a representative of the Orangeolo Company was going to stay at the N'Gor, I guessed he would be Radnitz's man. I arranged for him to have a room next to yours." He stared at her, then said, "That is another reason why I wanted you here. You are going to cultivate Girland. Do you understand?"

Janine nodded.

"You are going to do a thorough job on him," Malik went on.

"You should be sleeping with him by tomorrow night."

"I can do a job on him without sleeping with him!" Janine said, her eyes suddenly flashing. "I don't take that kind of an order from anyone!"

"You have no choice," Malik said. "You will sleep with Girland tomorrow night unless, of course, you want him to find out you are a double agent, passing information from the American Embassy to the Russian Embassy."

Janine stiffened.

"But you said Girland is working now for Radnitz. He has no reason to betray me."

"You say that because you don't know what this coloured woman had to sell. I'll tell you. Do you remember Robert Henry Carey?"

"Carey? Yes, of course. What has he to do with it?"

"Everything. Carey is in Senegal. Girland is here to talk to him. Dorey didn't realise this woman could tell him where Carey is hiding, but she has told Girland and he has told Radnitz. Before Carey left Russia he managed to get hold of quite a lot of very dangerous information. For instance, he has your Russian dossier. He has enough information on microfilm to send Radnitz to prison for life. Girland would give your dossier to Dorey. Even if he no longer works for Dorey, he is still an American, and Americans don't let Russian agents operate if they can stop them."

"If you know Carey is here," Janine said, sitting forward, "why haven't you caught up with him? Don't you intend to protect me? I'm useful to your people, aren't I?"

"I know he is here, but I don't know where he is hiding. Senegal is a big place. Girland will lead us to him if you handle him right."

"Why don't you take Girland somewhere and persuade him to talk?"

"You're being stupid. Girland can't know exactly where Carey is hiding. Carey must have a contact who arranged for this Senegalese woman to go to Paris. Girland must lead us to this contact who in his turn will lead Girland and us to Carey." He got to his feet and crossed over to the map of Senegal. "Come here." When Janine joined him, he pointed to a vast blank space on the map. "This is the bush. Unless you have actually seen the African bush, you can't imagine what it looks like. It is flat country. You can walk two miles and believe you haven't moved. Every tree, every

92

shrub, every clump of grass looks alike. Getting lost is the easiest thing in the world, and when you are lost in the bush, you are lost for good." He tapped the map. "Somewhere in this vast space, Carey is hiding. There are hundreds of villages, peopled by Africans, some big, some consisting only of three or four hovels. When he was a young man, Carey worked in Senegal. He knows how to handle the natives: he speaks their language. I am sure he is staying in one of the smaller villages and he can stay there as long as he likes."

"But why are you so sure he is in the bush?"

"We have been chasing him ever since he escaped from Moscow. We headed him off from Europe and he turned to Egypt. We nearly caught up with him in Cairo and he flew to Africa. He kept just ahead of us by using chartered aircraft. He took an airtaxi for Dakar, but something went wrong. The plane crashed ten miles outside Diourbel. We knew he was trying to reach Dakar and we were already in Diourbel. We drove out to the crash. The pilot was dead. Carey had vanished. There was nowhere else for him to go but into the bush. He's still there. I have men at Linguere, Bakel, Matam and Kadlack. He's hemmed in. I have hired thirty Arabs who know the bush and they are searching every yard of it, but unless they have some luck, Carey could still slip past them. A search like that could take months. We must find him quickly. Girland is our best bet. Now, perhaps, you understand why you must get onto intimate terms with him. You must persuade him to tell you who Carey's contact is."

Malik moved away from the map and lighting a cigarette, he sat down. After staring at the map for some moments, Janine came and sat near him.

"I'll do what I can," she said.

"Who is Kerman?"

Janine looked sharply at him.

"How do you know about him?"

"I make it my business to know such things. I had a copy of Dorey's cable to you before you had it. The code is like Dorey: simple and stupid. Who is Kerman?"

"He is one of Dorey's special agents."

"We don't want him at the N'Gor. He could spoil your chances with Girland. When he arrives, tell him to stay in Dakar. The less you see of him the better."

"It won't be that easy." Janine looked worried. "Kerman has very decided ideas of his own. He won't take orders from me."

Malik thought for a moment.

"Try to persuade him to stay in Dakar. If he becomes trouble-some, I'll arrange something. Your job now is to work on Gir-land."

"He spotted you were Russian," Janine said. "He wondered what you were doing here."

"I will keep away from the N'Gor. I will remain here. If you want me, telephone me." He gave her a telephone number. "Just say you want to see me and I'll send the car for you." He got to his feet. "Remember this is as important to you as it is to me. I want quick results."

Janine followed him to the front door. The Cadillac was waiting under the shade of a tree. The chauffeur opened the car door.

Without looking at Malik, she walked down the steps and got into the car.

Girland arrived back at the N'Gor Hotel a little after six. He had spent the afternoon in Diourbel. It had been roasting hot in the straggling, but pleasant little town. Madame Foucher had said Carey was in the bush outside Diourbel. It was only when Girland attempted to leave the main road and branch off into the bush that he realised how easily and quickly he could get lost. He found too that the Citroen wasn't the car to use on the narrow, sand packed lanes leading into the bush. Several times the rear wheels sank into the sand and he had a struggle that left him soaking with sweat and exhausted to get the car moving again. He hadn't driven more than a kilometre or two before he turned back and was thankful to regain the main road.

He entered his hotel room, threw off his clothes and took a cold shower. Dressing again in a light-weight suit, he took the lift down to the bar. As he walked down the long flight of stairs leading to the bar, he thought he hadn't wasted his afternoon. He now had a good idea of Diourbel, he had seen something of the bush and he had seen the difficulties that faced him of find-ing Carey. He decided he would go to the Florida Club that evening in the hope Enrico would be there.

As he moved to a table, he saw Janine sitting at a table at the far end of the big room. She looked cool and beautiful in a simple white frock. She waved to him as he looked in her direction and he joined her.

"Did you have a nice drive?" she asked as he sat down at her side.

"A little too hot for me," he said and when the African Waiter came to his side, he ordered a double gin and tonic. He saw she was drinking Campari soda with ice. "And you? Did you enjoy your afternoon?"

"Very much, thank you." She looked thoughtfully at him as he lit a cigarette. It was hard to believe this powerfully built, blond American could be the mysterious Girland.

They chatted, sipping their drinks.

"Will you keep me company for Dinner?" Girland asked. "I have a business date at half past eight, but if you don't mind eating early, I'd welcome company."

"That's lovely," she said. "I hate eating alone." She leaned back, arching her full breasts. "I'm not at all sure I've been wise coming out here on my own. I could get bored."

Girland grinned. "You won't. Not when I'm around."

"Are going to Dakar tonight?"

"Yes. Do you want a lift?"

She shook her head.

"I don't want to wander around Dakar on my own. No, I think I'll stay here. I have a good book."

Girland was tempted to ask her to come with him to the Florida Club, but decided she might be in the way if he had the luck to run into Enrico.

"Will you be back late?" she asked casually. "We might have a drink together before turning in."

"I don't know what time I'll get back," Girland said. "You know how it is with business men. Yak ... yak ... but I'll look for you here if it's anyth¹∿∿ like a reasonable time." He glanced at his watch. "Shall we go in and eat?"

"Give me three minutes," she said, getting to her feet, "and I'll be with you."

It would have shocked him if he had known what Janine did when she left him. Moving quickly, she shut herself in one of the telephone kiosks in the lobby and called Malik's number. He answered almost at once.

"My American business friend is leaving the hotel at 20.30 hrs. for Dakar," she said. "He expects to be back late," and she hung up.

95

Leaving the kiosk, she went to the Ladies' Room and touched up her face, then she returned to the bar. Seeing her coming, Girland got to his feet and joined her.

Together, they walked into the restaurant. They ordered smoked salmon and vodka, veal in a rich cream sauce and fruit. During the meal, they talked, and this time it was Girland who asked questions. He was now curious about this lovely looking woman.

"You live in Paris on your own?" he asked as he squeezed lemon juice on his smoked salmon.

"Yes. My father left me quite a lot of money and an apartment." She smiled at him. "I'm rather spoilt. I don't do anything but amuse myself, buy clothes and travel."

"Don't you get bored?"

"Sometimes, but not often. There is so much to do in Paris."

A few minutes to half past eight, after coffee and brandy on the terrace, Girland got to his feet.

"I hate to go, but I must. I'll look for you here tonight."

"I'll be here until eleven," she said. "Have a good time."

Leaving her, he went up to the reception lobby, handed in his key and then went out into the hot night air to his car.

He took his time driving to Dakar and arrived outside the Florida Club a little after half past nine. He was in a relaxed mood and off his guard so he didn't notice a black Dauphine car had been following him from the hotel to the club. The Dauphine, driven by a young African, passed him as he parked the Citroen. The driver noted that Girland walked across the road and entered the club. He then parked his car and getting out, he walked slowly towards the club. Tall and thin, wearing a shabby European suit, the African attracted no attention. He paused outside the club, then entered, going immediately to the bar where he hoisted himself on a high stool and called for tonic water.

Girland was already sitting at a table in an arched recess.

The club room was large and air conditioned. At one end was a dais on which a band of five Africans played expert swing. Around the room were tables and chairs. The dance floor took up the major part of the room. In a big alcove opposite him a number of African girls sat at tables chattering to one another with the incessant, noisy volubility of magpies.

A waiter brought Girland a whisky on the rocks, and Girland lit a cigarette, resigning himself to a long, boring wait.

People, mostly well dressed Africans, kept coming in. Some of them danced, but most of them preferred to sit at the tables, drinking soft drinks and listening to the band. Girland kept a sharp look out every time the door pushed open, but he saw no one remotely resembling a Portuguese.

Suddenly a tall, good looking African girl came from the opposite recess. Giggling nervously, she paused at Girland's table.

"Do you care to dance?" she asked, rolling her big, black eyes at him.

She was wearing a white dress over which she had draped pale green nylon, and on her head, she wore a turban, also of green nylon. Clattering on her thin, bony wrists were heavy gold bracelets and long gold ear-rings made a sparkling frame to her face.

"Why not?" Girland said and stood up.

All the other girls in the recess were giggling and pushing at each other as if it was the greatest joke in the world. As they moved onto the floor, the girl said, "They betted me I wouldn't ask you. You're American, aren't you?" She spoke in a sing-song French and she looked directly at him, showing him her magnificent white teeth in a happy smile.

"That's right," Girland said. He found she was an expert dancer, so light and quick to follow his lead, she made him feel slightly clumsy.

"I'm Awa. My sister's over there. She's Adama. We're twins. It is the custom in this country to call girl twins Awa and Adama. What is your name?"

"John," Girland said.

They lapsed into silence and gave themselves to the music. When the band stopped playing, they paused and smiled at each other.

"Have a drink with me, Awa," Girland said. "Keep me company."

She giggled, shooting a look of triumph across the room at the other girls.

"Yes. I would like to."

Returning to his table, they sat down and Girland signalled to the waiter. He ordered a Schweppes Orange for the girl and another whisky for himself.

It wasn't until they had had several more dances and more drinks that Girland said casually, "There used to be a girl here. She was tall and good looking. I don't see her here tonight."

"We're all here except Rosa," Awa said. "But you haven't been here before, have you?"

"No, I happened to meet her. She told me she worked here. Do you know where she lives?"

"With her father in Medina."

"Is that far?"

"No. It's just outside Dakar."

"What is her father's name?"

"Momar Arbeau. He owns a fruit stall."

"Doesn't Rosa have a boy friend? Enrico I think his name is." Awa nodded eagerly.

"Yes. He is very rich. He used to come here every night, but I haven't seen him now since Rosa went away."

"Where does he live?"

She shook her head, and he saw there was now an uneasy expression in her eyes. All these questions were beginning to worry her.

"I owe Rosa some money," Girland said, feeling some explanation was necessary. "If I can't find her, I would give the money to Enrico for her."

The uneasy expression went away and Awa smiled widely.

"I don't know where he lives. Rosa never told me."

"Do you know his other name?"

"No. Rosa always called him Enrico. I don't think she knows where he lived, otherwise she would have told me."

Girland experienced a deflated feeling of disappointment. He had been relying on the Florida Club to produce this Portuguese. Now, it seemed, his only lead was Rosa's father. If what Awa had said was true, why should Rosa's father know where Enrico lived if Rosa didn't?

"Listen, Awa," he said. "If you can find out where Enrico lives, I will pay you well." He felt in his trouser pocket and separated a thousand franc note from the roll of money he was carrying. He slipped the note across the table. "I'll give you three more of these if you find out for me."

Awa's slim black fingers snapped up the note so quickly that the tall, thin African who had been watching them in the mirror over the bar, failed to see the transaction.

"My name is John Gilchrist," Girland went on. "Will you telephone me at the N'Gor Hotel if you find him?"
She nodded excitedly.

"I'll find him. I'll ask all my friends. Someone will know where he lives."

"One more thing, Awa," Girland said. "Don't mention my name to anyone, and don't tell them that I want to meet Enrico. Do you understand?"

She began to look uneasy again, but the feel of the thousand franc note in her fingers gave her confidence.

"Yes."

"All right." Girland finished his drink. "I must go now. Try to find Enrico quickly."

He left the club and walked into the stifling night air. He paused to glance at his watch. The time was five minutes after eleven. Walking slowly, he crossed to where he had parked the Citroen.

In the club, Awa became aware of the tall, thin African coming towards her. His name was Samba Dieng. She knew him to be a wastrel who lived on the earnings of two old prostitutes who worked in the Arab quarter. She knew too he had been in and out of prison for petty theft. As he sat at the table, she looked at him with frank contempt.

"Who was the white man?" he demanded, his vicious eyes staring hard at her.

"I don't know. I asked him to dance and we danced. What is it to you, black boy?"

"What did he talk about?"

"Nothing. What do white men talk about?"

"Did he ask about Rosa?"

Awa got to her feet.

"He asked about no one," and with a contemptuous swagger in her walk, she crossed the dance floor and joined her giggling friends.

As soon as Girland had left the hotel, Janine had gone up to her room. She changed out of her white frock into a white blouse and black skirt, then she telephoned down for a taxi.

"I want to go to the airport and then to Dakar and then come back here," she told the Hall Porter. "I am meeting the Paris plane."

The Hall Porter said the taxi would be at the hotel in ten minutes.

She took the lift down to the reception lobby and sat in one of the lounging chairs, glancing through a day old copy of *France-*

Soir. After a short wait, one of the porters came over to her and told her the taxi had arrived.

It took only five minutes to reach the airport. Getting out of the taxi, she told the African driver to wait.

The girl at the information desk said the Paris plane was on time and would be arriving in five minutes. Janine sat down, lit a cigarette and waited.

A little after nine o'clock, she heard a plane touch down, and getting to her feet, she walked over to the arrival gate.

Some minutes later, passengers began to filter through the gate, and among the first of the arrivals was Jack Kerman. He was wearing a crumpled lightweight suit and was carrying a shabby hold-all. When he saw her, he waved.

"Hello there," he said, reaching her. "Phew! It's hot! Let's have a drink and talk."

She greeted him and fell into step beside him. They walked to the bar.

Janine was nervous of Kerman. She knew him to be the most shrewd and clever agent working for Dorey. He wasn't like Rossland. She told herself she would have to be very careful how she handled him.

She asked after Dorey.

"He's in a flap," Kerman said. He hoisted himself onto a stool by the bar. "What'll you drink?"

"I think a gin and tonic."

He ordered a beer for himself. At this hour the bar was empty, and the barman, having served them, went to the far end of the bar and opened a newspaper.

"Why is he in a flap?" Janine asked, holding her drink in her hand.

"Because he's dropped a clanger. You had a cable from him?" She nodded.

"Not very bright of him to let that woman get murdered, was it?" Kerman said. He drank some of his beer. "Obviously, she had vital information. Well, she's dead now, so she can't help us." He gave Janine a sudden searching glance. "Just why did you come out here?"

"I thought if the woman slipped through our net, I'd pick her up here," Janine said.

"That doesn't sound as if you have much faith in O'Halloran. You really thought she could get out of Paris?"

"I didn't know, but if she did, then I would be here."

"Well, since you are here, have you any leads?" Kerman shook a cigarette from a crumpled pack and lit it.

"Not yet."

He rested his elbows on the counter and peered at her.

"Got any ideas what to look for?"

She moved uneasily. How she wished Dorey hadn't sent this inquisitive little man out to Dakar.

"Not really. I was hoping this woman might . . ."

"Why don't you tell the truth?" Kerman said with a grin. "Why don't you admit you were fed up with Dorey and wanted a vacation?"

With an effort, she laughed.

"You can't expect me to admit that, Jack. Anyway, it's nice out here."

"Girland wasn't on your plane?"

The question was so unexpected, Janine slopped some of her drink. She was afraid to look at Kerman, aware he was watching her.

"Girland? I don't understand. He's dead," she said, finally.

"That's what Dorey thinks. Last seen, according to him, Girland was leaving the 'Allo, Paris' club with two of Radnitz's thugs. Know what I think? I think Radnitz made Girland an offer. Girland has never had any money. Radnitz could easily buy him, especially if he offered him no other alternative but to follow Rossland. It's my bet Girland is either here or he is coming here."

Janine touched her dry lips with her tongue.

"Well, it's an idea," she said, staring at her drink. "I have a description of him. I'll watch for him here."

Kerman grimaced.

"What's the matter with you tonight? I doubt if you would recognise him. Girland wouldn't come here as himself. When he does come, his own mother won't know him."

Janine sipped her drink. Her heart was beating rapidly. Kerman was getting unpleasantly near the truth.

"What do you suggest then?" She forced herself to meet his probing stare.

"Any lone American business men in your hotel?"

"A number of them."

"Any of them tried to get friendly with you?"

Janine swallowed, cleared her throat before saying, "Why, no . . . not yet."

"Well, watch out. Girland has one weakness ... pretty women."

"I see."

He finished his beer, sighed and wiped his mouth with his handkerchief.

"Another thing ... seen any Russians in your hotel?"

Janine's heart contracted.

"Russians? I haven't noticed any. What do you mean?"

"I've been thinking about this set-up. This woman must have got hold of some vital secret. Don't tell me Radnitz would have knocked her and Rossland off unless it was something really big. He's just back from Moscow. I'm sure the Russians must know about it and we must take them into consideration. I'll bet they are here now. Hence the question."

"I see." She felt it was an inadequate remark, but Kerman's astuteness was now frightening her. "I'll watch out."

He gave her a thoughtful stare, nodded and finished his drink.

"Yeah, you do that. Well, let's go to the hotel. I want to catch up with some sleep."

"You're not staying at the N'Gor, are you?"

"Why not?"

"I thought you would want to be more in the centre of things. I thought you would want to stay in Dakar. I can take care of this end. After all, the N'Gor is some kilometres from Dakar. If anything is going to happen, it'll be in Dakar."

"What makes you think that?" He swung around on his stool and regarded her quizzingly.

"Well, don't you think so?" she said. "There's nothing out here except the beach."

"And American business men." He thought for a moment, then shrugged. "Okay, maybe you're right. I'll make my headquarters in Dakar then. You watch the airport. Can I get a taxi?"

"Oh, yes." She was now determined not to go with him to Dakar. She had had enough of him for the moment. "There's a taxi rank outside."

She went with him to the rank and he paused before getting into the taxi.

"I'll be in touch with you tomorrow sometime. I'll give you a call and let you know where I am. So long for now," and giving her the same disturbing stare, he got in the taxi and was driven away.

She stood hesitating for some moments, then turning she re-entered the airport and shut herself in a telephone kiosk.

She called Malik.

Arriving back at the hotel, Girland picked up his key and then walked down the stairs to the bar. There were several American business men, drinking and talking, in the bar, but he couldn't see Janine. He guessed she had gone up to her room. He drank a Campari soda to quench his thirst, then took the lift to his room. He had a shower, then putting on a light dressing-gown, he walked out onto the balcony.

The full moon lit up the sea and the ornamental gardens below. With his hands on the balcony rail, he looked at the sea and was tempted to have a swim. He was trying to make up his mind if he could be bothered to take the lift down and then make the long walk to the sea, when he heard a movement on the next balcony to his.

The balconies were screened by a partition, but it was possible, by leaning forward to see around the partition. He listened, then heard someone sigh.

"Can't you sleep?" he said, knowing Janine was out on her balcony.

"Oh, you're back. No . . . it's too hot to sleep."

"I can't understand why they haven't air conditioning in an hotel of this standard."

"They have in some rooms. Did you have a nice evening?"

"As I thought: pretty dull. Too many drinks and too much talk."

There was a pause, then she said, "Seems silly for us to talk like this and not see each other."

Girland lifted his eyebrows. He caught hold of the top of the partition, hoisted himself on the balcony rail and dropped lightly onto her balcony.

"That's soon fixed, isn't it?" he said, smiling at her.

"You might have killed yourself," she said, looking up at him.

He sank into the other reclining chair, reached for a pack of cigarettes on the table and lit a cigarette.

"Isn't that exactly what Juliet said to Romeo?"

She laughed. Then looking away from him, she stared up at the moon. There was a long pause while he watched her, then she said, "I envy men. They have everything so much their own way.

They can do what they like and go where they like. A woman on her own is always suspect."

"Do you think so? I wouldn't have thought so these days. Fifty per cent of people travelling on their own today are women."

"Old women."

He studied her.

"Are you depressed about something?"

"No. It's just that I've been sitting here, thinking. I suppose I felt lonely. I'm not good at being alone."

She got to her feet and walked over the balcony rail. She stood, her hands on the rail, looking up at the moon. He watched her. He could see the outlines of her long legs through the thinness of her wrap. Silently he got up and walked over to her. He put his arms around her, his hands taking the weight of her breasts. She leaned against him and he bent and kissed the side of her neck. He felt her shiver, then she turned in his arms, offering him her lips.

Chapter Seven

THERE'S SOMETHING wrong about this set-up, Kerman was thinking as the taxi rushed him along the empty Autoroute towards Dakar.

Why had Janine been so nervy? He had never seen her like this before. Why had she nearly upset her drink when he had mentioned Girland? Why had she lost colour when he had talked about the Russians?

There was something wrong. Why had she come out here? Dorey had told him he hadn't sent her. He had said he was glad she had gone, but he hadn't sent her. So why had she gone at her own expense? She knew how thorough O'Halloran was. She must have known the Senegalese woman hadn't a hope of leaving Paris for Dakar. Yet she had said she had come out here to pick the woman up if she did slip through the net. It didn't make sense to come all the way out here.

Kerman crossed and uncrossed his legs. Something was wrong, he repeated to himself. The more he thought about it, the more convinced he became. He had considerable respect for Dorey's astuteness. Had Dorey purposely sent him out here to keep watch on Janine? Was Dorey losing faith in her at last?

Kerman told himself he had never really taken to Janine. He wondered thoughtfully if he were prejudiced against her because he had known at their first meeting he would never get anywhere with a woman like her. She had always been distant with him, not like the other women agents who worked for Dorey. She was, of course, in a class of her own, cool, off-hand and ... well, admit it ... with a suspicion of comtempt for his bohemian way of life. Was this why he disliked her or was it something deeper than that? Was it that after years of experience in this racket, meeting agents, assessing their value, he had come to the conclusion that Janine Daulnay wasn't entirely to be trusted?

He lit a cigarette, startled to realise that at last he had brought this thought up from his sub-conscious. Yes, that was it, he told himself. It's not that she is aloof. The fact is I have never really trusted her! But why? We've worked off and on together for the past four years. She is Dorey's favourite. He regards her as his best woman agent. What reason have I for not trusting her?

He could think of no reason why he shouldn't trust her. She had pulled off several first-class jobs. It was she who had exposed Nayland who had been feeding the Russians with Top Secret information over a period of years. That had been one of the smartest and cleverest pieces of counter-espionage in the records of the Embassy.

Kerman flicked ash off his cigarette.

But wait, he thought, although exposing Nayland had been a brilliant piece of work, it had been spoilt by Nayland's death. Had he really committed suicide or had he been conveniently silenced before he could be questioned?

Then there had been Bronson. She had exposed him too, but again, while trying to escape, Bronson had been silenced by a mysterious hit and run car: a car with false number plates and that had vanished as quickly as it had appeared.

Both Nayland and Bronson had done a lot of damage, but they were already suspected when Janine had exposed them. O'Halloran couldn't have failed to have caught up with them in the end.

But then in fairness to Janine, she didn't know these two men would be dead before they could be questioned. But it had been convenient for the Russians.

Convenient for the Russians. Kerman's eyes narrowed. Why had Janine lost colour when he asked her if she had seen any Russians at the N'Gor? Everyone had said it was bad luck that Janine's work had been wasted. It was because she had exposed both Nayland and Bronson that Dorey had made her his leading woman agent. So it had been also convenient for Janine.

Kerman stiffened. The way his mind is working, he thought, it could make Janine a double agent. You're getting fancy ideas or are you? Why is she so anxious for me to be away from the N'Gor? Is something going on there that she doesn't want me to know about?

The taxi slowed down and the driver said, "Dakar just ahead, sir. Where to?"

"A decent central hotel," Kerman said.

Well, all right, he said to himself as the taxi gathered speed, until I get a lead to the Foucher woman, it might pay off to watch Janine.

The taxi pulled up outside the Continental Hotel in rue Galandou-Diouf. An African porter came hurrying across the sidewalk and collected Kerman's hold-all as Kerman paid off the taxi. He followed the porter into the lobby.

He asked for a room and a bath and signed the register. Then crossing over to the Hall Porter he said he would want a hire-car without a chauffeur by eight o'clock the following morning. The Hall Porter told him that could easily be arranged and asked for his passport which Kerman gave him, then taking the lift, he reached the room which was air conditioned and pleasant on the second floor.

Taking off his coat, he began to unpack his bag, his mind very occupied.

Janine!

He just couldn't believe she was involved with the Russians. You're letting your mind run away with you, he thought, laying nylon shirts in a drawer. You're too damned suspicious of everyone.

He pushed the empty hold-all into the closet and sat on the bed.

He would go out to the N'Gor Hotel tomorrow morning and take a look around.

The sooner he could put Janine in the clear, the better for his peace of mind.

Samba Dieng pulled up outside the bungalow type house and got out of his battered Deux Chevaux. Two tall Africans appeared out of the shadows and converged on him.

"It's me," he said uneasily "Dieng. I have to report to Mr. Jenson."

One of the Africans ran his big hands over Dieng's clothes, making sure he had no gun, then led him into the bungalow.

Malik was sitting at the table, studying a map. Dieng paused in the doorway. A heavily-built man, completely bald with a savage, ruthless face made fiery red by drinking too much vodka stood behind Malik. He was known as Ivan. He was one of the best pistol shots in Russia. Malik and he made a team. One was always to be found with the other.

Malik looked at Dieng and motioned him to come to the table. Dieng came forward reluctantly. He was worried. He knew he hadn't had a successful evening, but he was anxious now to receive the money Malik had promised him.

"Well?"

"I followed him as I was instructed," Dieng said. "He drove to the Florida Club which is in rue Carnot. He spent the evening drinking and dancing, then he returned to the hotel."

Malik studied the African, his evil green eyes glittering.

"Is that all?" he asked in his guttural French.

Dieng lifted his thin shoulders in a gesture of resignation.

"All Americans drink and dance when they visit Dakar, sir," he said. "This one was no exception."

"Who did he dance with?"

Dieng shifted his feet.

"A coloured girl. Her name is Awa."

"She is there regularly?"

"Yes. She is one of the hostesses: a prostitute. She is always there."

"She would be a friend of Rosa?"

Dieng nodded.

"Yes. Rosa also is a hostess and a prostitute."

"Did this man dance with any of the other girls?"

"No. He danced only with Awa."

"How long was he there?"

"About two hours."

"You watched them all the time."

"All the evening in a mirror above the bar. The man didn't see me watching him."

"And they talked?"

"Yes. They talked."

"What about?"

"About nothing of any importance," Dieng said loftily. "I asked her when he had gone. They didn't even speak about Rosa."

"Did he give her any money?"

"No."

"So she danced with him for two hours for nothing?"

Dieng scratched one of his big ears.

"I didn't see him give her anything."

"So you really have nothing to report?"

"I did my best," Dieng said reproachfully. "Nothing happened."

Malik gave an irritable shrug. He took from his hip pocket a thousand franc note and gave it to Dieng.

"How well did you know Rosa?" Malik asked, reluctant to let the African go without squeezing some information out of him.

"I often spoke with her," Dieng said. "She was very high class. She was never friendly. Her protector was very rich and powerful."

"Her protector?" Malik leaned forward. "Who is he?"

"I don't know who he is, but I do know he has a lot of money."

"Have you ever seen him?"

"Yes. When Rosa was in the club, he came every night."

"What does he look like?"

"He is a Portuguese: fat with a moustache."

Malik stiffened.

"A Portuguese. Are you sure?"

"Yes."

Malik got to his feet.

"You can go," he said and crossed over to the steel safe that stood against the far wall.

Dieng looked helplessly at Ivan who waved him away. When he had gone, Ivan said, "What is it?"

Malik had opened the safe and now took from it a bulky folder. He carried the folder to the desk and sat down.

Ivan shrugged and poured himself a stiff drink of vodka.

"Something I remember reading in Carey's dossier," Malik said, going through the mass of papers in the folder.

Ivan drank the vodka and refilled his glass. He waited indifferently for some twenty minutes while Malik continued to read through the papers. Then Malik suddenly slapped the desk.

"Here it is!" he exclaimed. "In 1925, Carey worked as an engineer in an ice producing plant in Dakar owned by Enrico Fantaz, a Portuguese. The two men shared the same house in Dakar." He looked at Ivan. "This Fantaz could be the man who financed Rosa's trip to Paris. He could also know where Carey is hiding!"

"It is a long time ago. Is he still in Dakar?" Ivan asked.

Malik searched for the telephone book which he found under a pile of old newspapers. After checking, he said, "He's not in the book." He checked again. "But the ice plant is. Tomorrow we will go to Dakar and make inquiries." He stared at Ivan, his face a little flushed, his mouth a cruel line. "This could be the beginning of the end of Carey."

Janine came slowly awake from a relaxed, perfect sleep. She

opened her eyes and flinched at the bright sunlight that made a warm pattern on the tiled floor. Then she lifted her arm and looked at the tiny watch on her wrist. It was two minutes after seven.

She turned her head and regarded Girland, lying by her side. He was sleeping, and she studied him, her eyes examining every feature of his face wondering what he really looked like under this obviously expert disguise. As if aware that someone was watching him, he moved uneasily, reached out and slid his arm around her, pulling her to him.

Janine relaxed against him, her hand resting lightly on his naked chest.

She had known many lovers in her life. Men were necessary to her. The physical act of love at intervals was as essential to her as food. But so often she had been disappointed. She had grown cynical of the selfishness of men. They took what they wanted without thought of her, leaving her more often than not unsatisfied and frustrated, but not Girland.

No other man she had known had made love to her the way Girland had last night. He seemed to know the exact tempo at which to raise her desires, how to stimulate her passion and to bring the act to a momentous dual climax. It had been a shattering magnificent experience, Janine thought, leaving her drained of energy, but satisfied and fusing her body with well being. Nothing like that had ever happened to her before.

This experience she wanted again. She couldn't bear the thought of losing something so unique, and not for the first time since she had begun to work for Dorey and later for the Russians she bitterly regretted getting involved in this dangerous and one-sided game.

It was not as if she needed the money. What she had told Girland was true. Her father, who had made a fortune on the Bourse, had left her well provided for. But she had been bored with her clothes, her money and the endless hours of nothing to do.

She had met John Dorey at a dinner party and she had liked him. During the conversation they had together, it came out that Janine had many important contacts. She was rich and popular. She was continually at the various foreign Embassies, attending dinners and cocktail parties. The fact that her mother was American, the fact that she was wealthy and beautiful and gay, gave her an entrée wherever she wanted to go.

A few days later, Dorey had invited her to dinner.

"I want to talk to you," he had said. "There is something I might offer you if you are really as bored as you say you are."

How eagerly she had agreed to work for him. She had little to do but circulate, listen to gossip, rumours, and to the know-alls, and send in weekly reports. It had been amusing for the first year, and then she began to get bored again. She wanted excitement, even danger, but Dorey would give her no important assignment. She was more useful doing what she did, he told her.

Then one afternoon she had a call from a man who said his name was Dupont. She had met him on a *bâteau mouche* one evening and they had sat side by side as the boat took them along the Seine and he had talked softly in guttural French: a lean, dark man with deep set eyes and high cheekbones. He seemed to know all about her. That she was bored was a pity, he said. Unless she did something out of the ordinary, Dorey would never promote her. Had she hostile feelings towards the Soviet Union?

Janine had no hostile feelings against any nation. She gathered information about Russia since Dorey needed it. No, she would have no objection to gather information about America if the Russians could use her. Why not? She was in this business for the fun of it and after all, France was her country. Perhaps the Russians could make better use of her talents. Could they?

And so, as the years moved by, Janine became more expert, more professional and more involved. It was Dupont who had given her the information with which she had exposed Nayland and Bronson. It had been cleverly arranged and Dorey was completely deceived. He sincerely believed that it was Janine's cleverness and patient work that had exposed these two traitors: men who were no longer of any value to the Russians.

This began a new career for Janine. She now became Dorey's top woman agent, and this was when the Russians began to put on pressure. They gave her assignments instead of accepting the scraps of information she had previously given them: dangerous and difficult assignments. She only refused once to do this kind of work.

Dupont had stared fixedly at her.

"Your safety is in our hands, Mademoiselle," he had said. "Remember Nayland and Bronson: they too were double agents."

So the fun and the excitement exploded in her face. This was now no longer a game. It was for real as O'Halloran had once said. She was trapped and there was no wriggling out.

The shrill note of the telephone interrupted her thoughts.

Girland was sleeping on the side of the bed where the telephone stood on the night table. As he began to stir, she hurriedly lay flat across him, pinning him down and snatched up the receiver.

"Yes?"

"My place at nine," Malik said.

"But it's too early," Janine wailed. "I can't."

"At nine," Malik repeated and hung up.

Girland, awake, ran his hand slowly down Janine's long back. She rolled off him, sitting up, clutching the sheet to her breasts.

"Oh, damn!" she said. "I had forgotten. That was Hilda ... my friend. We had arranged to go for a car drive. I have to meet her at nine."

"Does she sing baritone in the choir?" Girland asked, lacing his fingers behind his head and smiling at her. "You know something? I thought Hilda sounded like a man."

"Well, she isn't! She just happens to have a cold."

"Poor Hilda." Girland suddenly reached out and took Janine in his arms. "Good morning, you beautiful, wonderful thing," and he began to kiss her eyes very gently so that she shivered and clung to him. His lips moved to her neck and she suddenly shook her head, and tried to push him away.

"You mustn't, darling. I've got to get up. You must go, really, John ... no ... oh, darling, please ..."

His lips closed on hers and she suddenly relaxed, sighing, as she felt the desire in her catching fire. Her arms tightened around him, her fingers feeling the hard muscles of his back.

Later, they lay side by side, looking at each other.

"Oh, it's so good with you," Janine said, lightly touching his face. "Nothing like this has happened to me before."

Girland smiled.

"I'm glad ... me too." He sat up and looked at his watch. "It's nearly eight. I'd better get back to my room." She watched him slide out of bed and walk to where he had left his wrap.

"Tonight, John? Will you be with me again tonight?"

"Of course. I don't know what's happening today. But sometime tonight, I'll be here. If I can, I'll look for you at lunch time on the beach."

When he had gone, she reluctantly got up and went into the bathroom. At twenty to nine, she went down to the reception lobby and then out onto the hotel terrace. She saw the black Cadillac, waiting. The tall African, his red fez at a jaunty angle, was chewing a strip of bamboo. She went down to him and he opened the car door, smiling broadly at her, giving her a little bow.

The drive to the bungalow took some twenty minutes, and during this time, she wondered what Malik wanted. She felt nervous and ill at ease. She would have been still more nervous if she had known that Jack Kerman who had driven out to the hotel and had arrived at half past eight had seen her get into the Cadillac. He hesitated about following her, but decided it would be too dangerous. Janine was a professional. She would quickly know that she was being followed. He was content to take the licence number of the car, and then getting into his hired Simca, he drove rapidly back to Dakar.

The Cadillac pulled up outside the bungalow and leaving the car, Janine walked up the steps and into the lobby.

Malik was waiting for her. They walked together into the main room.

"Where was Girland last night?" Malik asked, sitting down. "Did he tell you?"

"He said he spent the evening with business men drinking and talking," Janine said.

"He spent the evening at the Florida nightclub with a coloured woman who is a friend of Madame Foucher," Malik said. "You see? Do you need further proof that this man is not only Girland but is now working for Radnitz?"

Feeling cold, Janine said nothing.

"I have news," Malik went on. "It is now unnecessary for you to sleep with Girland tonight as arranged. I am almost certain we can find Carey without him. I shall know in a few minutes."

Janine looked sharply at him. "What has happened then?"

"I am sure Carey must have a contact here. I am sure too Girland is also trying to find this contact. It will be through the contact that he will find Carey. I am now pretty sure who the contact is: a man called Enrico Fantaz. Years ago Carey and he were friends. He . . ." He paused as Ivan came in. "Well?"

"Fantaz retired from the ice factory last year," Ivan said, looking at Janine, then looking away. "He now lives on L'Ile de Gorée, a small island three kilometres from the port of Dakar. The name of his villa is Mon Repose."

"How do you get to this island?"

"There is a regular ferry service. It takes only thirty-five minutes to get there," Ivan said and drawing up a chair, he sat down, his small sensual eyes going to Janine's legs.

"We will go there this morning," Malik said.

"Not both of us," Ivan said. "One of us. This may not be the man we want. It is unwise we should be seen together. I will go. I will take with me four good men. It is unlikely he will be willing to tell us what we want to know. It'll be a matter of persuasion."

"Yes. All right, Ivan, you go then." Malik looked at his watch. "When does the boat leave?"

"I'll take the eleven-thirty boat. I haven't time to catch the ten o'clock." He got to his feet, dragging his eyes away from Janine. "We could have found some luck at last."

When he had gone, Malik said, "If this man tells us where Carey is hiding, then we will get rid of Girland. You will suggest to Girland you both go for a drive. You will bring him here. Tell him it is where your girl friend lives. It'll be a very simple matter then to get rid of him."

Janine felt a cold clutch of fear at her heart.

"I'll do what I can," she said and stood up.

Malik looked at her, his green eyes probing, but she forced herself to meet his gaze.

"And Kerman?" Malik asked. "Last night when you telephoned you seemed to think he was suspicious of you."

"Yes, but I may have been mistaken," Janine said, opening and shutting her handbag nervously. "He asked so many questions. I told you. He is dangerous."

Malik's thin lips twisted into a smile.

"So am I. One thing at a time. First, we get rid of Girland, then Kerman. The vultures can look forward to a feast."

Back at the hotel, Girland had a leisurely breakfast, and then went out onto the balcony to consider what he would do with himself that day.

First, he thought about Janine. She was a remarkable woman, but he was a little uneasy about her. The look she had given him just before he left her warned him she might be falling in love with him. That wouldn't do. Girland had no intention of getting too involved with any woman. To him the act of love was a mutual appreciation of the senses. There had been times when women had become possessive and difficult, but the majority of them were content to give themselves to him for an hour's enjoyment, sensing that he was never to be captured.

Impatiently, he switched his mind away from Janine and instead, he thought of Radnitz. This was the third morning since his arrival and Radnitz would be getting impatient. It was too dangerous to put a call through to Paris. Maybe he had better send a cable. If he sent it from the Dakar Post Office it could not be traced. Then there was Rosa's father. Girland wondered if he would get any information from this man. He doubted it. Seeing him could do more harm than good. But what other lead had he? There was Awa, of course. She might find out who this mysterious Enrico was. Perhaps he had better wait another day just in case she did come up with something.

Just after ten, as he was deciding to go down to the beach, the telephone bell rang. Wondering who it could be, he picked up the receiver.

"A call for you, sir," the operator told him. "Hold on a minute, please."

He heard clicking on the line, then Awa's sing-song voice.

"Mr. John? Is that you?" She sounded excited.

"That's right. It's Awa, isn't it?"

He heard her giggle.

"I found him like I said I would, Mr. John. I know where he lives."

"You mean our Portuguese friend?"

"Yes. I got talking to the girls last night and one of them said her boy friend knew him. So I went on my bicycle this morning and he told me. I had to give him a hundred francs, Mr. John."

"That's all right. I'll let you have it back. Who is he and where is he?"

"I will take you to him." The telephone exploded into excited giggles. "Then you can give me the money you promised me."

"All right, but when?"

"Can you come now?"

"Yes, but where?"

"Meet me at the railway station. I am phoning from there. I'll wait for you. You'll have the money you promised me with you, won't you, Mr. John?"

"I'll have it. See you in half an hour." He hung up. For a moment he stood thinking, then he unlocked the closet and took out his suitcase. He opened the false bottom and took out the

115

.45 automatic. From another pocket in the case, he took a short, efficient looking silencer. He checked the gun to see it was loaded, then he buckled on the holster and adjusted the gun. He put on his jacket and examined himself in the mirror. The gun made a slight bulge under the thin coat, but it wasn't too obvious that he was armed.

He looked in his wallet to make sure he had enough money, then leaving his room, he hurried down the corridor towards the lift.

Jack Kerman pulled up outside the American Embassy, parked his car and entered the building. He asked the doorman for Lieutenant Ambler who was Captain O'Halloran's opposite number in Dakar.

Five minutes later, Kerman was seated before a big desk.

Ambler was a powerfully built, youngish man with an alert, clean-shaven face. His steady grey eyes regarded Kerman's crumpled suit, his dusty shoes, his string of a necktie with disapproval.

"Yes, we know about you," Ambler said. "We had a cable from Dorey. What can I do for you?"

"I want to know who owns a car with this licence number," Kerman said, laying a scrap of paper on the desk. "Can you fix that for me?"

"Oh, sure." Ambler reached for the telephone. He asked to be connected with Police Headquarters. He spoke to someone, held on while he lit a cigarette, then said, "Fine. Thanks. Yes, I've got it," and hung up. To Kerman: "It's a hire car rented from the Lotus Car Agency."

"Can you find out who rented it?"

"Yeah. These people know us." Again Ambler reached for the telephone. After a short conversation, he said, "Thanks. What? Oh, no; it's just routine," and replaced the receiver. "The car was hired for a month by Wilhelm Jenson, a Danish tourist. He's staying at a furnished villa just outside Rufisque."

"Jenson ... a Dane?"

"Yeah. He had a Danish passport."

"Would you know where this furnished villa is?"

Ambler got to his feet and crossed over to a large scale map of Dakar and district that was pinned to the wall.

Kerman joined him.

116

"There it is," Ambler said and pointed. "About twenty kilometres the other side of Rufisque, up this lane."

Kerman returned to his chair.

"You get any fresh dope on this woman Rosa?"

"Nothing new. All we were able to find out about her is she worked at the Florida Club."

"Yep . . . Dorey told me." Kerman paused, then went on. "Any Russians arrived recently?"

Ambler looked sharply at him.

"Not as far as we know. Why?"

"Just got the idea the Russians might be interested in this thing. I could be wrong. Janine Daulnay been to see you yet?"

"No. We know she's at the N'Gor, but she hasn't been here."

"Well, thanks for your help." Kerman got to his feet. "I'll have to talk to Dorey some time. Can I use your scrambler?"

"Any time you want," Ambler said and walked with him to the door.

Girland found Awa waiting for him at the railway station. Giggling excitedly, she got in the car and directed him to the *Bassin Ouest*. She said her brother had a motor-boat and would take them across to the island.

"You pay my brother a hundred francs." She looked happily at Girland. "He will wait for you. You got my money?"

"Yes," Girland said, slowing down as he passed through the open gateway that led to the quay.

She pointed.

"Leave the car there."

He drove into the covered parking lot, got out, locked the car and then walked with her to where a line of fishing boats bobbed in the water.

Awa's brother, who told Girland his name was Abdou, was a powerfully built African with a cheerful ebony coloured face and who wore an electric blue robe that reached to his enormous-splayed feet.

He led Girland to a fast looking motor-boat. Boarding the boat, Girland sat in the stern. Fluttering and giggling, Awa sat opposite him while Abdu cast off. He started the engine, and once clear of the shipping, he opened the throttle and the boat surged forward.

It took less than half an hour to reach the small island. Abdou steered the boat past the Ferry station and moored alongside the mole. As Girland clambered out of the boat he glanced at his watch. The time was eleven forty-five. In the distance, he could see the Ferry steamer coming from Dakar. Had he known that Ivan was on board, he would have hurried, but the mid-day sun was so hot, he was content to take things at a leisurely pace.

"My brother waits here," Awa said. "I come with you. The house is not far."

They walked down the mole together and across a sandy plaza. The surrounding buildings were old and shabby and the streets narrow. Swarms of coloured children, some naked, some wearing dirty white shifts stared curiously at Girland as he walked with Awa, keeping to the meagre shade.

A five minute walk through the narrow, bakingly hot lanes brought them suddenly to the sea again. Awa paused and pointed. "There's his house. That one with the high walls."

Girland could see little of the house except for the red sloping roof. The white surrounding walls hid the house from view.

"I wait here," Awa said, sitting on a rock. "You will give me the money when you come back?"

"Yes," Girland said and set off at a brisker pace towards the house.

Heavy wooden gates guarded the entrance and when he lifted the iron latch, he found the gates locked. He stepped back, wiping his sweating face with his handkerchief, then seeing a hanging iron chain, he pulled it. From somewhere in the hidden garden, he heard the bell toll and again he waited.

There was a long pause, then a judas window in the gate opened and a black face showed itself.

"I would like to see Mr. Fantaz," Girland said.

Close-set black eyes studied him, then the man shook his head. "Mr. Fantaz is not in."

"I have important business with him. When will he be in?"

"Sometime after six this evening."

"Will you say I will be here at half past six and that I am a friend of John Dorey? Will you remember that?"

The man nodded and closed the Judas window.

Girland walked back to where Awa was sitting. She looked anxiously at him.

"Why didn't you see him?" she demanded. "He lives there. I know he does."

"He isn't in. I have to come back this evening."

"Then you give me my money?"

118

He gave her the three thousand francs he had promised her. She smiled happily as she put the money in her bag.

"You want to see the island? It is very interesting. There is a very interesting museum and a slave house. You will like it all very much."

"Not right now," Girland said. "Is there anywhere good were I can have lunch?"

"A very good hotel." Awa stood up. "I will show you. My brother will wait all day."

Girland decided now he was here, he might as well explore the island. He followed Awa down a narrow lane. For no reason at all, he felt an urge to look behind him. He stopped and turned. He was in time to catch a glimpse of Ivan as he walked slowly past the mouth of the lane, heading towards Fantaz's house.

"Wait here," Girland said sharply to Awa, and moving quickly, he walked to the end of the lane. He paused and cautiously looked around the wall.

Ivan was standing outside the gates of Fantaz's house, his fiery red face a mask of sweat. Girland watched him pull the bell chain.

As Ivan waited in the sun, Girland examined him. A Russian! he thought, feeling a prickle of excitement. So he had guessed right. The Russians were in on this. He watched Ivan talk to the gatekeeper, then step back as the Judas window shut. There was a snarling expression of rage on Ivan's face as he walked slowly to where Girland was concealed.

Girland looked around. Close by was an open doorway leading to a rubbish strewn courtyard. He stepped into the courtyard and concealed himself behind the open door. Through a crack in the door, he had a limited view of the bottom of the lane.

Ivan appeared and paused, wiping his face as he looked down the lane and then to right and left. A short, emaciated Arab, wearing a dirty robe and an even dirtier piece of cloth wrapped around his head, joined Ivan.

Ivan said, "He is not there and won't be back until this evening. Surround the house and wait for him to come. Keep out of sight. I am going to the hotel. As soon as he returns send one of your men to the hotel. Do you understand?"

The Arab bowed his head.

"Which is the quickest way to the hotel?"

The Arab pointed down the lane where Awa was still waiting.

Ivan's voice came clearly to Girland and he pressed himself against the wall as Ivan passed the courtyard. He waited several minutes, then moved cautiously into the lane. There was no sign of Ivan. Awa was squatting on her heels with native resigned patience. Seeing him, she stood up.

Girland joined her. He told her to take him to the hotel.

A ten minute slow walk brought them within sight of the hotel that overlooked the sea.

Girland said, "You can go back to Dakar now with your brother." He gave her money to pay her brother.

"My brother will wait if you want him."

"No. Tell him to go. And you: remember, don't talk about me."

She nodded, then turning away, she walked with long, lazy strides towards the mole.

Girland continued on to the hotel. He wondered if he were taking risks, letting the Russian see him, but decided it was safe enough. There were a number of white people on the beach and several Americans sitting at tables outside the hotel. He would be just another American tourist to the Russian.

He found a vacant table and sat down. There was no sign of the Russian. Glancing around, Girland found he was able to look through the windows into a small bar and there he saw him, leaning up against the bar, a bottle of Scotch and a half filled glass before him.

A waiter came languidly over to Girland. He ordered a beer. When the waiter returned a few minutes later, Girland asked him when lunch would be ready.

"It is ready now, sir. Upstairs." The waiter pointed.

"I'll go up in a minute." Girland turned to watch the Russian who was pouring himself another drink. He saw the Russian beckon to the barman and there was a brief conversation, then the Russian went back to his drinking.

Having finished his beer, Girland went up the stairs and into the L-shaped restaurant. There were only a few tourists in the restaurant and the waiter led Girland to a table so placed he could see both arms of the room.

He ordered the set meal and a bottle of Muscadet. It was while he was eating the hors d'oeuvres that Ivan came into the restaurant. He sat at a table near the entrance and looked around with the quick searching glance of a man who misses no details. Girland looked away as the Russian's eyes reached him. The next time Girland glanced in his direction, the Russian was studying the menu.

As Girland waited for his second course, two men came into the restaurant. The first man was bald and thin. He carried with him a briefcase, and as he followed the waiter to a secluded table, he took off his green sunglasses.

But it was the second man who held Girland's attention. He was tall and bulky. His face was round and fat. He wore a black moustache and dark glasses. He looked extraordinarily like ex-King Farouk. Glittering on the little finger of his left hand was a large gold signet ring.

Girland had no doubt that this heavily built man, walking towards him, was Enrico Fantaz.

Chapter Eight

A NUMBER of gaily dressed Africans, walking in single file, converged on the Ferry steamer as it manoeuvred into position alongside the mole.

Girland watched them from the window of the restaurant. He had finished his meal, and was now idling over his coffee. The Russian had gone. Girland had overheard him ask the waiter where he could find Room 12, and Girland guessed he was going to sleep off his heavy lunch.

From time to time, he glanced at Fantaz's table. The fat Portuguese had consumed an enormous lunch while he talked in low tones to his companion. Both men were now smoking cigars; coffee and brandy on the table.

"That's the boat," Fantaz said, slightly raising his voice and pointing at the steamer. "We have plenty of time. It doesn't leave until two o'clock."

The other man said, "You are sure you can spare the time, Mr. Fantaz? It is not really necessary to come all the way."

Fantaz waved a fat hand.

"Of course, I'll come. I have nothing to do this afternoon."

Listening, Girland finished his coffee and signalled to the waiter for his bill. He paid, then pushing back his chair, he left the restaurant and walked slowly through the intense heat to the steamer.

Now that he had found Fantaz, Girland was determined not to lose him. He decided to follow him until he parted with his companion, and then he would approach him.

He bought a ticket and went on board. He chose a seat that would enable him to get off the steamer quickly when it arrived at Dakar, and he settled down to wait.

Five minutes before the steamer was due to sail, Fantaz and his companion came across the sand, still talking. Fantaz, from time to time, gesticulated with his fat hands, his gold ring glittering in the sun.

They came on board, brushing past Girland and taking seats in the shade.

The half hour trip to the port of Dakar allowed Girland time for thought. What worried him particularly was he had no proof to give Fantaz that he did come from Dorey. It wouldn't be easy to persuade him to tell him where Carey was hiding. He would warn him about the Russians. This information might inspire confidence in him.

As the steamer bumped against the side of the mole, Girland, already on his feet, was the first off, followed by a crowd of chattering, laughing Africans.

He hurried to where he had parked his car, unlocked it and slid under the driving wheel, cursing at the oven-heat that had built up in the car. Lowering the windows, he started the engine and waited.

Fantaz and his companion, still talking, made their way towards a black Buick. The African chauffeur opened the car door and both men got in.

The car slid away, and Girland drove after it. Five minutes later, the Buick nosed its way through the traffic, swirling around Place de l'Independence, and double parked outside *Banque Internationale pour le Commerce et l'Industrie de Senegal.*

Girland drove past the stationary car, and watching in his driving mirror, saw Fantaz and his companion leave the Buick and enter the bank.

A car pulled out of a parking bay and Girland took its place. From where he sat, he could see the entrance to the bank, and although his car was parked in the full sun, he reluctantly settled down to wait.

The Buick drove away. After ten minutes, Girland, unable to stand the heat any longer, left the car and took shelter in the shade of the bank's arcade. He bought a newspaper and propping himself up against a pillar, he spent the next half hour glancing at the paper and watching the bank.

He was so preoccupied that he did not notice Janine coming towards him. The sound of her voice startled him.

"Why, hello," she said. "What are you doing here?"

Girland started.

"What are *you* doing here?" he asked, folding his newspaper and smiling at her. Again, he glanced at the entrance to the bank. He mustn't miss Fantaz, he told himself.

"I came in on the hotel bus. I've been shopping. Are you waiting for someone?"

Girland hesitated, then said, "Yes." He waved towards the bank. "One of my business contacts went in there and I just missed him. I'm waiting to talk to him."

Janine showed her disappointment.

"I was hoping we could go in your car and explore the town."

"I'm sorry. I have to talk to this guy . . . you know how it is." Girland grimaced. "Business."

Janine looked away. Her eyes were suddenly suspicious. Was this man who had gone into the bank someone who knew about Carey? she wondered.

"Oh, well never mind." She smiled up at him. "I must show you what I have just bought." She opened her bag and took from it a tiny, beautifully carved ivory idol. "The man who sold it to me . . ."

Girland saw Fantaz come out of the bank alone.

"Excuse me," he said quickly. "There's my man. I'll see you at the hotel tonight."

Janine was looking after Fantaz as he began to walk away from them.

"That's all right," she said. "I mustn't keep you. *Au revoir* then until tonight."

Girland touched her hand and then set off after Fantaz. Janine watched him. When Girland was only a few metres from Fantaz, he slowed his pace. He followed Fantaz around the corner and into rue Carnot.

Janine hesitated, then started after him. A dry, hot hand closed around her wrist, stopping her. She turned with a startled gasp to find Malik at her side.

"Leave him to me," Malik said curtly and pushing past her, he walked quickly after Girland.

Janine remained still for a long moment, her heart racing. She was sure now that the fat man was Fantaz. She was sure also Girland was in danger. There was no knowing what Malik might do if he got these two men in a lonely place.

It was then she realised how much in love she was with Girland. Ever since he had left her that morning, she had thought of him. She had never before been in love. Infatuated, yes, but she had never before experienced this feeling for a man that sent the blood coursing through her body every time she thought of Girland.

The thought of losing him was unbearable, and she realised she couldn't go on with this hunt for Carey. Whatever the consequences, she told herself, she must now side with Girland. She must warn him that Malik knew who he was. Even at the almost certain risk of losing her life, she would change sides if Girland would have her.

Moving quickly, she went after Malik.

Some way down rue Carnot, she caught sight of his silver blond head. She quickened her pace, dodging around the slow moving Africans who looked at her in surprised amusement.

Girland kept behind Fantaz who seemed in no hurry. Fantaz waited on the edge of the kerb for a break in the steady flow of traffic. Girland also waited behind him. Fantaz glanced at his watch, then crossing the road, he entered a corner café. Nodding to the barman, he made his way to a table at the end of the big room and sat down.

Girland crossed the road and paused outside the café. He saw Fantaz speak to the African waiter, then take a cigar from a leather case.

From across the street, Malik stopped to look in a shop window, his eyes shifting from the window to Girland. Further down the street, Janine stepped into a shop doorway, watching Malik.

When the waiter had brought a beer to Fantaz's table, Girland walked into the café. He wandered down the long room and took a seat at a table next to Fantaz who glanced at him, then looked away.

Girland ordered a beer and lit a cigarette. He waited until the beer was before him and the waiter had gone, then shifting his chair closer to Fantaz, he said quietly, "I called at your house this morning. I wanted to speak to you."

Fantaz drew on his cigar and let smoke drift out of his small. mouth. Sowly, he turned his head. From behind his black sunglasses, his eyes scrutinised Girland. His fat face remained placid and expressionless.

"Yes?" Fantaz's voice was husky and effeminate.

"John Dorey sent me to see you."

"John Dorey?" There was no reaction. "An unfamiliar name, Mr. ... Mr. ...?"

"I'm Mark Girland."

Fantaz picked up his beer and studied the tiny bubbles that rose in the glass.

"Another unfamiliar name," he said and shook his head. "What did you want to speak to me about?"

Girland glanced around the half empty café. There was no one who could overhear what they were saying. Lowering his voice, he said, "Robert Henry Carey."

Fantaz lifted his black eyebrows.

"Now that is a familiar name. How extraordinary! Some twenty-five years ago, when I was a very young man, Robert Carey and I were friends."

"Does that mean he isn't your friend any longer?"

"Twenty-five years, Mr. Girland, is a long time. We do sometimes out-grow our friends." The heavy fat shoulders lifted in a shrug. "Still, it would be interesting to meet Carey again. From what I can remember of him, he was an agreeable person to know."

Girland took another cigarette from his pack and lit it.

"Rosa told me you had seen Carey within the past two weeks."

"Rosa ... another familiar name," Fantaz said and sipped his beer. "You met her?"

"I was told to meet her by Dorey. I paid her seven thousand dollars for information she gave me. She was to have collected another three thousand dollars, but unhappily, she was not able to."

There was a long pause, then Fantaz said, "Most interesting. Just why wasn't she able to collect the rest of this handsome sum, Mr. Girland?"

"A gunman hired by Herman Radnitz shot her at Orly airport as she was leaving for Dakar."

The beer slopped a little in the glass Fantaz was holding.

"Is she dead?" The voice was huskier.

"She's dead," Girland said. "We were leaving in the same plane. I came on alone."

A trickle of sweat ran down Fantaz's face. He took out a crisp white handkerchief and dabbed at his cheek.

"And who is Radnitz?"

"The infamous Radnitz: there is no other. He also wants to find Carey."

"Why did he have Rosa shot?"

Careful, Girland warned himself. He mustn't get the idea I am working for Radnitz and not for Dorey.

"She was no longer of any use to him. He had bribed her to give him your name. He too is looking for you."

The black sunglasses were directed at Girland.

"And how do you know all this, Mr. Girland?"

"There's not much Dorey doesn't know. He told me."

While they were talking, Janine had finally made up her mind. She walked away from where Malik was standing and turning left at the end of the street, she came to a café bar. She entered and asked the barman if she could use the telephone.

Fantaz was saying, "All this is very interesting. It is also mysterious. What is expected of me?"

Girland began to lose patience.

"Dorey employed an agent to contact Rosa," he said, an edge to his voice. "This agent told me to handle it. Radnitz caught up with this agent. I found him with the nails of his fingers torn out and very much dead."

Fantaz slumped a little in his chair.

"That still doesn't answer my question, Mr. Girland. What is expected of me?"

Girland became aware that the bell of the telephone standing on the bar was ringing. He saw the barman answer, frown, then look around the café. His eyes met Girland's and he signalled to him.

"Excuse me for a moment," Girland said and crossed to the bar.

"You Mr. Gilchrist?" the barman asked.

"That's right."

The barman handed him the receiver.

"Someone wants you," he said.

Puzzled, Girland took the receiver and said, "Hello? This is Gilchrist."

Over the open line, he could hear the busy roar of the traffic, then a woman's voice, slightly muffled, said, "The blond Russian is following you. He is outside the café where you are now," and the line went dead.

Girland stood for a long moment, staring out into the sun baked street, then slowly he replaced the receiver. He was sure the woman who had spoken to him was Janine, and yet he could scarcely believe it. He remembered the big blond Russian he had seen on the N'Gor beach. He had a sudden tight feeling across his chest. If the Russian was really following him, he must know who he was. It was possible too the Russian had recognised Fantaz.

Girland went back to where Fantaz was sitting.

Fantaz had finished his beer and now looked up as Girland joined him.

"You will have to excuse me, Mr. Girland," he said. "All this is very interesting, but I have an appointment."

"A few minutes after I had called on your house, a Russian agent also called. At this moment your house is being watched and another Russian agent is outside watching this café."

Fantaz's mouth twitched and his face lost colour.

"How am I to know you are speaking the truth, Mr. Girland?"

"Call your house and ask your doorman if two men haven't been asking for you."

Fantaz didn't move. His forehead was creased into a frown as he thought.

"Where can I contact you?" he asked finally.

"I'm at the N'Gor. I'm registered there under the name of John Gilchrist. What do you intend to do?"

"That is my affair." Fantaz got to his feet. "I may contact you later."

"Don't go back to your house," Girland warned. "And watch out. You could land up very dead."

"I am able to take care of myself," Fantaz said. "Please remain here. I am leaving by the back way."

Girland watched him walk behind the bar, nod to the barman, then disappear through a door, screened by a dirty red curtain.

Girland finished his cigarette and his beer. Five minutes later, he saw Malik walk slowly past the café and glance in.

Girland resisted the temptation to wave to him.

Janine stood in the shade, waiting for the hotel bus to take her back to the hotel. She was surprised at her own calmness. She knew if Malik had the lightest suspicion that he had warned Girland he was following him, Malik would wipe her out with no more hesitation than killing a fly. But she had made up her mind now to side with Girland, and no threat of danger to herself would stop her.

It came as a shock, however, when Malik's black Cadillac pulled up by the kerb and she saw Malik sitting in the back seat.

His green eyes regarded her as he beckoned. Her heart beating rapidly, she crossed the sidewalk as he opened the car door.

"Get in," he said curtly. "I'm going back now. I will drop you at your hotel."

"Thank you," she said and settled herself beside him.

"The N'Gor," Malik said to the chauffeur who pulled away from the kerb.

"What happened?" Janine asked. "Who was the fat man? Were you able to find out?"

Malik stared straight in front of him, his thin lips in a tight line.

"It was Fantaz: the contact. He left the café where they were by the back way. I lost him."

"And Girland?"

"I left him there. He's now talked to Fantaz. I don't know if Fantaz has told him where Carey is hiding or not, but I intend to find out. Ivan is watching Fantaz's house. When he returns sometime tonight we'll have him. I have a job for you." He looked suddenly at her and she felt herself flinch at the cold expression in his eyes.

"Yes? What is it?" she asked, looking down at her bag, unable to meet those evil, probing eyes. She opened the bag and taking out a handkerchief, she dabbed her nose with it.

"Tonight, you will bring Girland to the bungalow," Malik said. "We will find out what he knows and then we will get rid of him."

Janine turned cold.

"I don't know if I shall see him tonight," she said, trying to steady her voice. "He comes in at all hours. Besides, what am I to say to him? Why should he come out to the bungalow?"

"I told you. Your friend Hilda is throwing a party. You want him to go with you. He'll go."

"But if he's late?"

"He won't be late," Malik said. "He had nothing to do now but to wait until Fantaz is ready to take him to Carey. Fantaz will first make inquiries about him. Girland will come back to the hotel to wait. You will bring him to my place at eight o'clock tonight. Do you understand?"

Janine nodded.

"I understand."

"Don't forget it is as important to you as it is to me that we find Carey. You don't want to spend ten years in a French prison, do you?"

Janine flinched.

"No."

"Well then."

The car slowed down and stopped as the traffic lights turned to red. Neither Malik nor Janine noticed Jack Kerman sitting in his Simca at the far traffic lights, but Kerman saw them.

He had been out exploring the country and was returning to Dakar. He stiffened at the sight of Janine and then his eyes went to Malik. He recognised the Cadillac. Was this the mysterious Dane? he wondered. He couldn't see Malik well through the windscreen of the Cadillac.

The lights changed to green and the Cadillac swept past him. With a shocking piece of driving, Kerman shot in front of two cars, drove too fast round the round-about and went tearing down the Autoroute in pursuit of the Cadillac.

Once in the straight, he saw the car, a half a kilometre ahead of him, moving very fast. He couldn't hope to overtake it, but he managed to keep it in sight. After a few kilometres, the Cadillac was forced to slow down and finally stop to let a herd of goats, driven by three grinning Africans cross the Autoroute. This stop gave Kerman a chance to catch up and by the time the Cadillac was moving again he was just behind it.

He was still behind it when the Cadillac swept up the drive into the hotel. He pulled into a parking bay and watched Janine leave the car and enter the hotel. Kerman got out of his car as the Cadillac pulled slowly away. He looked directly at Malik who glanced indifferently at him.

A Dane? Kerman thought. Oh, no. This was no Dane. He had seen too many Russians in his time not to be able to spot one when he saw him. This silver blond giant was a Russian!

Kerman ran up the steps and into the hotel. Janine was coming away from the reception desk, carrying her room key.

"Hello, there," Kerman said, coming up to her.

Janine started and lost colour. Her smile was forced as she looked at him.

"Where did you spring from?" she asked.

"I sprang. I want to talk to you. Let's go to the bar."

She went with him, her mind busy and uneasy. Had he seen her with Malik? she wondered. He must have done. Well, all right, she could cope with that situation. Had she aroused his suspicions? She knew she had lost colour at the sight of him and she knew too Kerman never missed a detail like that.

They sat down at a quiet table and Kerman ordered a beer. She said it was a little early for her to drink. She settled for a cup of coffee.

While they waited for the waiter to bring them their order, Kerman came straight to the point.

"Who was the man you were with in the Caddy?"

She had control of herself now and she looked mildly surprised.

"My dear Jack, why so intense? I was waiting for the hotel bus and he kindly offered to give me a lift."

"Is that right?" Kerman paused while the waiter put his beer before him and set down the coffee things. When the waiter had gone, Kerman went on. "He introduced himself, didn't he? What's his name?"

Janine's face hardened.

"You sound as if you were cross-examining me. I don't think I like that."

Kerman smiled.

"Nothing of the kind. I have an idea I have seen him before. He's a Swede, isn't he?"

She looked thoughtfully at him. She mustn't arouse his suspicions, she thought as she said, "I believe he is. He looks Swedish, doesn't he? His name is Bergman and he is here for a few days on business."

Kerman drank some of his beer. She was lying, of course, he told himself. If she really hadn't known this man it was obvious he would have introduced himself to her as Wilhelm Jenson. And as for looking like a Swede, she had enough experience to see that he had Russian written all over him.

"Don't you think he might be a Russian?" he asked.

Janine's eyes opened wide.

"You know that never occurred to me ... come to think of it, he could be, couldn't he?"

"Did he ask you any questions?"

"Just the usual. Was I enjoying my stay? How long was I staying ... that's all."

Kerman thought for a moment, then shrugged.

"The trouble with me is I'm too suspicious." He laughed. "Well, let's forget him. Any news?"

"No." She looked at her watch. "In a few minutes, I'm taking the bus to the airport. The four o'clock Paris plane is due in. Maybe Girland will be on it."

Kerman got to his feet.

"Okay, then I'll get going. Can I drive you to the airport?"

"I want to go to my room first." She stood up. "No, don't wait for me, Jack. Keep in touch."

"You bet," he said and leaving her he walked up the stairs and into the reception lobby.

Girland had just come in. The two men passed each other, Girland going to the desk for his key, Kerman going out into the hot sunshine to his car. He stood by his car, thinking.

He was now sure that his first suspicions were right. Janine was a double agent. She was working for Dorey and also for the Russians. Kerman had no doubt on whose side she would come down on under pressure. He must alert Dorey. Then he had a sudden idea. He walked away from his car and took up a position behind another parked car where he could see the entrance to the hotel. He waited.

Five minutes crawled by and he saw the hotel bus pull up outside the hotel. Several people came from the hotel and buying tickets from the driver, got into the bus. The driver waited a further five minutes, then got into the bus, slammed the door and drove away.

Kerman nodded to himself. So she wasn't even watching the airport. Another nail in her pretty coffin. He returned to his car and drove fast to Dakar.

Girland had driven back to the hotel, his mind puzzled and confused. He now had little doubt that Fantaz would contact him some time that night at the hotel. Fantaz would first get into touch with Carey to make certain Carey wanted to see Girland. Once he got the all clear he would stop being mysterious.

But Girland was worried about Fantaz. This blond Russian had seen him and Fantaz wasn't the kind of man you could miss on the streets. Girland only hoped that Fantaz hadn't been bluffing when he said he could take care of himself.

But what really puzzled Girland was the mysterious telephone call. Had it been Janine's voice? If it had been Janine, then what was the explanation?

Keep it simple, he told himself as he speeded along the Autoroute. She could have seen this Russian, recognised him and watched him follow me. Knowing him to be Russian she had become alarmed and had gone to a telephone and warned me. She must have seen me go into that café. That could be the explanation, but he wasn't satisfied.

Could Janine be an agent? He wondered. They had met so

casually and so conveniently, the way a trained agent hooks up with a prospect. If she were an agent, who was she working for? Dorey?

He was still puzzling over this as he collected his key, and then moving to the lift, he saw Janine coming from the bar.

She looked pale and worried, and she gave him only a fleeting smile as she came up to him.

"John, I must talk to you. Will you come to my room?"

"Sure," he said. "Something on your mind?"

They entered the lift and he pressed the button to the seventh floor.

"Yes. Let's wait until we get to my room."

Leaving the lift on the seventh floor, they walked in silence down the long corridor and down the few steps that led to her room. They entered and she locked the door.

She moved away from him, then turned and faced him.

"I know who you are," she said quietly, "you are Mark Girland."

Girland rubbed the back of his neck, frowning, then he took off his coat, undid the gun holster that was shaffing his ribs and laying the gun and coat on the table, he sat down.

"Well, go on. Let's hear more about this before I do any talking."

"I am U 2260," Janine said, dropping on the bed. She kicked off her shoes and opened her bag, took out a cigarette. "Mean anything to you?"

Rossland had once told Girland that Dorey had a very special woman agent working for him.

"She's quite a girl from what I hear," Rossland had said, with his leering grin. "I've never met her, but I've seen some of her reports. She's known as U 2260."

"So you work for Dorey," Girland said. "Yes, I've heard of you. Well, thanks for the telephone call."

Janine waited, but as Girland remained silent, his face expressionless, she said, "Do you know why I am here?"

"It's pretty obvious. Dorey sent you out here to keep an eye on me. Why have you suddenly decided to come into the open? You had me fooled."

"Did I?" She lifted her shoulders. "You had me fooled too. I really thought you were John Gilchrist, an American business man."

Girland frowned.

"I'm not with you. Didn't Dorey send you out here to watch me?"

"Dorey didn't send me here at all. It's a lot more complicated than that. When I told him I was going to Dakar, he was pleased, but it wasn't his idea. He thinks you are dead." She tapped ash off her cigarette. "You are working for Radnitz, aren't you?"

Girland smiled at her.

"You're doing the talking. I don't have to say anything."

"Please, Mark, don't be hostile," she pleaded. "I'm not trying to trap you. I've been stupid enough to fall in love with you."

Girland kept his face expressionless, but he moved uneasily.

"I'm sorry. I'm a bad person for any woman to fall in love with. I mean that, Janine. I had an idea that might be happening. I should have left you alone."

"Oh, no. I'm not blaming you. This sort of thing does happen. I thought I could sleep with you and get away with it as I've done often enough with other men. Why did you have to be such a perfect lover?"

"Is that why you have fallen in love with me?"

"That and other things."

"Well, I'm sorry. Do you want to go on with this, Janine? If I cleared out and stayed in Dakar would you have to tell Dorey you've spotted me?" Then he looked sharply at her. "Just how did you spot me?"

"I was wondering when you were going to ask me that," she said and hesitated. "Do you love me at all, Mark?"

"I don't know. Frankly, I don't think I'm capable of loving any woman. You interest me. I often think of you. I have a feeling of affection towards you. I can't go further than that."

"Well, at least, you are truthful." Her smile was bitter. "You wouldn't want to spend the rest of your days with me?"

"I couldn't spend the rest of my days with any woman. Look, Janine, do we have to go on with this? I hate hurting you, and that's what I'm doing."

She dropped back on the pillow and stared up at the ceiling. Well, she knew the truth now, she thought, but it doesn't make any difference except it hurts and hurts. I couldn't let him walk into Malik's trap. I couldn't bear anything bad happening to him.

"You asked me how I knew who you were," she said, drawing on her cigarette. "It was quite simple. Malik told me."

Girland stiffened.

"Malik. Who's he?"

"Haven't you heard of Malik? Surely Rossland or someone has told you about him."

"You mean the Russian agent?" Girland leaned forward. "That blond hunk of beef? Is he Malik?"

"Yes. That's Malik."

"*He* told you? Why? What's he to do with you?"

"U 2260 is a double agent, Mark."

Girland got to his feet and went over to where his coat was lying on the table. He took from one of the pockets his pack of cigarettes. By the time he sat down, he had his face under control. He lit a cigarette, then asked, "Why are you telling me this, Janine?"

"Because I love you I suppose."

This word love, Girland thought impatiently. Women *will* use it. It is like a sharp hook they try to sink into you: a barbed hook they hope won't come out.

"Malik has orders to find Carey," Janine went on. "Carey has vital information the Russians can't afford to let him pass on. Malik sent for me to come out here. He knows much more than Dorey does. Actually, Dorey knows practically nothing. He does know he made a mistake in not dealing with the Foucher woman direct. He does know now she had important information to sell, and he is still trying to find out through me and Kerman what that information is." She looked across at Girland who was tense and listening. "Kerman is here. I think he is beginning to suspect that I am working for the Russians. He saw me with Malik this afternoon." She made a helpless little gesture with her hands. "I think I am coming to the end of my career as an agent." She paused, then went on very quietly, "I think I am coming to my end."

"What else does Malik know?" Girland asked.

"He knows about Fantaz, but you have guessed that, haven't you?" She half sat up to stub out her cigarette. "He knows about Kerman too." She looked at him. "You are working for Radnitz, aren't you?"

Girland stared at the glowing end of his cigarette, frowning.

"Malik knows that too," Janine said.

"He's quite a bright boy, isn't he?" Girland said, an edge of anger in his voice. "Well, he's right. Yes, I am working for Radnitz. I didn't have much choice. Not that I'm excusing myself. I'm sick of working for a mean little miser like Dorey. Radnitz has offered me fifty thousand dollars to find Carey. Carey has a microfilm that Radnitz wants. Why should I care? He's willing to pay for it. Dorey would never offer money like that."

"Money means a lot to you?"

He nodded.

"I have wasted ten years of my life fooling with people like Dorey. I have about five hundred dollars in the bank to show for those years. Yes, money means a lot to me."

"I have money, Mark. You and I could go away and get lost. You wouldn't have to take Radnitz's money. You might even learn to love me."

"Stop it," Girland said, gently. "You know that wouldn't work out."

She lifted her slim hands and studied them. Her lips were trembling.

"I suppose you're right. I really don't know what I'm going to do . . . now."

Girland stared at her, suddenly realising her position.

"Do you think Kerman will report to Dorey his suspicions that you are a double agent?"

"I suppose so. He is shrewd. He can tell Dorey enough for Dorey to check on me, but I'm not really worried about Dorey."

"But Malik doesn't know you're telling me all this. Do you have to worry about him?"

"I'm supposed to take you to his place tonight. It's an order. I am to tell you my friend Hilda is throwing a party and she wants to meet you. Now Malik knows Fantaz is Carey's contact, he plans to get rid of you."

"Some time tonight or tomorrow morning, Fantaz will contact me," Girland said. "Tonight, I am tied up with a business meeting. I will be happy to come to Hilda's place tomorrow night. By then I should be on my way to find Carey. Tell Malik that."

"He wants you there tonight. It's an order."

"Tell him I will come tomorrow night," Girland repeated. "He'll wait. It won't be your fault I am tied up. He'll see you can't press me without raising my suspicions."

"Yes. All right." She stared up at the ceiling. "I want to get away from all this, Mark, but I don't see how I can do it." She gave a resigned shrug. "Well, I'm not going to bother you with my troubles."

Girland got up and sat on the bed by her side.

"Why in the world did you hook up with the Russians?" he asked, taking her hand.

"You've never been bored, have you? They say the devil finds work for idle hands. I turned to the Russians because I was so bored with Dorey. I wanted adventure and danger ... well, I have them now." She smiled at him. "I don't like them as much as I thought I would."

"Why don't you take tomorrow's plane back to Paris? Just chuck it. Tell Dorey you're not working for him any more. If Malik contacts you, tell him the same." He knew he was talking nonsense. Once an agent always an agent until those you worked for had no further use for you, but he couldn't think of anything else to say to her.

"I might." She slid her arms around his neck. "Love me a little, Mark. It won't be for much longer. Don't talk any more ... just love me."

The hidden microphone that had transmitted every word they had said to the revolving spools of a tape recorder in the room next door now recorded her soft moans of pleasure as Girland joined his body with hers.

Chapter Nine

A LITTLE after four o'clock, the Paris plane touched down and taxied to the arrival centre. A few minutes later, passengers began passing through the Police Control.

Two men ... one tall, dark and hatchet-faced, the other short and fat ... moved along with the crowd, each carrying a light hold-all, their cheap tropical suits ill-fitting and obviously bought in a hurry.

The fat man as he moved towards the Police Control was staring around him with rounded eyes. He particularly gaped at the massively built African women who were waiting beyond the barrier to welcome their friends coming off the plane. Their brilliant clothes, their gold ornaments and their ceaseless chatter seemed to intrigue him. His companion, his cold dark face expressionless, didn't even look at them. This was the first time Borg had been to Africa. Everything he saw delighted him.

Once through the Police Control and the Customs, the two men walked side by side out of the airport building and into the violent afternoon sunshine.

"Did you see those women?" Borg asked excitedly. "Man, oh, man! All that black meat! Imagine ..."

"Shut up!" Schwartz said without looking at him. He set down his bag and looked from right to left. An African, wearing a red uniform approached.

"The N'Gor Hotel, sir?" he asked.

Borg nodded.

"The bus is waiting," and the African pointed. "Leaving in five minutes."

The two men walked to the bus, bought tickets and climbed in. There were several other people in the bus, mostly American and French business men.

Borg settled himself beside Schwartz and stared out of the window.

Late the previous evening Radnitz had received a cable from

Girland. Its contents had been so vague and unsatisfactory, he had called Borg to the George V Hotel.

"You are to go with Schwartz to Dakar on the morning plane," he said. "Find out what Girland is doing. He's wasted enough time. Report back to me by cable when you have talked to him."

Borg now wished he had a better travelling companion. He was prepared to enjoy himself, but how could anyone hope to enjoy himself with this kiss of death in his hair?

During the short drive to the hotel, he gaped at the hawks floating just above the sea, at the herds of goats moving slowly along the beach, at the flat fishing boats and at the women. Every now and then, he whistled softly and punched his fist into the open palm of his hand.

But it was no good attempting to share his excitement with Schwartz who stared stonily ahead of him, not looking at the view, his mind preoccupied with his own mysterious thoughts.

At the hotel, Borg checked in. Radnitz's secretary had already telephoned for two reservations and there was no difficulty.

As Borg completed the police cards for them both, he asked, "Have you got Mr. Gilchrist staying with you?"

"Yes, sir." The clerk turned to look at the keyboard. "He should be in."

"Call him, will you?"

The clerk picked up the telephone receiver and rang Girland's room.

It was at this moment that Girland, in Janine's room, had taken her in his arms. He didn't hear the telephone bell ringing in his room. If he had, he would have let it ring.

"I'm sorry, sir," the clerk said, hanging up. "There's no answer. It is possible, Mr. Girland is on the beach or has gone out, taking his key with him."

"Okay," Borg said. "I'll be up in my room. When he comes in, call me, will you?"

"Certainly, sir."

A girl wearing a bikini, an open beach wrap over her shoulders came up to the desk and asked for her key. Borg stared at her, then pursed his lips with a soundless whistle.

As he followed the porter to the lift, Schwartz moving behind him, Borg decided he was going to enjoy himself here.

Lieutenant Ambler led Kerman into a small room, equipped with a desk, two chairs and a green telephone.

"That's the scrambler," he said. "Shut yourself in. You won't be interrupted. Anything else you want?"

"Not right now, Lieutenant, maybe later," Kerman said as he sat down.

"Just say the word." Ambler nodded and left the room.

Kerman put a call through to Dorey's office. Then taking out a notebook and putting a pencil on the desk, he waited impatiently for the connection.

Three minutes later, he heard Dorey's voice, coming clearly to him from Paris.

"Kerman. I'm calling from the Embassy, Dakar. Let's scramble, Mr. Dorey." He pressed the scrambler button.

"I'm scrambled," Dorey said. "What's been happening?"

"Plenty." Kerman lit a cigarette. "I'll try to give this to you as it happened. Stop me if you want to ask questions." Carefully and with detail, he told Dorey of his meeting with Janine at the airport and then all the subsequent happenings.

He could hear Dorey's light breathing and now and then a rustle of paper as if Dorey were taking notes.

"Give me a description of this so-called Dane," Dorey broke in suddenly.

"He's quite a boy. About six foot four, big with it, silver blond hair, green eyes, good looking, and if he's a Dane, then I'm General de Gaulle."

There was a long pause.

"That's Malik," Dorey said finally. "One of the top Russian agents. I've seen him. It's Malik all right."

"Well, there you are," Kerman said. He knew Malik by reputation as most American agents did. "So . . . what do you think?"

"Janine was actually with him?"

Kerman moved impatiently.

"I saw them in the car together. We've got to face facts, Mr. Dorey. Looks like Janine is a double agent, and you can bet your last dollar which side she'll come down on when the red light goes up. What do you want me to do?"

Dorey, sitting at his desk, his files spread out before him, had a sick cold feeling in the pit of his stomach. Janine! A double agent! He couldn't believe it. He had trusted her utterly during the past year. He and she had discussed Top Secret problems. He had shown her files meant only for his eyes. His fingers gripped the telephone receiver until they began to ache.

There was still a chance that Kerman had been mistaken.

Perhaps Malik had known she was an American agent and was trying to get friendly with her. Maybe it was only that. To condemn her because she had been seen in a car with Malik ... then he remembered what Kerman had said. She had been to this mysterious bungalow. So this was the second time she had seen Malik. Again he tried not to accept the evidence. Janine fell for handsome powerfully built men. She could have fallen into a trap set by Malik. It was possible she thought Malik was a tourist and was having fun with him.

"Mr. Dorey!" Kerman said impatiently. "What do you want me to do?"

"You haven't real proof that she is working for Malik," Dorey said desperately. "I know her better than you do. She's unstable with men. She might have fallen for Malik not knowing who he is."

"How come she isn't watching the airport then? That's her job out here. Why did she lose colour when she saw me after her drive with Malik?"

"There could be an explanation," Dorey said. "I can't believe she is working for them, Kerman. I just can't believe it."

"I'm giving you the facts. It's your business and your responsibility how you interpret them ... not mine. What do you want me to do?"

"Go to the hotel right away, Kerman. See her. Tell her she is to come back here by tomorrow's plane. Tell her I have another job for her to work on and I'm sending out a replacement. Don't say anything to make her suspicious. Be friendly. Say you happened to be in the Embassy when I called and I told you to give her the message. Understand?"

"Suppose she won't go back? Suppose Malik won't let her?"

Dorey wiped his sweating forehead with the back of his hand.

"Then get Ambler to arrest her and have her flown back under escort."

"Can do ... will do," Kerman said and hung up.

The telephone bell brought Janine awake. She sat up, her heart beginning to pound. She looked with frightened eyes at Girland.

He half raised himself on his arm, blinking a little, then nodded to the telephone.

"You'd better answer it." He glanced at his watch. The time was twenty-five minutes to six.

141

Janine picked up the receiver.

"A Mr. Kerman asking for you, Madame," the clerk told her. Janine hesitated, then said, "Ask him to wait in the bar. I'll be down in twenty minutes."

Girland was already off the bed and dressing.

"Who is it?" he asked, slipping into his short-sleeved shirt.

"Kerman."

"Think he's been talking to Dorey?"

"I suppose so." Janine got off the bed and walked into the bathroom. Raising her voice above the sound of the shower, she said, "I'm not worrying about him. It's Malik who worries me."

Girland lit a cigarette and sat on the edge of the bed. He waited until she came back, wearing bra and panties.

"Stall him for tonight," he said. "Then do what I said: get the hell out of here. Go back to Paris."

She looked at him, forcing a smile.

"You're staying, Mark?"

"Yes. Now look, I'd better get off in case they're watching the hotel. As soon as you get rid of Kerman, phone Malik. I'll go into Dakar and I'll be back sometime tonight. We'll meet and see how it is working out. Okay?"

She went to him and put her arms around him.

"I love you Mark. You're the first and you'll be the last. You don't know it but you're the most wonderful thing that's ever happened to me. I don't care now what becomes of me."

He looked at her, worried, then he kissed her. She clung to him for a brief moment, then pushed him away, smiling.

"Goodbye, Mark. Think of me sometimes."

"Don't get dramatic." He frowned at her. "Nothing's going to happen. By tomorrow I'll be out of here with any luck and you'll be on your way to Paris."

"Yes."

They looked at each other, then Girland went to the door, opened it cautiously, looked back at her, smiled and went quickly across the lobby to his room.

He strapped on the gun holster, put on his coat, checked to see if he had money and cigarettes, then left his room and took the lift to the reception lobby. As he handed in his key, the clerk said, "Excuse me, Mr. Gilchrist, two gentlemen were asking for you. Mr. Borg and Mr. Schwartz. Do you wish me to call their rooms?"

Girland kept the surprise from his face. So Radnitz was getting impatient, he thought. These two thugs could complicate things.

"Not right now," he said. "I'm in a hurry. I'll see them when I get back. I'm expecting a telephone call. If anyone asks for me will you tell him I shall be in the bar of La Croix du Sud Hotel?" He took a fifty franc note from his wallet and slid it to the clerk. "Don't tell my friends upstairs where I'll be. This is an important business date and I don't want to be interrupted."

"I'll take care of it, sir, and thank you."

As Girland was leaving the lobby, he saw Janine, wearing a lemon coloured sleeveless frock come out of the lift and make her way down to the bar. He hesitated, then with an irritated shake of his head, he left the hotel and crossed to where he parked his car.

Janine found Kerman sitting in the shade on the terrace, drinking beer. He grinned at her as he got to his feet.

"Hello there," he said. "What will you drink?"

"Oh, I suppose a gin and tonic." She sat down.

When Kerman had given the order to the waiter, he said casually, "No one on the four o'clock plane?"

"No."

"I have a message for you."

The waiter set down her drink and went away. Janine, a little tense, was staring at Kerman who seemed quite at his ease.

"A message for me?"

"I was in the Embassy this afternoon when Dorey called." Kerman paused to drink some of his beer, noting that Janine's hand had turned into fists. "He wants you back. A job's come up he wants you to handle. He's sending a replacement out here by tomorrow's plane. He wants you back in Paris tomorrow. Okay?"

"If I can get a reservation."

"I've fixed that." Kerman put an Air France envelope on the table. "There's your ticket. All you have to do is to pack."

"Well, all right. I'll be sorry to leave. It's not been a very satisfactory job, has it?" Janine sipped her drink.

This was working out better than she had thought. Even if Kerman had told Dorey she was a double agent, she was sure they had no real proof. She was equally sure she could handle Dorey. She had always been able to talk him into her way of thinking.

"No, it's been a waste of time," Kerman said. "I have an idea we'll never find out what that woman wanted to sell. Just another foul up."

"Are you staying on?" she asked, looking at him over the rim of her glass.

"For a few more days. I have nothing to work on, but you know Dorey ... he expects miracles." He got to his feet. "Well, I'll be moving. When you see Dorey tell him I'm wasting my time out here and I'd just as soon be back in Paris."

"I will."

"*Bon voyage.*"

With a wave of his hand, Kerman ran up the stairs and disappeared from her sight.

She finished her drink and lit a cigarette. She sat thinking for five minutes or so, her face expressionless, her eyes cloudy, then she got to her feet and returned to her room.

The time by her watch was twenty-five minutes past six. It was time to call Malik.

She sat staring at the telephone, aware of fear in her heart. It was some minutes before she forced herself to pick up the receiver. She gave Malik's number and waited.

Malik came on the line.

"Yes?"

The sound of the deep voice made Janine flinch.

"I have seen Mr. Gilchrist," she said, trying to make her voice sound casual. "I asked him to the party tonight, but he can't come. He has a business date which he can't break. I thought it better not to try and persuade him. He will be very happy to come tomorrow night so I have arranged to come with him at eight tomorrow."

There was a pause on the line, and she drew in a long, shuddering breath.

"I said tonight," Malik said softly.

"I know, but he can't come tonight."

Again that pause, then he said, "Well, never mind. We're wasting time, but tomorrow night will have to do. I've sent the car for you. It will be outside the hotel by now. I have something to talk to you about," and the line went dead.

She sat there, holding the receiver, her body cold, her heart thumping and her mouth dry. Slowly, she replaced the receiver, got up and walked to the window.

The black Cadillac stood before the hotel. The African

144

chauffeur, his fez at a jaunty angle, was chewing on a bamboo stick.

She went to her closet and took a handbag from it. She unscrewed the ornamental knob on the clasp of the bag and shook from the hollow recess a tiny glass phial, no bigger than the nail of her little finger. She held it up to the light. It was filled with a colourless fluid and she wondered if the fluid had gone stale. She had had it some time. Dorey had given it to her.

"You better have this," he had said. "It's part of the equipment. One never knows. If you're unlucky ever to get into a really bad spot, crush the phial between your teeth. You'll be dead in seconds."

She put the phial in her mouth and with her finger, she lodged the phial between her gum and the inside of her cheek. It felt quite comfortable there and looking at her white frightened face in the mirror, she could see no tell tale sign that the phial was hidden in her mouth.

Then picking up her bag, she went out of her room and locked the door. Walking briskly, her head held high, she made for the lift.

Borg blew out his fat cheeks and let the air escape in a whistle of boredom. He was standing by the open window of his room, looking down on the drive-in to the hotel. He had been standing there, watching the arrival of various cars for the past half hour.

"There's a black Caddy just come in," he said to Schwartz who was sitting away from the window, smoking and reading a newspaper. "Some job! The Wog driving it is wearing a god-damn fez! Now, I wonder what I'd look like in one of those gimmicks. Think I'll buy myself one. It'd kill my piece of tail."

Schwartz turned a page of the newspaper. He wasn't listening.

Borg growled at him.

"I could do with a drink. You coming?"

"No," Schwartz said.

"Well, I'm going. I'll be in the bar..." Borg broke off and leaned forward to stare out of the window. "Goddamn it! There he is! Here, quick!"

The urgency in his voice brought Schwartz out of his chair and to his side. The two men peered out of the window.

They saw Girland walk down the steps of the hotel, cross to a D.S. Citroen, slide under the driving wheel and then the car moved swiftly away and headed towards Dakar.

"What do you know?" Borg said in disgust. "Why didn't that damn Wog tell him we were here?"

"How do you know he didn't?" Schwartz's eyes still followed the Citroen as it moved swiftly along the stretch of Autoroute.

Borg looked suspiciously at him.

"Think he's double-crossing us?"

"How do I know?"

Borg hesitated, then shrugged.

"No use sticking around here. Come on, for Pete's sake, let's have a drink."

Schwartz folded his newspaper and the two men took the lift down to the reception lobby.

The clerk who Borg had spoken to wasn't behind the desk. Borg asked one of the porters where the bar was. He and Schwartz went down the stairs and into the bar. Borg ordered a double whisky on the rocks and Schwartz a beer.

As Borg was finishing his drink, a porter came around calling, "Mr. Gilchrist, please, Telephone."

Borg got to his feet.

"Stick around," he said to Schwartz and walked casually up to the reception lobby. He saw one of the clerks holding a telephone receiver and looking around the lobby. Borg moved up to the desk and pretended to be examining a selection of Postcards in a rack on the counter.

The clerk said into the receiver, "I'm sorry, sir, Mr. Gilchrist has gone out." He listened, then said, "Hold on a moment, sir, I'll see." He reached for a pad and thumbed back a few pages. "Yes, sir, there is a message. Mr. Gilchrist will be in the bar of La Croix du Sud this evening. That's right," and the clerk hung up.

Borg wandered over to the doorman.

"What's La Croix du Sud?"

"A hotel in Dakar, sir."

"I want to go there. Get me a taxi."

"Certainly, sir. It'll be here in five minutes."

"I'll be in the bar," Borg said and hurried back to where Schwartz was waiting. Borg signalled to the waiter to bring him another drink, then said to Schwartz, "Girland got a call just now. He's on his way to a hotel in Dakar. I've ordered a taxi. You want another beer?"

Schwartz shook his head.

Borg waited impatiently until the waiter brought this drink

and he paid the check. Then swallowing the drink in a gulp, he led the way up the stairs back into the lobby.

The two men stood on the top of the steps in the fading evening sun until the taxi arrived. Having tipped the doorman, Borg climbed into the taxi, followed by Schwartz. He told the driver where to go and sat back, mopping his sweating face.

As Girland entered the bar of La Croix du Sud, an African pageboy was wandering around the bar, calling, "Mr. Gilchirst, please. Telephone."

"That's me," Girland said, going up to the boy. He dropped a franc piece into the boy's hand.

"First booth on the left, sir," the boy told him and pointed. Girland shut himself in the booth and lifted the receiver.

"Hello? This is Gilchrist."

"Ah, Mr. Gilchrist." Girland recognised Fantaz's husky, effeminate voice. "I was beginning to think I had missed you. It would be interesting if we had another little talk. You have a car?"

"Yes."

"Could you come to Diourbel?"

"Yes."

"Excellent. You will be most careful? You know what I mean? As you enter the town, you will see on your left a large open space with trees. A yellow Fiat will be waiting. Shall we say nine o'clock, Mr. Gilchrist?"

"I'll be there."

"Good. Until then, Mr. Gilchrist."

Girland returned to the bar. Glancing at his watch, he saw he had time for a quick dinner and another drink.

He was sitting up at the bar, drinking whisky, when a familiar voice said, "Hello, palsy: long time no see."

He turned to find Borg grinning at him. Behind Borg, was Schwartz.

As Jack Kerman left the N'Gor Hotel and was crossing to his car, he saw the black Cadillac come up the sweep of the drive and park before the entrance to the hotel.

Without pausing, he continued to his car, unlocked the door and got in. He lowered the windows, lit a cigarette and waited, his eyes on the Cadillac.

He didn't have long to wait before Janine appeared. The sun had set and it was difficult to see much of her in the fading light, but he was convinced that it was Janine. She got into the Cadillac, nodding to the driver who held the car door open for her. The driver slid under the driving wheel as Kerman started his car engine. He followed the Cadillac until it took the branch road to Rufisque.

Then in case Janine suspected she was being followed, he continued on along the main road. As soon as the Cadillac was out of sight, he pulled up, U-turned and went after the Cadillac.

As he drove he wondered if Janine would tell Malik she had orders to return to Paris, and if she did, how Malik would react.

He finally came to the sandy secondary road that Ambler had pointed out to him on the map. By the cloud of dust, slowly settling, he knew the Cadillac had passed this way recently. He pulled up and surveyed the scene. He would take no risks, he told himself. He wouldn't drive past the bungalow. He would wait. He backed the car off the road and into the bush. It would be dark soon and the car would be invisible if anyone passed. Getting out of the car, he sat with his back to a tree and settled himself to wait.

Janine got out of the Cadillac as the driver opened the car door. During the drive to the bungalow, she had been asking herself why Malik had wanted to see her. Was he suspicious of her? Had she been seeing too much of Girland? Had he an idea that she planned to leave tomorrow? Trying to reassure herself, she thought probably he had a job for her.

She walked into the hall, and then through to the big lounge.

Malik, alone, was sitting in an easy chair. He was wearing an open neck white shirt and a well fitting grey tropical suit. He had a pile of cables on a table beside him and he was decoding a cable which he held in his hand. He glanced up, nodded and waved to a chair.

"I won't be long," he said.

Gripping her handbag, Janine waited. Minutes crawled by. Malik worked steadily. Finally, after what seemed to Janine an eternity, he dropped the cable on the pile on the table and turned to stare at her. His green eyes were impersonal, his face expressionless.

"So you talked to Girland and he couldn't come tonight," he said. "Why couldn't he come?"

"I told you. He said he had a business date."

"And did you guess what the business date was?"

"Fantaz?"

148

"Of course. He won't come here tomorrow night because he hopes by then to be with Carey."

Janine didn't say anything.

"But he won't be with Carey because I have four men watching him, and at a convenient moment, they will kill him."

Janine flinched inwardly, but she had enough control over herself to keep her face expressionless.

"Will you be sorry?" Malik asked, continuing to stare at her.

Janine stiffened.

"Sorry? Why should I be?"

The sudden evil in his eyes frightened her.

"I just wondered. I would have thought you would have been sorry." He got to his feet and crossed over to a cupboard. From it he took a tape recorder which he set on the table. He plugged the lead into the mains and switched the machine on. "This will amuse you," he said. "It amused me." He pressed the play-back button, adjusted the volume knob and then moved away, his eyes on Janine's face.

From the loudspeaker of the recorder, she heard herself say, "I know who you are. You are Mark Girland."

She closed her eyes, feeling the blood drain out of her face, her body turning cold.

"All right," she said. "Turn it off. I don't want to listen."

The loudspeaker was saying, "Well, go on. Let's hear more about this before I do any talking."

"No, we'll listen to it. The sighs and moans at the end are very amusing," Malik said.

This was her end, Janine thought. How could she have been so stupidly careless not to check to see if her room had been bugged? She shut her ears to the sounds coming from the recorder. She didn't want to die. She was frightened of death, but she knew there was no mercy to hope for from Malik. She had betrayed him too thoroughly.

Finally, she became aware that the recorder was silent, and she looked at Malik who stood by the recorder, watching her.

"I am surprised," he said, "you could have been so stupid to have fallen in love with a man incapable of love." He shrugged. "Well, this is the end for you. In some ways, you have been useful, but we have never entirely trusted you. You have the mind of a whore. We have kept track of your various men friends. I felt sooner or later you would meet a man who would make a fool of you." He looked at his watch. "Come with me."

Janine got to her feet.

"What are you going to do with me?" she asked huskily.

"You'll see. Follow me."

He turned and moved to the door.

For one panic stricken moment, she had the urge to rush past him, out into the hall, through the doorway and into the darkness of the night, but she knew she wouldn't get even as far as the door. She would be helpless in the grip of this man. If she was going to die, she would try to die with dignity.

Bracing herself, she followed him out of the room, across the hall and into a small bedroom. He stood aside to let her pass.

There was only a bed in the middle of the room and an upright chair by the wall. The wooden shutters were locked across the windows.

She stood by the bed, trying to control the fluttering muscles in her legs. She kept her hands behind her so he couldn't see that her hands were trembling.

He shut the door and leaned against it.

"Take your clothes off, please," he said in a quiet, polite voice.

She stiffened, jerking up her head.

"No!"

"I have five Arab servants who work in the garden," Malik said, his expression bored, "If you don't do what I ask, I will call these men who will take an unhealthy pleasure in stripping you naked. Please, undress."

Her tongue touched the glass phial and she hesitated. Should she use it now? Yet even at this moment, life was still precious to her. She hesitated and was lost. With shaking fingers, she undressed, looking at him from time to time, terrified that he could watch her with such bored, detached eyes. He was as impersonal as a doctor waiting to make an examination.

When she stood naked before him, he pointed to the bed.

"Lie on the bed, please."

She sat on the bed, her hands hiding her breasts and looked pleadingly up at him.

"Can't you just shoot me? Do you have to do this to me? I have been useful to you. I . . ."

"Lie flat, please."

As she dropped back on the pillow, he moved so swiftly she had no chance of realising what he was doing until it was done. Her ankles were locked into the rings of handcuffs attached to the bed posts and then as she tried to sit up, screaming to him not to touch her, he fastened her wrists to the top of the bed.

He moved away and looked down at her, spread-eagled on the bed.

"I'll leave you now," he said. "I'm late for an appointment. I have told my servants to make use of you in my absence. You've lived like a whore so you must be prepared to die like one."

She lay there, panting, fighting back the scream that rose in her throat.

"There are seven of them," he went on. "None of them are very clean. They know I will be away all night. No doubt they will tell their brothers and their cousins what is to be had in this room. You should have a very busy and disgusting night. I can't think of a more suitable way for you to end your love life, can you?"

She closed her eyes.

There was a long pause and then she heard the door shut. She made one hopeless and desperate effort to slip out of the handcuffs, but only succeeded in tightening them. She heard a murmur of voices, then the sound of the Cadillac starting up, then silence.

As the door opened a few inches and a brown, rat like face appeared around the door and two black beady eyes alighted on her, she gave a shuddering sob and crushed the glass phial between her teeth.

Chapter Ten

GIRLAND'S CARE-FREE grin, as he shook hands with Borg, masked a feeling of dismay. How had these two tracked him here? he wondered as he said, "Well, where did you drop from?" He ignored Schwartz who stared stonily at him. "Have you just arrived?"

Borg got up on a stool beside Girland and signalled to the barman.

"Gimme a big whisky on the rocks," he ordered, then to Girland, "The boss is getting the ants. He wants to know what the hell you are doing." He reached for his drink, nodded to Girland and drank. "Just what *are* you doing, palsy?"

Girland said, "Do you think this is a good place to talk about that?"

Borg looked around the room, saw a vacant table in a corner and nodded to it.

"Over there do?"

Girland got off his stool and the two men, carrying their drinks, crossed the room to the table and sat down. Schwartz joined them, pulling out a chair and sitting, he faced them.

"I couldn't give Radnitz the full dope in a cable, and it wasn't safe to use the telephone." Girland leaned forward and lowering his voice, went on, "the Russians are in on this. They have two agents right here in Dakar and they are watching every move I make . . . except the ones I don't want them to watch."

Borg's eyes bugged out.

"You mean they know who you are?"

"They know that all right, and they know I'm working for Radnitz. And another thing, Dorey's got a man out here too. He's on to me as well."

"So you're having fun, huh?"

"You can call it that. The set-up is tricky. I've found Carey's contact: a Portuguese. He imagines I'm working for Dorey. Tonight, I have a date with him and I think he'll take me to Carey."

"That's something!" Borg said excitedly. "That's what the boss wants, isn't it?"

"But I've got to handle this alone, Borg. If Fantaz sees you two, he won't play. As it is, he's suspicious of me. As soon as I've talked with Carey and got what Radnitz wants out of him, I'll contact you two."

Borg hesitated.

"I don't know about that. The boss said . . ."

"We stay with you," Schwartz said. "The boss said from now on, we work together and we stick together."

"Well, yes, that's right," Borg said. "That's what the boss said, palsy. We'll keep out of sight, but we're sticking with you."

"How do you do that and keep out of sight?" Girland asked impatiently. "If Fantaz spots you, he won't play."

"Then I'll persuade him to," Schwartz said.

Girland thought for a moment, then shrugged. Maybe these two might be useful, he told himself. If Malik moved in, he might not be able to handle him on his own.

"Well, okay," he said. "I have a date with Fantaz at nine o'clock at Diourbel. It's about an hour's drive from here. If you come with me, you've got to keep out of sight when I meet him. Is that understood?"

Borg nodded.

"Well, I'm hungry," Girland said. "We have time for a quick snack. There's a place just around the corner."

The three men left the hotel and made their way to a café bar.

A thin African, wearing a shabby European suit watched them enter the café, then he walked down a narrow street to where an old, dusty Buick was parked.

Samba Dieng sat at the wheel, a cigarette drooping from his thick lips. Two other Africans, also in European dress sat in the back of the car, also smoking. They all looked at the thin African as he poked his head into the car and began to talk rapidly to Dieng.

"Three of them?" Dieng looked startled. He turned to the other two sitting at the back. "He has two others with him."

"What's it matter?" The African who spoke had a knife scar down the side of his face. The expression in his black eyes was vicious. "We can handle them," and his black hand rested lightly on the machine gun he had across his knees.

153

"Get in," Dieng said to the thin African and started the car engine.

The thin African obeyed, slamming the car door. Dieng drove past the café, glanced in, catching a glimpse of Girland as he leaned against the bar, eating a sandwich. Dieng was aware of two other men with Girland but he had no time to see them properly.

He found a parking space further down the street and stopped. The thin African got out and walked back until he was opposite the café. He lolled against the wall and waited.

At a quarter to eight, Girland paid for the sandwiches and nodded to the other two.

"Let's go. I have a car across the way."

As the three men walked over to the Citroen, the thin African returned to the Buick. He climbed in and Dieng started the engine. He watched the Citroen pull out and turn the corner and he followed. There was a certain amount of traffic on the road and he had no fear that the men in the Citroen would suspect they were being followed. The time to worry about that would be when they were in open country.

Girland drove in silence, but when they reached the Autoroute, he said, "Watch out behind. We don't want to be tailed."

Borg shifted around in his seat and stared back at the long stretch of dark road.

"Three cars and a truck behind us."

Girland reduced speed.

"We'll let the cars overtake."

A few minutes later, two cars roared past.

Borg said, "The truck and a car. The car is keeping behind the truck."

"Watch it," Girland said and once again increased speed.

"The car's coming out now from behind the truck. It's coming after us."

Girland continued to drive fast for the next ten minutes, then he began to slow down.

"We're coming to the turn off." He braked slightly and swung the car onto the Rufisque-Diourbel road.

After a minute or so, Borg said, "Looks like a tail, palsy. The same car still with us."

Girland slowed down.

"He's slowed," Borg reported.

"We'll stop at Rufisque. Let's see what he'll do then," Girland said and again increased speed.

When they reached the crowded main street of Rufisque, Girland pulled up, got out of the car and walked over to a cigarette stall. As he was buying a pack of cigarettes, he saw a dusty Buick drive rapidly past. He caught a glimpse of four men in the car before the car disappeared into the darkness.

"That the one?" he asked Borg as he walked back to the Citroen.

"That's it," Borg said.

"We have a little time in hand. We'll stick around here for five minutes. They were all Africans in the car as far as I could see. Maybe they weren't following us."

He stood by the car, breathing in the hot night air while Borg and Schwartz remained in the car.

Borg said, "This place kills me. Look at those Wogs. What have they got in their mouths?"

"Bamboo sticks," Girland told him. "That's how they keep their teeth so clean."

He got back into the car.

"Watch out," he said as he engaged gear. He drove slowly out of the town. When once clear of the horse-drawn carts, the swarm of unsteady cyclists and the slow moving crowds, he increased speed.

"The next town is Thies, then Diourbel," he said.

Later, after they had driven through Thies, Borg said sharply, "We have our tail back."

"Then they know we are going to Diourbel," Girland said. "You two got guns?"

"What do you think!" Schwartz said. This was the first time he had spoken during the whole drive.

"The car's coming up," Borg said and pulled a Colt automatic from his holster. "It's coming up like a goddamn streak."

Girland kept glancing in his driving mirror. The Buick flashed on its headlights, and Girland edged off the centre of the road, his off-side tyres leaving the tarmac and biting into the sandy verge of the road.

The Buick went roaring past. Borg saw the outlines of four men in the car. None of them looked their way, and then the Buick was ahead. Driving at well over a hundred and eighty kilometres an hour, its tail lights began to disappear into the darkness.

"What do you make of that?" Borg said, putting his gun back into his holster. "False alarm, huh?"

"Could be." Girland flicked on his headlights. "Don't relax. The road is straight and narrow for some kilometres. They could be going on ahead to fix an ambush."

"Then don't drive so fast," Borg said, hauling out his gun again. "We don't want to run into them."

Ten minutes crawled by. Girland was now driving at a steady sixty kilometres an hour. Suddenly, the Citroen's headlights picked out something in the road ahead of them.

Girland's sharp eyes saw it was a car parked across the road, forming a barrier.

He slammed on his brakes and the car screeched to a standstill.

"Out!" he exclaimed and opened his door. He rolled out of the car, hitting the sandy verge with his shoulder and then flattened down in the sand. His hand jerked his gun free from its holster.

Both Borg and Schwartz also threw themselves out of the car, both darting for cover along the side of the road.

They had scarcely dropped flat before there was a burst of machine gun fire. They heard the windscreen of the car shatter and the car heaved as bullets slammed into the back of the seats where the three men had but seconds ago been sitting.

Schwartz's .45 crashed into sound. There was a yell and a shadowy figure rose up from behind the bonnet of the Buick and fell forward.

Girland heard the machine gun clatter to the road. He began to crawl forward. In the uncertain light of the moon, he saw something move and he took a snap shot at it, his gun barking spitefully. There was a howl of anguish and a tall figure straightened up, clutching his arm. Schwartz's gun banged again and the man dropped, spreading out on the road.

The other two men had had enough. They turned and ran, keeping low. Girland heard their pattering footfalls as they dashed for shelter, then he heard them crashing through the thickly growing shrubs. Cautiously, he stood up and with Schwartz, advanced towards the car. Borg remained flat in the sand, sweat running off his face, his breath coming in short gasps.

Reaching the Buick, Girland kicked against the machine gun which he picked up. Schwartz was bending over the fallen men. He grunted and straightened. Girland joined him.

"They've wrecked our car," he said. "We'll take theirs. Let's get going."

Satisfied it was now safe to move, Borg scrambled to his feet and ran up.

"Jeeze! That was close," he panted. "What do we do now?"

Girland got in the Buick.

"Hurry up! They may come back."

Borg got in so quickly, he hit his head on the frame of the car half stunning himself.

Schwartz was already in the back seat, his gun in his hand, peering through the open window at the darkness of the bush.

Girland straightened the car, then sent it surging forward.

"Well, they tried," he said. "They can't follow us now." He looked at his watch. He had ten minutes in which to reach Diourbel and he squeezed down on the gas pedal.

Rubbing his head, Borg said, "Think there is going to be any more of it? Goddamn it . . . a machine gun!"

"You ought to have thought of that," Schwartz said. "Why didn't you fix it we had one?"

"Yeah? We'd have looked pretty crummy trying to smuggle a machine gun through the Customs, wouldn't we?"

Girland wasn't listening. He was thinking that there were no means for the two men who had got away to alert Malik the ambush had failed . . . anyway, for some time. With luck, he would now reach Carey without having to worry about any opposition.

Ahead of him, he could see the street lights of Diourbel, and he slowed down.

"You two stay with the car. I'll handle this on my own."

"You're welcome," Borg said. "You could walk into a mouthful of slugs."

Schwartz said, "I'm telling you, Girland. You try to lose me and you'll end up dead."

"Do what you like, but keep out of sight." Girland pulled up between street lights and got out of the car. "Just remember, Radnitz will love you two if you queer my pitch."

Leaving the car, he walked quickly down the road until he came to the open space on the left as described by Fantaz. In the shadowy moonlight, he could make out a parked car.

His hand slid inside his coat and his fingers closed over the butt of his gun. He walked slowly towards the car, a little tense and very alert.

157

Whoever was in the car saw him. The car door swung open and a man got out. It wasn't Fantaz. This man was short and slim and looked youthful. He came towards Girland who kept moving and the two men met in the open space away from the trees.

Girland could see now that this man was dark and swarthy. He had black curly hair and seemed less than twenty years of age. He smiled at Girland.

"My uncle told me to meet you," he said, offering a lean, hard hand. "I am Gomez."

Girland shook hands, relaxing.

"Had a little trouble on the road. I'm a little late."

"Trouble?"

"I'll tell your uncle about it. Where is he?"

Gomez glanced around.

"Excuse me. I don't see your car. Are you alone?"

"Fortunately, no," Girland said. "If I had been, I wouldn't be here now. I have a couple of men with me. They're waiting for me just round the corner."

Gomez stood for so long in silence, staring at Girland that Girland asked sharply, "What are you hesitating about?"

"My uncle said you would be alone."

"Well, so I am alone. I'm leaving my men here."

He hoped Schwartz would have the sense not to show himself if he did follow behind.

"Very well. Will you come with me?" Gomez turned and walked back to the yellow Fiat.

"Is it far?" Girland asked, falling into step with him.

"It's no distance."

They got in the car and Gomez started the engine, turned the car and headed down the main street. Girland resisted the temptation to see if the Buick was following.

"It's hot here," he said. "Much hotter than Dakar."

"It's inland," Gomez returned. He was driving slowly. The road was crowded with Africans, wandering aimlessly along and talking to one another. The acetylene lamps above the food stalls attracted the insects that swarmed and buzzed around the hard white light.

After a two minute drive, Gomez turned down a sandy road and pulled up outside a white house, surrounded by a wire fence on which was growing a dense creeper.

They got out of the car and Girland glanced back in time to

see the Buick drive slowly past the entrance to the road.

He followed Gomez into the small garden and up the steps. Gomez took a key from his pocket and unlocked the front door. He stepped into a dimly lit hall, then opening a door on his right, he motioned Girland to enter.

Girland walked into a large room, lit only by a red shaded lamp that stood on the table. The far end of the room was in darkness.

Sitting by the table, smoking a cigar, was Fantaz. As Girland came closer to the light, he was aware that there was someone else there: someone concealed in the heavy shadows at the far end of the room.

"Well, here I am," he said to Fantaz. "I had a little trouble getting to you."

There was a movement at the other end of the room and then a girl came into the light. She was a tall blonde, wearing a bush shirt and fawn slacks, and in her right hand, she held a .38 automatic which she levelled at Girland.

"You idiot!" she said to Fantaz. "This isn't the man ... this isn't Girland!"

Then with a shock of surprise, Girland recognised her: the girl who had been wearing a *New York Herald Tribune* sweater when last he had met her: the girl who called herself Tessa.

A gun jumped into Gomez's hand and he moved around so he could cover Girland who was smiling at Tessa.

"Hello, baby," Girland said. "You certainly disappointed me, running out on me like that: I was expecting great things from you. Where did you spring from?"

The girl peered at him, a puzzled expression coming into her eyes.

"A pretty good disguise, isn't it?" Girland went on. He removed the two cheek pads. "Take off the moustache and forget the blond rinse, and it's your boy friend once again."

Slowly, she lowered the gun.

"Why yes, I recognise you now." She still seemed very suspicious of him. "Why are you wearing a disguise?"

Girland wandered over to an armchair and sank into it.

"Dorey thought it safer," he said airily. "My handsome face is known to the Russians." He lit a cigarette and leaning forward went on, "Pardon my curiosity, but exactly where do you fit in here?"

159

The girl moved further into the light and sat down on an upright chair by the table. She looked at Fantaz who lifted his fat shoulders in a shrug.

"I'm Tessa Carey," she said. "I am Robert Henry Carey's daughter."

Girland let out a whistle of surprise.

"Why didn't you tell me that when we first met in Paris?"

"I had my reasons. I wasn't ready to tell you."

"Why did you search my apartment?"

"I wanted to be sure who you were. Then when I was convinced you were the man my father told me contact, I had to leave. I had a cable from Enrico telling me to come here at once."

Girland looked puzzled.

"Your father told you to contact me?"

"Yes. He wasn't sure Dorey would co-operate. He wanted you as a second string."

Girland thought of Malik.

"Do the Russians know you are out here?"

"I don't think so."

"Why have you come out here?"

"I'm looking after father."

"One of the Russian agents working here is a man known as Malik," Girland said. "He's a character to be avoided. If he finds out who you are and gets hold of you, it'll be too bad for you and your father."

"Someone has to look after father," Tessa said.

"What's the matter with him?"

"He's ill. He's very sick." She looked away, her lips trembling. Girland turned to Fantaz.

"What's wrong with him?"

"We don't know, but it's something bad," Fantaz said. "He keeps wasting away. We can't get a doctor to him. He won't hear of it."

"And he's cooped up in an awful little hut. He can't get out," Tessa said. "There are a number of Arabs in Russian pay searching for him. They have been searching for him now for over a month. They keep getting closer and closer to where he is hiding."

Girland rubbed the back of his neck, frowning.

"Suppose you take me to him? We used to know each other ... not well, but we liked each other."

"But you can't go looking like this," Tessa protested. "If I

160

didn't recognise you, how do you imagine he will?"

"Get me a hair dye and I'll be my normal self in five minutes."

"We can't get that until tomorrow."

"I'm not waiting until tomorrow. Get me a hat and a burnt cork: that'll do until you get me the dye."

Gomez went out of the room and returned a few moments later with a straw hat, a cork from a bottle, a candle and matches.

"I'll get this moustache off first," Girland said. "Where's the bathroom?"

Ten minutes later, wearing the straw hat, Girland was recognisable as himself.

"All right now?" he asked Tessa who had turned on all the lights in the big room and was looking at him.

"Oh yes. He'll know you now."

"We ran into a little trouble on the way out here," Girland said.

Tessa stiffened.

"We? Aren't you alone?"

"Dorey sent two of his men out here yesterday. He wants this job wrapped up quickly. You needn't worry about them. They will keep in the background. Without them, I wouldn't be here now," and Girland told her briefly about the ambush.

He was quick to see Fantaz had lost colour and was sweating by the time he had come to the end of his recital.

"I don't like this," Fantaz said. "I shouldn't have brought you out here, Tessa. None of us will be safe. I know these Russians."

"Don't let's waste time. How long will it take to reach your father?" Girland asked Tessa.

"It's a good three hours' drive from here."

"What are we waiting for?" He got to his feet. "Let's go." He looked at Fantaz. "You coming?"

The fat man shook his head.

"I'm staying here." He glanced at Gomez. "You stay too."

Gomez hesitated.

"Perhaps I should go with them. Suppose they run into trouble? Three are better than two."

"What about me?" Fantaz's voice went shrill. "I'm not staying here alone! It's your duty to remain with me. I have taken too many risks already."

"Stay with him," Girland said, then turning to Tessa, he asked, "Have you a car?"

"It's at the back. I have an African guide waiting."

"Do we have to take him?"

"We'd be lost in five minutes without him. He used to be my father's house-boy. It is he who is hiding him."

"Well, okay. Then let's go."

"What about your two men?"

"They're watching the main road. Better leave them there. If your father is as bad as you say he is, he won't want them around. Come on, let's go."

She led him through the kitchen and out into the dark, hot yard, through a gateway to where a Deux Chevaux stood waiting.

A stooped, grizzled-haired African got out of the car and bowed to her.

"This is Momar," Tessa said. "Momar, this is Mr. Girland. He is here to help father."

Black suspicious eyes stared at Girland, then the old African grunted. He climbed into the back seat of the little car.

As Tessa was about to get in the car, a hoarse voice demanded. "Hey, palsy, just where do you think you're going?"

Tessa spun around as Borg appeared out of the darkness. She stared at the fat man who was gaping at her.

"Who's this?" Borg asked. "What's all this about?"

"Where's Schwartz?" Girland asked, moving up to Borg. He caught hold of his arm and began to lead him away from the car.

"He's watching the front," Borg said. "Wait a minute. What are you shoving me around for? What's going on?"

"Keep your voice down," Girland said. He kept pushing Borg further into the darkness. "I told you if you queered my pitch, I'll tell Radnitz."

"You're running out on us," Borg protested, coming to a halt. "Now look palsy; I like you but that doesn't mean I trust you. We stick together ... understand? Who's the girl?"

Girland stepped back slightly to give himself room, then his fist flashed out in a crushing punch to Borg's jaw.

Borg grunted and began to fall forward. Girland hit him again, then lowered him to the ground. He turned and ran back to the car.

"Let's go!" he said. "Come on, come on, let's go!"

Tessa started the car engine.

"What's happened? Who is he? Did you hit him?"

"Never mind! Drive!"

The car moved forward; bumping over the uneven ground; then slowly gathering speed. There was no road, only shrub and loose sand. Tessa reached for the headlight switch, but Girland struck her hand down.

"No lights!" He peered back, but could see only darkness.

"I can't see where I'm driving," Tessa wailed. "We'll hit a tree or something."

"Keep going," Girland said. "We won't hit a thing."

Tessa slowed the car and leaning forward to peer through the windscreen, she guided the car through the tall shrubs, avoiding the trees as they loomed out of the darkness until after a ten minute, nerve-racking drive, she reached the main road into the bush.

"There you are ... not a tree damaged," Girland said cheerfully. "You can put on the lights now."

Tessa stopped the car and swung around to face him.

"Who was that man? I've seen him before somewhere. Who is he?"

"One of Dorey's boys, and as useful as a hole in the head. Forget him. Come on, we're wasting time."

"But I've seen him before ... in Paris."

"So what? He lives in Paris. Get moving!"

A puzzled expression still on her face, Tessa drove the car through the loose sand covering the road and into the wastes of the bush.

Hearing the sound of a car engine, Schwartz, watching the front of the house, hesitated, then ran around the house to the back entrance. He was in time to see the car, without lights disappearing into the darkness of the bush. He lifted his gun, then paused. Maybe it was some crazy African driving home. Where was Borg?

A strangled grunt made him turn and he saw what looked like the body of a man lying in the shadows. He went over and found Borg slowly gaining consciousness from the two punches Girland had given him.

Cursing, Schwartz kicked Borg savagely.

"Get up, you jerk," he snarled. "What's happened?"

"Nearly bust my goddamn jaw," Borg moaned, sitting up and nursing his face. "Never gave me a chance."

Schwartz kicked him again and Borg hurriedly staggered to his feet.

"Lay off!" he whined. "Girland nearly bust my jaw."

Schwartz spun around, looking into the dark bush. He could still hear the car, but he no longer could see it.

"Where did he go?" he demanded, grabbing Borg and shaking him.

"I don't know. He had a girl with him. I caught them getting into the car, and then Girland went for me."

"A girl?"

"Couldn't see much of her . . . a girl all right."

"You slob!" Schwartz was beside himself with rage. "He's going after Carey and we've lost him! We haven't a hope in hell to follow them in the bush."

"It wasn't my fault."

"You should have shot him."

Borg leaned against a tree. He was still feeling dizzy and his jaw ached.

Schwartz turned and stared at the white house. He could see a light coming through a chink in the shutter covering one of the windows.

"Someone's in there," he said, lowering his voice. "We'll see who it is."

Without waiting for Borg to argue, he went around to the front of the house and moving like a black shadow, he crept into the garden and then up the steps to the front door.

Borg followed him, his gun in his sweating hand.

Schwartz gently turned the handle of the door and pushed. As the door swung open, he paused to listen. He could hear voices. He looked back over his shoulder at Borg and nodded, then he crept into the dimly lit hall.

He let Borg pass him, then he silently shut the front door.

He heard a man say, "I don't like them going off like that alone, uncle. I should have gone with them."

"I've done enough for Carey," a husky voice replied. "I was crazy to have helped him in the first place. If I'd known the risks, I wouldn't have done it. Now the girl's here to look after him, we're going to keep out of it."

Schwartz nudged Borg, nodded and silently stepped to the half open door. He moved into the room, his gun threatening the two men who faced him.

Fantaz was in the arm-chair. He was in the act of stubbing out his cigar. Gomez was sitting on the edge of the table.

At the sight of Schwartz and Borg, Fantaz dropped the cigar

butt on the floor. His fat face sagged, turning a yellowish green. Gomez stiffened, his eyes going to his gun on the table near him.

"Don't move!" Schwartz barked. "Get the gun," he went on to Borg who moved to the table and snatched up the gun which he stuffed into his hip pocket.

"All right," Schwartz said, staring at Fantaz, "now we'll talk. Who's the girl who has just left with Girland?"

Neither Fantaz nor Gomez said anything. They remained motionless, staring at Schwartz.

"You want me to soften you up, fatso?" Schwartz asked and began to move towards Fantaz, sliding his gun through his fingers until he was holding it by the barrel. Fantaz watched him, horror growing in his eyes.

"Wait!" he gasped. "I will tell you. She is Carey's daughter." Schwartz stood over him.

"Carey's daughter? Have they gone to him?"

"Yes."

"Where is he?"

"In the bush."

"I know that, you fat fool." Schwartz hit Fantaz on his knee with the butt of the gun. Fantaz groaned, but didn't move. "But where?"

"I know," Gomez said. "Leave my uncle alone and I'll take you to Carey. You'll never find the place on your own. It's a three hour drive into the bush."

Schwartz and Borg exchanged glances, then Schwartz nodded.

"Okay, you come with us." He turned to Fantaz who was clutching his aching knee. "You stay here. If you want to see your boy friend again, don't do anything smart. Understand?"

Fantaz nodded. He looked at Gomez whose dark face was expressionless.

Borg gave Gomez a shove.

"Come on. You got a car?"

"Yes, but I'm low in petrol." Gomez seemed calm and at ease. "There's nowhere here to buy petrol until tomorrow morning."

"Well take the Buick," Schwartz said to Borg. "Go and get it."

Borg nodded and went out of the room.

Schwartz moved away from the other two and leaned against the wall. They waited in silence until they heard the Buick pull up outside the house, then Schwartz jerked his head at Gomez who gave Fantaz a fleeting smile before he walked out of the room.

"Watch it!" Schwartz warned, staring stonily at Fantaz. "You start something and you won't see him again."

He went out and joined Borg and Gomez. He got in the back seat of the Buick, motioning to Gomez to get in the front seat beside Borg who was to drive.

"Which way?" Borg asked, starting the engine.

"Three kilometres up the main road and then you take the first on the left," Gomez said, settling back in his seat.

Borg looked at him suspiciously.

"That's not the way they went."

"We have to use the bush road. Their car is light. If we go through the sand as they did, we'll get stuck."

This made sense to Borg. He reversed the car and drove onto the main road.

Schwartz touched Gomez's neck with the barrel of his gun.

"You try anything funny, Buster, and I'll make a hole in your head."

Borg drove through the crowds that were wandering in the road. Several smiling Africans hopefully tried to thumb a ride, but Borg kept the car moving. At last they were through Diourbel and once again on a clear road.

"Just ahead to the left," Gomez said. "You'll have to drive fast. Don't drop below sixty or we'll get stuck."

The headlights picked out the narrow road that seemed to Borg to be a track of loose white sand. On either side of the road, the flat bush spread out in wastes of sand and scrubby shrubs.

As Borg drove, he felt the rear wheels of the car slipping occasionally. The night air was stifling and his hands were slippery with sweat. It was a drive he wasn't enjoying.

As kilometre after kilometre disappeared behind them into the darkness, Borg began to experience the uncanny feeling that, in spite of the speed at which they were travelling, they weren't moving at all. It was like being on a fast moving belt on which he was running but because of the speed of the belt, he could make no forward progress. The sand, the shrubs, the trees and the flatness of the terrain were identical: the scenery never changed. It began to worry him.

After they had driven for over an hour, Gomez said, "We'll have to leave the road now. You must be careful how you drive. Don't accelerate suddenly. Keep a constant speed or we'll get stuck." He leaned forward to peer through the windscreen. "Turn off just here. Don't slow down."

Muttering, Borg swung the wheel and steered off the road into the bush. He let the rear wheels slide to the left. He steered into the skid, resisting the temptation to accelerate. The car shuddered, slowed, then picked up speed and began bumping over the knots of grass, shaking the three men about in their seats so they had to hang on.

Suddenly an enormous tree with spreading arms appeared in the beams of the headlights. Startled, Borg swung the car away from it, his foot automatically pressing down on the brake. The car slowed, the engine jerked and stalled. The car stopped.

Borg cursed.

"Well, get on!" Schwartz shouted at him.

Borg started the engine again and engaged gear. He let in the clutch and gently accelerated. The rear wheels spun in the sand, but the car didn't move.

Schwartz opened the car door.

"Stay where you are. I'll push." He went around to the back of the car and put both hands on the boot. "Now!"

Borg again let in the clutch and Schwartz pushed with all his strength, but the wheels of the heavy car settled further into the sand and Schwartz's feet sank into the sand up to his ankles.

"Go and help him," Borg said to Gomez who got out and joined Schwartz who was panting and swearing.

But even Gomez's added weight failed to move the Buick. The wheels now had sunk down to their hubcaps. Schwartz moved back, wiping the sweat streaming down his face with his shirt sleeve.

"We must collect wood and leaves," Gomez said. "Then we must level the sand around the wheels and pack the wood and leaves around the tyres. In this way we will be able to move the car again."

Borg joined them. He looked at the sunken rear wheels and felt a twinge of fear. The wheels looked as if they would never climb out of their twin, sandy graves.

"Come on!" Schwartz snarled at him. "You heard what he said." And he began tearing up small shrubs and throwing them in a pile by the car. Borg moved further away and began to collect dead branches that were scattered over the sand. Gomez walked over to the big tree and began stripping leaves from the lower branches.

167

They worked for some ten minutes, then Schwartz straightened and looked around. He couldn't see either of his two companions in the darkness and he became alert. He had been so occupied that he had forgotten the other two until now.

"Hey, Borg!" he shouted.

Borg came out of the darkness, carrying a pile of branches.

"Where's the punk?" Schwartz demanded.

Borg gaped at him.

"He was with you, wasn't he?"

"He was with you, you slob!" Schwartz snarled. He peered towards the enormous tree some twenty yards to his right. "He was there."

Throwing down the branches, Borg ran to the tree, but he could see no sign of Gomez.

"Hey! Where are you?" he bawled. "Come back here!"

Gun in hand, Schwartz joined him.

"He can't have gone far. Come on!" and he broke into a run, his feet sinking into the hot sand, making progress difficult and slow. "I'll beat that jerk to a jelly when I get him!"

Panting at his side, Borg kept stumbling over clumps of brown dried grass. The heat was like a smothering damp blanket. Sweat turned his shirt black.

Finally, exhausted, he stopped running and stood gasping for breath. In no better state, Schwartz ran on for a few more metres, then also stopped.

The two men listened, but they could hear nothing but the violent thumping of their own hearts.

"He's got away," Schwartz said and raised his clenched fists above his head. "We'll go back to the house and I'll cut that fat pig to pieces. Come . . . back to the car!"

Scarcely able to drag one foot after the other, Borg followed him.

The darkness worried Borg. He could only see a metre or so ahead of him, and he kept running into prickly shrubs that seemed to spring out of the ground before he could avoid them.

They moved past the tree, but after walking a few steps, Schwartz stopped and peered into the darkness.

"Where's the car?" he demanded.

"It must be just here," Borg said.

"Well, it isn't!" Schwartz looked at the tree and then at the place where the car should have been. "You don't think he came back and took the car?"

"How could he?" There was a quaver in Borg's voice. "It was sunk up to its hubcaps."

"Well, it's not here now." Schwartz put his gun back into his holster and stared at the tree again. "Think this is the right tree?"

"I don't know. Looks like it, but the place is lousy with trees."

"It all looks the same to me," Schwartz muttered. "Did you notice that on the way here?"

"Yeah ... think we're lost?" Borg licked his dry lips.

"It's the dark." Schwartz refused to panic. He walked to the tree and sat down, resting his back against the tree. "We'll wait until it gets light. I'll bet as soon as it's light we'll see the car. Then we'll go back and I'll teach that fat slob to monkey with me."

Borg joined him, settling his heavy body on the sand with a grunting groan.

"Even if we manage to dig the car out, think we can find our way back?"

"Of course, you fool. We'll have left wheel tracks in the sand. All we have to do is to follow them back."

"Yeah. I hadn't thought of that." Borg paused, then said, "Judas! I could do with some beer!"

"Shut up!" Schwartz snarled.

Around three o'clock in the morning, a brisk, hot wind got up. It blew steadily for the next two hours, smoothing and flattening the sand and obliterating the wheel tracks of the Buick.

Chapter Eleven

THE HEADLIGHTS of the Cadillac lit up a parked car by the side of the road and two Africans in European clothes, standing dejectedly beside it.

There was something familiar about one of them, and Malik snapped an order to his driver. The Cadillac slowed and stopped a few yards beyond the parked car and Malik got out.

One of the Africans came hurriedly towards him and he recognised Samba Dieng.

"What are you doing here?" Malik demanded.

Dieng, his eyes rolling fearfully, told Malik of the failure of the ambush.

Malik restrained his fury with difficulty.

"How long have they been gone?"

"Some time . . . an hour perhaps."

"What were these other two men like?"

Dieng described Borg and Schwartz.

"If it had not been for them, we would have succeeded sir," he said, aware of Malik's restrained fury. "It was not our fault."

"Get in the car!" Malik said.

The African with the scar on his face whose name was Daouda, joined them and he and Dieng got in beside the driver who glanced at them and wrinkled his nose.

Malik got in the back.

"Diourbel and fast!" he told the driver.

As the Cadillac began to move, Malik considered what he had to do. Fantaz had vanished. He had had word from Ivan that Fantaz had not returned to his villa. He had told Ivan to come back as fast as he could and they would meet at Diourbel. Girland must be on his way to meet Carey. Fantaz must have told him when they had met in the café where Carey was hiding. These black fools had let Girland slip through their fingers. The situation was bad, but not hopelessly bad. Girland would be going into the bush where Malik had thirty men who knew the bush backwards, watching for him and for Carey. Even if Girland found Carey, it was unlikely he would be able to get Carey out of the bush without being caught.

They reached Diourbel ten minutes after Borg, Schwartz and Gomez had driven into the bush. The Cadillac pulled up outside a small villa set back from the main road that Malik had rented and used as his advance operations headquarters.

Leaving the car, and followed by the two Africans, Malik climbed the steps to the front entrance of the villa. He knocked three times on the door. A judas window opened and eyes stared at him, then the door was opened.

"Smernoff here?" Malik asked the broad-shouldered African who had opened the door.

"Yes, sir."

Motioning to Dieng and Daouda to remain where they were, Malik walked quietly down a passage and into a room where a man sat at a desk, headphones clamped to his ears. His fingers turned the dial of a walkie-talkie set, an expression of concentration on his flat Slavonic face. This was Boris Smernoff, a man of forty-five, thickset, dark and squatly built, who was the most persistent and ruthless hunter of men in the Soviet Secret Service.

He looked at Malik, gave a warning shake of his head, and went on moving the dial of the radio.

Malik pulled up a chair and sat down. He reached for a bottle of vodka that stood on the desk and poured himself a drink, using one of the number of glasses on a tray. He sipped his drink while he watched Smernoff who was now consulting a large-scale map that was spread out before him.

"You will wait for further orders," he said into the microphone and then switched off. He looked at Malik. "The net tightens. The lights of a car were seen just now ten miles from our nearest look-out. He was in a tree otherwise he wouldn't have seen the lights. The car is heading east. Probably it is taking supplies to Carey."

"No, taking Girland to Carey." Malik got up and went around behind Smernoff to look over his shoulder at the map. "Where was the car seen?"

"About here." Smernoff pointed. He picked up a pencil and began making little crosses on the map. "Here and here and here are our men. The car is moving in this direction." He drew a line with his pencil. "You will see our men form a half circle to this line. So somewhere here," the pencil tapped the map, "Carey must be hiding."

Malik studied the map and nodded.

"You have enough men to complete the circle?"

"Widely spaced, they could complete the circle, but if Carey moved out at night, he could still slip through."

"Can we get more men?"

"I have already arranged for that. They should be in place by tomorrow morning."

Malik returned to his chair. He finished the vodka and poured another.

"So Girland knows where Carey is now?" Smirnoff said. "Girland is a dangerous man. He could fight his way through. These Arabs have no stomach for a fight."

"I'm waiting for Ivan. As soon as he arrives, we'll go into the bush. You'll come too. We mustn't leave anything to chance."

The radio crackled into life and Smernoff again adjusted the dial. He listened and Malik saw him frown. "Hold on," he said into the microphone. "Another car's been sighted," he went on to Malik. He studied the map. "It is heading south-east. It passed one of the lookouts about ten minutes ago. It's an old Buick with three men inside."

"That's Girland!" Malik said, jumping to his feet. "He stole Dieng's car."

"Well, if it is, he's heading the wrong way. Then who is in the other car . . . going the right way?"

"Could be as you said . . . supplies going in for Carey."

"What do we do about Girland?"

"Leave him. If he hasn't a guide, he'll get lost and that'll save us the trouble of getting rid of him."

Just then the door opened and Ivan came in.

"You're in time," Malik said. "We're going into the bush."

"And Fantaz?"

"We can forget him. We now know within ten miles where Carey is. By tomorrow morning, we'll have him."

Smernoff had finished speaking into the microphone and now he picked up the set and carried it out to a waiting Jeep.

Malik and Ivan followed him.

"You'll both come with us," Malik said to Dieng.

Their eyes rolling uneasily, Dieng and Daouda followed them out into the hot, dark night.

Tessa had been driving now for some two hours. The springs of the little car were scarcely adequate to cope with the dips and holes in the sand they crashed through before she could avoid them and the car behaved like a small boat in a wild sea.

It was a nightmarish journey for Girland who was not used to driving in the bush. Although he hung on, he got thrown about in his seat, and soon his body was aching and bruised.

Several times they got stuck in the sand and had to get out. He and Momar lifted the little car out of the sand and pushed until the car was moving again. It was exhausting work in the humid heat.

"How much further have we to go?" he asked as once again the rear wheels of the car sank into a patch of deep loose sand.

"About eighty kilometres ... another hour," Tessa said, getting out of the car. She stretched, trying to ease her aching muscles.

With Momar's help, Girland heaved the car onto harder ground, then he came around the car and joined Tessa.

"Our headlights are worrying me. If Malik's men are as close as you think and on the lookout, they could spot us a kilometre away. I think we should stop right here and wait until it gets light enough for us to drive without lights."

"But I can't leave father alone all night," Tessa protested.

"Safer to leave him than to lead these boys to him, and that's what we are doing right now. Up in a high tree, a lookout could see a long distance over this flat ground."

Tessa hesitated, then nodded.

"I hadn't thought of that. All right, we'll wait." She peered at her wristwatch. "It won't be light for another six hours."

"Then we'll wait six hours." Girland sat down on the sand. "Phew! I could do with a drink!"

Tessa said something to Momar who brought from the car a large vacuum flask and glasses. Leaving them, the old African moved to the other side of the car, settled himself on the sand and almost immediately fell asleep.

Tessa sat beside Girland and poured ice cold orange squash from the flask.

"Pity there's no gin in it," Girland said, after he had sipped from the glass, "but it's a lot better than nothing." He leaned back and regarded her. "How did you learn to drive a car like this?"

She smiled, pleased with the implied compliment.

"I lived in Diourbel until I was eighteen. I was always driving into the bush with Momar. You soon get used to the technique of driving in sand."

"Were you out here with your father?"

"No. My father had gone back to France three months before I was born, leaving my mother here. The war had started and he wanted to be in it. I've only known my father to speak to these past few days. After the war, he went to America." She picked up a handful of sand and let it trickle through her fingers. "We didn't have much money. Enrico managed father's business here, but without father, it didn't prosper. The next thing we heard of father was, he was a spy and had defected to Russia. That came as a horrible shock. My mother died soon after, and I went to Paris. I always kept in touch with Enrico and he knew where I was in Paris. I didn't have any money, but I did all kinds of jobs, including selling the *Tribune*. I had really a lot of fun. Then suddenly out of the blue, Rosa Arbeau turned up at my one room apartment. She and I went to school together. I knew she was Enrico's mistress. She gave me a letter from my father. This was the first time I had heard from him since I was born. Rosa acted mysteriously. She wouldn't tell me anything. She just gave me the letter and went away."

Girland lit a cigarette.

"Sure it was from your father?"

"Yes, there was also a letter from Enrico. My father said he had escaped from Russia and had important information he wanted Dorey to have. I didn't know who Dorey was. He said that Dorey might not trust him, but that I should contact a man he had met years ago who could be trusted. He said this man's name was Girland but he couldn't remember his first name. He did live in Paris and I was to be careful I found the right man. In Enrico's letter, he said father was seriously ill. I didn't know what to think. I found your name in the telephone book. I followed you one night and ... well, you know the rest." She smiled at him.

"Your father said nothing else?"

"He mentioned a man called Herman Radnitz. He warned me against him. One of my newspaper friends often talked to me about Radnitz. I knew he lived at the George V Hotel so I watched there one evening, hoping to see him but I didn't. I ..." She broke off, her eyes opening wide. "Now I remember where I saw that fat man who you hit!" She turned to stare at Girland.

"He was outside the George V with another thin, horrible looking man."

"That's likely," Girland said mildly. "Dorey spent a lot of time having Radnitz watched. Don't ask me why. He never learned anything about Radnitz, but he was always hoping."

"There was also a young man with a beard. I remember them distinctly now. Who are they?"

"They all work for Dorey." Then changing the subject, Girland asked, "Did your father give you any idea what kind of information he has for Dorey?"

"Oh no, he wouldn't discuss that with me."

"You have told him you contacted me?"

"Yes, I told him that. He said you were the only one of Dorey's men he could trust."

"Now I wonder why he said that," Girland said, frowning.

She looked sharply at him.

"He can trust you, can't he?"

Girland forced a smile.

"Of course he can."

There was a pause, then she said, "Tell me about yourself, Mark."

He looked at her and shook his head.

"There's nothing to tell."

"There is. I want to know how you became an agent. Are you married?"

"Me? My work and marriage wouldn't mix."

"I told you about myself. Why are you being so secretive?"

He laughed.

"Only because its so damned dull. I am the black sheep of my family if you must know. My mother was French and my father was a very learned American Judge. As soon as I could leave home, I left. We lived then in Miami in a tiresome and enormous house full of stuffy and tiresome servants. I always wanted to live in Paris, so when I was eighteen, I packed a bag, got on a cargo boat and finally arrived in Paris. I had a very thin time trying to ape Hemingway, writing the most dreadful stuff and starving. My father died and left me thirty thousand dollars. I spent it all in two years and began starving again. Then Harry Rossland appeared and persuaded me to work for him. That was about six years ago. I've been an agent ever since."

"Do you like it?"

He shrugged.

"It's all right. No money in it of course, but I get around. Yes, it's all right."

"Do you like living alone in that apartment of yours? I should have thought you would have been lonely."

He thought of the very few times he had been alone in that apartment which now seemed to be very far away. There were always girls willing to share it with him: girls who stayed a night, a week, but never more than a month. After a month, he had grown tired of them.

"I'm too busy to be lonely," he said and stretched himself out on the sand. "Let's take a nap. We have a long day ahead of us."

She lay back.

"What's going to happen tomorrow? Do you think you'll be able to persuade father to leave?"

"It might not be safe for him to leave just yet."

"But he can't stay there much longer."

"Once he gives me the information for Dorey, he'll cease to be of value to the Russians or to Radnitz. Then he'll be able to come safely out of hiding. You go to sleep."

He shut his eyes, but his mind was too busy for immediate sleep. He wondered what Borg and Schwartz were doing. He wondered about Malik. He thought of Janine. There were so many things to think about. His final thought before he dozed off was of Carey and he remembered what Tessa had said: *He said you were the only one of Dorey's men he could trust.*

A streak of pale light across the sky brought him awake and he sat up. There was a brisk wind blowing and he felt gritty all over.

At his movement, Tessa who was curled up near him, blinked, raised her head, then sat up.

"Time we got moving," Girland said. He looked at his watch. It was a few minutes after four o'clock. He yawned and stood up. "I feel like hell."

Momar was making coffee on a small wood fire. He brought two steaming cups over to them and they drank gratefully.

"Oh, that's better!" Tessa said. "A cigarette now and I think I'll survive. This sand! It drives me crazy!"

They lit cigarettes and smiled at each other. In spite of her dishevelled appearance, Girland thought she still looked sensationally attractive. He rubbed the stubble of his beard and grimaced.

176

"Not even a toothbrush," he said. "Well, come on. Let's go."

Momar was already in the back seat of the car and they climbed in. Tessa consulted the old African and he pointed in the direction she was to go. She started the engine and once again the car banged and bumped over the uneven ground, heading further into the bush.

After a few kilometres, they saw in the distance a large village, surrounded by a bamboo and straw wall. A blue clad African was squatting at the gate of the wall. He stared indifferently at them as they drove past.

"Do you often come this way?" Girland asked.

"No. We never come the same way. I have only been to Diourbel twice since I came out. You're thinking the villagers might talk?"

"They could, couldn't they?"

"They just wouldn't be interested which way we were going. I think it is safe enough. It has to be. There are things we can't get along without and I have to get them in Diourbel."

They continued to drive further and further into the bush and Girland was struck by the variety of brilliantly coloured birds that flew out of the bushes and shrubs at their approach. Miniature parrots with blue and yellow plumage particularly caught his attention and they sat in the sandy track and only flew away when they seemed about to be run over.

During the next fifty kilometres, they got stuck four times and now the sun was up, the labour of lifting and pushing the car was exhausting. Girland was thankful that Tessa had had the foresight to bring two vacuum flasks of ice cold drink with her.

"How much further is this goddamn place?" he asked as he climbed into the oven hot car for the fourth time.

"Another five kilometres."

Eventually they saw ahead of them three bamboo and straw huts, shielded from the wind and sand by a wall of dried grass and bamboo sticks. To the right of the huts was a large mound of straw and brown shrubs.

"Here we are," Tessa said. "We hide the car under that straw. This is Momar's home."

As the car pulled up, three tall grinning Africans came out of the wall gate, followed by four excited children.

Tessa shook hands with them all and they then turned to Girland, nodding and giggling, to shake hands with him. Momar curtly told them to unload the car and get it hidden.

"I'll tell father you have arrived," Tessa said. "Have a drink and sit in the shade. I'm afraid you'll find it all very dirty and smelly, but this is real Africa."

"That's all right," Girland said doubtfully. "If you can survive, I guess I can."

He was disgusted to see the mass of flies that swarmed over the back of Tessa's shirt. There were flies everywhere and when he put his hand to the back of his own shirt, a great cloud of startled flies buzzed around his head before settling on his back again.

He followed her through the gate. Two small huts stood to the left of the open space which was littered with rusty, open cans and other rubbish. To the right, further away, was a bigger hut.

A fat, cheerful looking African woman with a wrinkled face was pounding millet with a heavy wooden pole. Girland guessed she must be Momar's wife. Two young African women peered at him from the shelter of one of the huts and then withdrew, giggling into the darkness.

He found some shade and squatted down, watching Tessa walk over to the big hut and enter. Momar came over to him carrying a glass of orange squash that Girland accepted gratefully. There was a long pause. Girland kept waving away the flies, wondering how long he would have to remain in this hellhole.

After a ten minute wait, Tessa came to the entrance of the hut and beckoned to him. He got to his feet, aware of a feeling of growing excitement. Now at last, he thought as he joined her, he was to come face to face with Robert Henry Carey.

"Go in," she said quietly. "He is waiting for you."

He moved past her into the airless, sweltering hut. It was some moments before his eyes became accustomed to the dim lighting that filtered through the straw roof and he saw a man sitting on a low stretcher type of bed, an upturned wooden chest that served as a table before him.

Girland paused, staring at the man. He was wearing a patched bush shirt that seemed too big for his bony frame and frayed, stained khaki trousers. His face was pale and almost skull-like in its thinness. The sunken eyes looked feverish, the mouth was a tightly drawn line, but Girland knew this shadow of a man was Carey. He remembered the photograph Rosa had shown

178

him. During the short time since the photograph had been taken, Carey had lost a lot of flesh and looked much more ill.

"Girland?" The voice was low and strengthless.

"Yes." Girland moved forward and held out his hand. "I came as fast as I could."

Bony, dry fingers touched his hand for a brief moment, then Carey let his hand drop limply back in his lap.

"Sit down."

Girland looked around, found a small wooden stool and lowered himself carefully onto it.

"I thought Rossland would be coming," Carey said, his feverish eyes examining Girland.

"Rossland's dead," Girland said. "I've taken his place."

"So Rossland's dead." Carey passed his bony fingers across his forehead. "Well, we all have to come to it. How did he die?"

Girland was reluctant to mention Radnitz. He said quietly, "He was found strangled. No one knows who killed him."

Carey lifted his shoulders in a resigned shrug.

"I liked Rossland. He wasn't clever and I didn't ever trust him, but there was something about him that was likeable." He looked up at Girland. "Rossland said you were his best man. You have a face of a man who can be trusted. I remember thinking that when I first met you. I believe in first impressions."

Girland moved uncomfortably. He didn't say anything.

"How did Dorey react when Rosa told him about me?"

"He told me to come out here at once and make contact with you."

"Did he pay the girl the money? I told Enrico he wouldn't. Ten thousand dollars is a lot of money to Dorey. Did he really pay her?"

"I don't know," Girland wasn't going to involve himself in too many lies.

"She is a shrewd girl for an African. He must have paid her otherwise she wouldn't have told him about me."

"I guess so."

"Did you come back with her?"

"I started to come back with her. She was shot dead at the airport."

Carey lowered his head and stared down at his hands. There was a long pause.

"Rossland and then Rosa?" he said finally. "How is it Radnitz allowed you to come out here?"

"Radnitz? Why bring him into this?" Girland asked, his voice sharpening.

"There is no one else who would kill like that. Even the Russians wouldn't have done it. Doesn't Dorey know about Radnitz? Don't you know?"

"I hadn't even heard of Radnitz a couple of weeks ago. Rossland mentioned him, but he didn't go into details."

"What did Rossland say about him?" Carey suddenly looked up. There was an expression on his wasted face that made Girland think of an Impressionistic portrait of the Prophet he had seen in the window of a Paris art gallery.

"He said something about Radnitz looking for you," Girland said cautiously. "We were talking in a car and I was driving. I didn't pay much attention." He wondered uneasily how much longer he could go on lying convincingly. "Why is Radnitz looking for you?"

"I did a deal with him: a Faust and the devil kind of deal," Carey said. "Radnitz never trusts anyone. He is afraid I will blackmail him."

Girland thought of the deal he had made with Radnitz. "Could you take that further?" he said, "or isn't it my business?"

"For you to understand this thing, I must take it further. Five years ago, I was a successful agent working for the American government. Someone high up had the smart idea that I should defect to Russia, learn all their secrets and then defect again to America, plus the secrets. Everyone seemed to have confidence in me and the idea except me. However, I was finally persuaded. Somehow Radnitz got to hear what was being planned. He is a man who gets to hear State secrets without difficulty. The night before I left for Moscow, he came to my apartment." Carey hesitated. When he continued his voice was so low Girland had to lean forward to hear what he was saying. "Radnitz wanted to get hold of certain papers relating to a man whose name was Henrich Kunzli which were held by the Soviet Secret Service. He thought once I was in Moscow, I could get hold of these papers. He offered me three million dollars in exchange for the papers. I was tempted by this enormous sum and I saw no reason why I shouldn't make such a deal with him. I agreed. He paid into my bank account ten thousand dollars as a goodwill gesture: the rest of the money was to be paid when I handed the papers to him. It took me nearly four years to get them and when I did get them, I found out what kind of man I

180

had made a deal with. I found out that Radnitz and Kunzli were one and the same: as evil a man as you could imagine."

"How . . . evil?" Girland asked.

"The papers he wanted were contracts signed by him and the Nazi and Japanese Governments, contracts that dealt with the manufacture of soap, fertilisers and gun powder. That seems harmless enough, doesn't it? But in the contracts the Nazis and the Japs agreed to supply the raw materials for these products. The raw materials were the bones, the hair, the fat and the teeth of the murdered millions from concentration camps. Radnitz laid the foundation of his fortune by turning into money the dead bodies of Jews and other victims of the Nazis and the Japanese. The Russians had found these contracts and they were holding them until the time was ripe to use them as a black-mail weapon against Radnitz. Among the papers is Kunzli's dossier. This man has used his enormous wealth in dozens of ways to the detriment of the free world. It was he who sold weapons that began the first trouble in North Vietnam. He started the Congo affair. He encouraged the Hungarians in their suicidal attempt to cast off the Russians. The list is endless. I have the contracts and the dossier on micro-film. When I left Moscow, I left the originals still in the Russian's hands. I now want the micro-film to go to Dorey. It will be the finish of Radnitz."

Girland felt his mouth was dry. The salty sweat that trickled from his forehead made his eyes smart. He felt deflated. If what Carey said was true, and he couldn't doubt him, then he, like Carey, couldn't take Radnitz's money.

"I have several fims for Dorey," Carey went on. "During the years I was in Moscow, I didn't waste my time. Among the many important things, I have a list of thirty-five Russian agents working in France and America: among them is Dorey's special pet . . . Janine Daulnay."

"Why didn't you give them to Rosa? She could have taken them to Dorey."

"Radnitz knows I am somewhere in Senegal as the Russians do. I could not trust Rosa. Radnitz had only to offer her a large sum of money and she would have made a deal with him. I am glad you have come, Girland. You wouldn't make a deal with Radnitz."

Girland shrugged. All along he had planned to double cross Radnitz, but he had had hopes of laying his hands on the fifty thousand dollars Radnitz had promised him. Well, it wasn't to be. Now he had the tricky task of getting out of Senegal and reaching Dorey. He wondered how Dorey would treat him.

"It won't be easy," he said. "Apart from Radnitz, the Russians also know you are in the bush."

Carey nodded.

"Every day they get closer. I know they are very close now. The sooner you go, the safer for you. I have everything ready for you. Momar will guide you out of the bush. If you can reach the American Embassy they will give you protection to get to Paris. I want you to take Tessa with you. She should never have come out here. That fool Fantaz lost his head."

"And you? You'll come with us too?"

"I intend to stay here. I am not strong enough to face the journey."

Girland looked sharply at him.

"Do you think Tessa will leave you here? I don't."

"Oh, she will." Carey drew in a long breath of weariness. "Don't let her fall into Radnitz's or the Russians' hands. A bullet is cleaner and better than that. You understand?"

Girland frowned.

"You're putting a lot of responsibility on me, aren't you? I'd rather travel alone."

"Then how is she to get away? I'm relying on you, Girland." With a painful effort, he stood up and walked to the end of the hut. "Perhaps you could help me? The films are buried here . . . an unsafe place to hide them, but after all the trouble I have taken, I could not bear them out of my sight."

Girland joined Carey. When Carey showed him a patch of loose sand, Girland knelt down and scooped the sand away. In a few seconds, he lifted a small tin box out of the sand and stood up.

"Not much to show for four years' dangerous work, is it?" Carey said, "but in place of quantity, it has great quality. Don't wait about, Girland. I would be glad if you would prepare Tessa. Tell her I wish her to go with you. She's a sensible girl." He paused, then went on, "I don't expect to live much longer . . . a week or two, not more. I have here," he touched his body, "a killer that is much surer than Radnitz. Tell her that. She'll understand."

"You'll have to tell her yourself," Girland said. "I'll take her with me if she'll go, but I'm not going to force her. It's up to you to convince her. I'll leave in ten minutes."

"Very well. You are right, of course. I'll convince her," Carey said and held out his hand. "Goodbye, Girland, and good luck."

Girland put his hand into Carey's dry, bony grip.

"I too nearly made a deal with Radnitz," he said. "I wasn't going to tell you, but you may as well know. That makes two of us."

Carey nodded.

"I knew about that," he said quietly. "That's why I was frank with you. Fantaz's nephew was here early this morning. He told me about these two men. Schwartz has worked for Radnitz for years. I recognised his description. Money is a temptation, isn't it," and he smiled.

"Yes," Girland said. "You can trust me, Carey."

"I know. Goodbye."

Girland went out of the hut into the blinding heat and the flies. He paused, blinking, then seeing Tessa sitting in the shade, he walked over to her.

"I have what I want," he said as she jumped to her feet. "We'll be leaving in ten minutes. Your father wants to speak to you."

As Tessa started towards the big hut, there came a loud bang of a gun shot. She came to an abrupt halt and stood staring at a wisp of smoke that drifted through the open door of the hut.

Chapter Twelve

THEY HAD been driving now for the past half hour. From time to time, Girland glanced at Tessa. Her stony expression and the shocked look in her eyes warned him to keep silent.

As she had begun to run towards the hut after the shot, he had realised what had happened and had caught her wrist.

"Don't go in!" he had said sharply. "He had come to the end of his road. He was dying fast anyway. I'll go."

She had turned to stare at him, horror in her eyes.

"You mean he's – he's shot himself?"

"Wait here."

Leaving her in the hot sunshine, Girland had gone into the hut. He came out again a few minutes later, carrying an automatic pistol he had picked up by Carey's side. Carey had lived efficiently and he had died efficiently. He had made no mistake. The bullet had killed him instantly.

Girland nodded to Tessa who turned away, hiding her face in her hands.

The Africans stood uneasily at the doors of their huts and stared at Girland. Old Momar walked slowly to the big hut and peered in, then he walked with dignity over to his sons and spoke to them.

Girland waited until he had finished, then he joined him.

"We must leave at once," he said. "It is dangerous for Mademoiselle to stay here. Get the car and be ready to leave in five minutes."

Momar nodded and went through the gateway and over to where the car was hidden.

Girland moved over to Tessa who was looking towards the big hut, a lost expression in her eyes.

"We're leaving," he said gently. "He wanted you to leave with me. They'll take care of him." He knew Carey hadn't hesitated to hasten his death so that Tessa would leave, but he didn't tell her so. "Come on ... let's go."

Momar's wife came over carrying a water skin and a bag containing food. The old African was weeping. No one spoke. Girland took the water skin and the bag and then catching hold of Tessa's arm, he drew her towards the gate.

She pulled away from him, but she went with him across the hot sand to where the Deux Chevaux was waiting.

Under the shade of a tree, Momar's sons were digging a grave. The two men didn't look around as Tessa got into the car. Girland handed Momar who was already in the car the bag and the water skin, then he climbed in beside Tessa.

Now, after thirty minutes of driving, they came to a water hole around which were some two hundred goats and cattle.

Momar leaned forward.

"I will speak with these men," he said.

Tessa pulled up and Girland got out to let Momar out. He stood watching the old African walk over to the three Africans tending the herd and salute them. They talked together. One elderly African kept pointing to the east. He seemed agitated.

Momar came back. There was an expression on his face that brought Girland alert.

"What is it?"

"They say they have seen three armed Arabs: strangers with rifles about two miles to the east. That is our direction."

"They are sure about the rifles?"

"They are sure."

"We must avoid them. How do we do that?"

"To the east is the quickest way. We can go north and then make a circle to the east, but it will take time and the ground is very bad."

"We must avoid these men," Girland wasn't going to risk matching his Colt automatic against three rifles.

They got back into the car.

Tessa said, "Arabs in pay of the Russians?"

"I guess so. Anyway, we mustn't take chances. Let's go."

Momar showed Tessa the direction and again she sent the little car banging and bumping over the sand.

They soon found that Momar was right about the ground being bad. They hadn't driven more than ten kilometres before the sand became so loose the rear wheels of the car began to slide and Tessa had difficulty with the steering.

"Like me to take over?" Girland asked.

"Not yet." She wrestled with the steering wheel and suddenly the engine stalled and the car stopped. "Oh, damn!"

Girland and Momar got out. The rear wheels were hub deep in the sand. Sweating, they lifted the wheels onto more solid ground and by pushing frantically once again got the car moving, but Tessa was afraid to stop and the two men had to run after it.

A hundred metres ahead was solid ground again and Tessa was able to stop. As Girland approached the car, he heard something like an angry bee zip past his head. This was followed by a distant rifle shot. He spun around, his hand flying to his gun. A half a mile to his right was a clump of trees. He caught a glimpse of something white in the trees and saw a flash of flame as the half hidden gunman fired again. This time Girland didn't hear the zip of the bullet. He lifted his automatic, then lowered it, the distance was too great.

He heard a scream and he spun around to see Tessa, out of the car, running towards him.

"Momar!" she screamed. "Look!"

Momar had been to Girland's left and behind him. The old man was lying face down in the sand.

Both Girland and Tessa reached him together. Girland turned him over and then let the lifeless body drop back.

Again the rifle cracked and a spurt of sand less than a metre from Tessa showed the accuracy of the shooting.

Girland grabbed Tessa by her arm and began rushing her back to the car.

"We can't leave him!" she protested, trying to shake Girland off. "We can't leave him!"

He bundled her into the car, then sliding under the driving wheel, he started the engine and cautiously engaged gear. As he let in the clutch, the wheels slipped, but bit and the car began to move. Using the gas pedal as if it were made of glass, Girland gradually built up speed until once more they were jolting and bumping over the sand.

He heard the rifle crack again. He kept driving, aware that Tessa was hunched up in her seat, her hands covering her face, crying quietly.

If only this cursed bush wasn't so flat, he thought. That sniper up in his tree can watch us for kilometres. He'll know which way we are heading.

Girland suddenly felt a cold empty feeling of fear. Which way *were* they heading? Up to now, Momar had directed Tessa, and Girland had blindly accepted the way. Now he realised

186

every bush, shrub and tree looked alike. There was no road. They could be driving in circles for all he knew.

"Tessa!" he said sharply. "Pull yourself together! You've got to help me!"

She straightened, wiping her eyes with the back of her hand.

"He was the nicest and kindest person I've ever known," she said unsteadily. "Oh, the devils!"

"They'll do the same to us if we don't watch out," Girland said roughly. "Do you know where we are?"

"No, but we must keep the sun to our right. If you get lost in the bush, you must do that otherwise you go in a circle."

Girland looked at the petrol gauge. The tank was three-quarters full. That at least was encouraging, he thought. We have water and food. We could still get out of this mess.

"Well, watch the sun," he said. "But we are driving north and we want to go east. Shouldn't we head east now?"

"There's a road somewhere ahead of us ... about ten kilometres. Momar was heading for that. If we can find it, it will take us to a village and we can get a guide."

But after driving fifteen minutes or so, Girland came to the conclusion that they had somehow missed the road. He stopped the car under the shade of a tree.

"Do you think we should turn back?" he asked.

Tessa got out of the car and looked around the flat endless waste.

"We might have missed it by a kilometre or twenty kilometres. If we go back we might run into that gunman."

Girland looked at his watch. The time was half past ten. It didn't seem possible so much had happened in so few hours.

"Think there's another village further ahead?"

"There are villages all over the bush. We might be lucky."

"Okay, then we'll go on. Let's have a drink first." He got out the water skin and carefully poured a little of the water into the cap of the vacuum flask. They both moistened their parched mouths. "Hell!" Girland went on, grimacing, "I would settle for that orange squash without the gin now."

He put the water skin back in the car and got under the wheel. Tessa got in beside him, and once again they drove over the uneven ground.

A further ten minute drive brought them to a circle of Baobab trees.

"This is where they used to practice black magic," Tessa said.

187

"When you see these trees in a circle you know what they were used for and are still sometimes used for. The trees are hollow. When they die, witch doctors are buried inside the trees as they believe they will foul the land."

"As long as no one buries me in one of them," Girland said. He glanced again at the petrol gauge, then felt a cold chill run up his spine. The needle of the gauge showed they had now only a quarter of a tank of petrol left. "For God's sake, look at that! We couldn't have used all that gas!" He pulled up. "Maybe we're losing gas." He went around to the back of the car and inspected the petrol tank. He swore under his breath when he saw the neatly drilled hole in the lower part of the tank. The last rifle shot he had heard had been devastatingly effective.

Tessa joined him.

"We're in trouble," he said. "A quarter full. How far do you think that'll take us?"

"Thirty kilometres," Tessa said, watching Girland as he plugged the hole with a .45 bullet covered with his handkerchief. "We might find a village by then."

He looked sharply at her.

"You're not frightened?"

She smiled at him.

"It's no good being frightened, is it? We have food and water. When the gas runs out, we must get in the shade and wait for the sun to go down. We can't walk in this heat."

He nodded.

"Okay. Well, let's get going."

They climbed into the car and drove on into the burning waste land that seemed to have no ending.

Malik with a map on his knees sat beside Smernoff who was operating the walkie-talkie. Dieng was at the wheel of the Jeep with Ivan at his side. Daouda sat on the roof in the full glare of the sun, a rifle across his knees.

They had been driving some time and now the walkie-talkie crackled into life.

Smernoff listened to the excited voice that buzzed and hummed through the headphones. Whoever was calling had a lot to say and Malik kept glancing impatiently at Smernoff. Finally, the voice ceased and Smernoff said, "Alert Post Three," and took off the headphones.

"A girl, a man and an African, driving a Deux Chevaux

188

reported on square ten of your map." He leaned against Malik and pointed. "That would be about forty kilometres from here. They were shot at and the African was killed. It is unlikely the girl and her companion will get far without a guide. The African came from a small settlement on square nine of your map. Carey could have been hiding there. The girl and the man are heading towards three of our best snipers. They've been alerted. What do we do now . . . follow after them?"

"Who's the girl?" Malik asked frowning. "Would the man be Carey?"

Smernoff didn't say anything. It was Malik's job to make the decisions.

"We'll go to the settlement," Malik said. "We must be certain that Carey isn't there still." He leaned forward and gave Dieng a change of directions. Once again the Jeep increased speed, tearing through the bush and sending clouds of sand rising in the air in its wake.

"Get Post Three," Malik said suddenly. "Tell them the man isn't to be killed. If it's Carey I want to talk to him."

Smernoff raised Post Three on the walkie-talkie and gave the operator Malik's instructions.

"Cripple the car and take them alive," he concluded. "I don't care how you do it . . . do it!"

A ten minute drive brought them in sight of the three huts with their surrounding straw and bamboo wall. The Jeep pulled up at the gate. Gun in hand, followed by Ivan, Malik walked into the small compound.

Three Africans faced him uneasily. They made a protective circle before one of the huts where their wives and children tried to hide themselves in the semi-darkness.

"We are looking for a white man," Malik said to Momar's eldest son, Cheickh. "Where is he?"

The green evil eyes frightened Cheickh. Monsieur Carey was beyond the reach of these men now. He saw no reason to antagonise them.

"He is dead, monsieur. We have just buried him."

Malik's mouth tightened. "Where?"

Cheickh moved forward and pointed through the gate.

"Under the tree."

Malik snapped an order to Dieng who walked over to the tree and picking up a shovel that leaned against the tree, he reluctantly began to dig.

189

Ivan had gone into the big hut. After some minutes, he came out and joined Malik.

"That's where he's been hiding. There's a small hole in the ground as if something had been buried there. It's not there now."

Malik turned away and walked over to where Dieng, now helped by Daouda, had opened the grave. He stood looking down at Carey's dead face. Ivan came over.

"Shot himself," Malik said. "Damn him! He was always one move ahead." He leaned forward and spat in the dead man's face.

Ivan said, "These other two must have the films."

"Tell Smernoff to raise Post Three again. They are to stop them at all costs," Malik said. "If they can't stop the car, they are to shoot them. Hurry!"

As Ivan ran over to the Jeep, Malik returned to the compound.

"Who is the white woman who was here?" he demanded, walking up to Cheickj.

The African shuffled his feet.

"I don't know, monsieur."

Malik hit him across his face with the barrel of his gun. Cheickh staggered and recovered his balance.

"Who is she?" Malik repeated viciously.

"I don't know, monsieur."

Malik turned to Dieng.

"Go in there and get one of the children. If this man doesn't talk, cut the child's throat."

The women in the hut began screaming. Dieng had to fight his way through them to grab one of the crying children. Momar's youngest son whose child it was, rushed forward, swinging his fists. Malik shot him through the head.

There was a long pause and silence, then the women and children began wailing. One of the women threw herself on the fallen African, pulling at his clothes in a frenzy of grief.

Malik paid no attention: his eyes were fixed on Cheickh.

"Who was the woman?"

Dieng was holding the struggling child, a short bladed knife in his hand.

Cheickh hesitated, then said, "The daughter of Monsieur Carey."

"And the man?"

"They called him Girland."

Malik signed to Dieng to release the child, then he walked out of the compound and breaking into a run, reached the Jeep.

"It's Girland and Carey's daughter," he said to Smernoff. "Anything from Post Three yet?"

Smernoff was twiddling one of the dials. He raised his hand for silence as he listened to the crackle coming through the headphones. Then an excited voice began speaking.

He listened and then said, "Shoot them. They must be stopped."

Taking off the headphones, he said to Malik, "They've been seen. They are about two kilometres from Post Three and driving straight towards it."

Malik snatched up his map.

"Where are they?"

"Square eleven. About thirty kilometres from here."

Malik looked at the gate leading into the compound.

"We don't want trouble with the police," he said and walked back to where Ivan was standing. "Get rid of this lot. They could make trouble. Hurry!"

Ivan grinned. This was an order he liked and could execute efficiently. He drew his gun and moved into the compound.

Malik returned to the Jeep. Dieng was already sitting behind the wheel. Daouda was perched on the roof.

The two Africans flinched when the shooting began. One skinny child, his black eyes rolling in terror, darted out into the hot sunshine and began running frantically away from the Jeep.

Malik lifted his gun and squeezed the trigger.

"Good shooting," Smernoff said as the child rolled in the sand. "That gun of yours throws a little to the left, doesn't it?"

"I make allowance for that," Malik returned and slid the gun back into its holster.

Ivan, smoking gun in hand, ran out and climbed into the Jeep. There was a relaxed, satiated expression on his fat, red face.

The Jeep moved off, gathering speed.

A lone vulture swooped out of the sky and settled its heavy body awkwardly on the branch of a tree. It surveyed the scene with its beady eyes. Other vultures appeared circling in the sky. Then one after the other they dropped to the ground and began to move slowly and awkwardly towards the compound.

*　　*　　*

Tessa was driving and the going was bad. It needed all her skill and experience to keep the car moving. At her side, Girland stared through the dusty windscreen. From time to time, he glanced at the petrol gauge. The needle kept flickering to 'Empty'. Any moment he expected to hear the engine cough and stop.

He had no doubt that they were completely lost, but at least, he was sure they weren't driving in a circle. Although they had changed their direction and were heading east, he was certain they were miles and hopeless miles from Diourbel and safety.

The hawks that floated motionless overhead worried him. They must know that sooner or later there would be a feast to share with the vultures and they kept circling the car, waiting with sinister patience.

The little car lurched. The rear wheels spun and the engine stopped.

This was the seventh time they had had to lift the car out of the loose sand.

They looked at each other, then wordlessly, they got out of the car and walked around to the back. Girland paused to glance up at the circling hawks, then he caught hold of the rear bumper and with Tessa's help, heaved the car onto more solid ground.

"Want me to drive?" he asked, trying to moisten his dry lips with an even dryer tongue.

"It's all right. We'll be walking soon."

"How about a drink?"

"I think we should wait. In this heat the water will evaporate. We may need every drop before we are out of this." He caught a note of despair in her voice and he forced a grin.

"We'll get out of it."

"If we could only find a village . . ." She paused and stared into the distance. "I thought I saw something move out there."

Girland followed the direction in which she was looking. The flat waste land with its trees and shrubs shimmered in the heat.

"It's the heat," he said and opened the car door.

"No! Something moved!" Tessa exclaimed, shading her eyes with her hand. "To the right of that tree."

Girland stared and this time he caught a glimpse of something white move and then disappear.

"Get behind the car!" he said sharply.

Tessa moved back, putting the body of the car between herself and the distant tree. Girland crouched down so that he could

192

look along the bonnet of the car. He pulled his gun from its holster.

The insufferable heat beat down on them. Again Girland saw the movement. This time he was sure a man had risen up out of the sand, advanced a few quick paces and then dropped down again.

"There's another to the left," Tessa said who was peering around the side of the car. "And another further to the left."

Girland saw the three Arabs now. They were carrying rifles and advancing in small rushes, but covering the ground. They were not more than five hundred metres away.

He took Carey's gun from his hip pocket.

"Can you use this?" he asked, and moving back, he offered the gun to Tessa.

"Yes. I can handle it." She took the gun and slid off the safety catch. He was pleased to see her hand was steady and her eyes calm.

He moved back to his original position and in doing so, exposed his head and shoulders above the bonnet of the car.

A rifle shot rang out and Girland felt the bullet fan his cheek. He gave a loud, gasping groan, threw up his hands and dropped out of sight behind the car.

He heard Tessa scream.

"It's all right," he hissed. "Don't move!"

Two of the Arabs stood up. They made perfect targets against the brilliant blue sky.

"The one on the left is yours," Girland said, paused for a brief moment and fired. A split second later, he heard Tessa's gun snap spitefully. Both Arabs fell forward as the remaining Arab, hidden behind a shrub, fired.

Girland felt a searing pain in the biceps of his left arm. He moved further back. Blood ran down his arm and onto the sand. He caught a glimpse of white as the Arab began to snake forward. Before he could lift his gun, Tessa's gun snapped again.

A small, wizened man in dirty white robes sprang up, clutching his shoulder and dropping his rifle. He started a mad rush towards the car as Girland shot hit through the head.

Tessa came around the car. She was white and shaky, but she quickly pulled herself together at the sight of Girland's injured arm.

"Is it bad?"

He shook his head.

"It's nothing . . . just a scratch."

"I'll fix it." She ran back to the car and came back carrying a First Aid kit. Quickly she washed the wound, using a little water from the water skin, then strapped up the cut the bullet had made.

Girland walked over to the dead Arabs and picked up their rifles. Each man had a cartridge belt around his waist. Tessa helped him collect the three belts.

"Now we can hit back," Girland said grimly. "Come on, let's get moving."

They climbed back into the car and drove forward once again into the burning heat.

"I wonder how many more of them are ahead of us," Girland said. He looked at his watch. The time was twenty minutes past three. He realised neither of them had eaten since daybreak, but he wasn't hungry. His throat and mouth were dry and he longed for an ice cold drink. "The gas must be nearly used up," he went on, looking at the gauge.

"Is your arm all right?"

"Getting stiff, but it's all right. You okay?"

"Yes."

"You're quite a girl. When we get out of this, we'll celebrate. I'd like to get to know you a lot better."

"Do you think we're going to get out of this?"

"We can but hope."

She was silent for a long moment, then she said, "How will we celebrate, Mark?"

"We'll start the evening in the Plaza Athene bar. Vodka martinis, very dry and very, very cold. Then we will take a taxi to the Grand Vefour and we will eat oysters and partridges with a 1949 Claret. We will then go to my apartment where I will show you my collection of Abstracts."

"I've been to your apartment. You haven't any Abstracts."

"I know but it won't matter. If you can't admire my Abstracts, at least, I will be able to admire you. It could be quite an evening."

"But we have to get out of this first."

"Yes." He leaned forward to peer through the windscreen. "Look what we are running into."

They found themselves facing an endless waste of hard sand that seemed to stretch with the flatness of a yellowing, tightly stretched bed sheet to the distant horizon. It was as if the trees and the shrubs had abruptly lost courage and had refused to advance any further.

"It looks like a dead sea," Girland said. "We'll never get across that."

"I remember Momar telling me about this place," Tessa said, her voice excited. "On the far side is a watering place for cattle. If we can get across, we're certain to find a guide."

"We haven't the gas."

"We must try, even if we have to walk."

Girland hesitated, then headed the car onto the hard solid plane of sand. The little car surged forward as its tyres found at last something concrete to bite on. They were no longer bumping and banging about in their seats. The ride had become miraculously smooth.

"You have no idea how far across it is?" Girland said. "It could go on forever by the look of it."

She shook her head.

"I don't know. I do know there is a water hole the other side."

Girland again looked at the motionless needle of the petrol gauge. How accurate was it? Did they have enough gas to get across? The heat of this exposed plane was scorching and relentless. A spark of panic began to grow in his mind. To be stranded in this shadeless death-trap could only end in one way. Again he looked up at the metalic blue sky where the hawks circled above him.

He increased the speed of the car.

"Don't drive so fast." Tessa said sharply. "The faster we go the more gas . . ." She stopped as the engine began to splutter.

Girland pushed the gas pedal to the boards, but there was no response. The engine spluttered again and then died. The car slowly rolled over the sand for a few metres and then stopped.

The hawks overhead hung motionless. Their shadows made large black splashes on the white sand.

With forced casualness, Girland patted the hot steering wheel.

"Well, that's it. We have three hours to sunset. We'll stay right here until the sun goes down, and then we'll walk."

Tessa stared at the black shadows on the sand.

"I'm glad you are with me," she said huskily. "I couldn't face this alone."

"That makes two of us," Girland said, and put his hand on hers.

Smernoff had been fiddling with the dial of the walkie-talkie for some minutes. Watching him, Malik saw his impatient tension gradually mounting.

"I'm getting no reply from Post Three," Smernoff said finally. "Something's wrong."

"Try Post Four."

"They're too far to the north to know anything. Post Three said they were driving straight towards them. They must have intercepted them by now."

"We can't be more than ten kilometres from them," Malik said, after studying the map. "Drive quicker," he went on to Dieng.

The Jeep increased speed and the four men had to cling to their seats. Daouda, on the roof, was nearly thrown off. He wailed his alarm as he clung to the roof support.

They drove like that for ten minutes, then Ivan said sharply, "Something over there . . . to your right."

Dieng reduced speed. Malik peered out of the Jeep. He saw something white in the sand. At his order, the Jeep headed towards it and pulled up.

They all scrambled out of the Jeep and went over to the three dead bodies lying in a little group in the sand.

There was a long pregnant silence, then Smernoff said, "I warned you Girland was dangerous."

"He's got their rifles," Ivan said.

Malik turned away and stared across the waste land. Faintly in the soft sand he could make out the tracks of a car.

"They went that way," he said and walked back to the Jeep. He picked up the map and studied it. His green eyes were unnaturally bright: the only sign of his rage and disappointment.

Smernoff joined him.

"Post Four is here. Is that right?" Malik asked, pointing to the map.

"Yes."

"Then they have broken through the circle. We'll have to go after them. They are heading into the bush and not out of it, but none of the Posts can intercept them now. We'll have to keep after them until they run out of petrol. How is our petrol?"

"We have half a tank full and two spare Jerry cans. We have plenty," Ivan said.

"And water?"

Ivan grimaced.

"Not as much as we should have. It keeps evaporating in this damned heat. We'll have to watch it."

Malik looked at his watch.

"It'll be dark in about four hours. We will have to catch them before then. We'll have to be careful how we approach them. Ivan, you'd better have the rifle. You're the best shot."

Ivan turned to Daouda.

"Give me the rifle."

The tall scarred African shuffled his feet in the sand. He giggled with embarrassment, covering his gold filled teeth with his hand.

"It fell off the roof when we went so fast," he said. "I would have fallen too if I hadn't been so strong."

Ivan's fiery face turned purple.

"You mean you've lost the rifle?" he said, his voice rising to a shout.

"It fell off the roof."

Malik came up and caught Ivan's arm as he was about to strike the African.

"Wait. How far back did you drop it?"

Daouda shrugged his shoulders.

"Back there," and he pointed.

"We'd better go back for it," Smernoff said in Russian.

"We'll never find it," Malik said also in Russian. "We could pass within a metre of it and not see it." He paused, then went on, "Every minute we waste gives them a chance of getting away." He turned to Daouda. "Go back and get it. We will wait here."

Daouda shook his head.

"It is too far, monsieur. I would get lost."

"Go and get it!" Malik said, pulling his gun.

Dieng came up.

"Excuse me, monsieur, but this man is my friend. If he goes he will get lost and he will die."

"Then go with him," Malik said, and the gun swung towards Dieng. "Go!"

Dieng stared into the green glittering eyes and sweat sprang out on his black face.

"I have said nothing, monsieur. I will stay. He will go."

"You both go!" Malik said, and he thumbed back the safety catch on the gun.

The two Africans turned and began to run back the way they had come. Malik sent a shot above their heads and they increased speed, stumbling in the loose sand, their arms waving frantically.

"As we are running short of water," Malik said, walking back to the Jeep, "the less mouths to drink it the better."

The three men got in and Malik, taking the wheel, sent the Jeep once more moving through the loose sand.

"I don't like this," Ivan said uneasily. "Now Girland has a rifle, we are in a bad position. He'll have the range of us."

"There are three of us," Malik said. "One of us will draw his fire while the other two circle him and get within range."

Smernoff stared ahead at the monotonous scene.

"We could miss him. The wind's getting up and it's wiping out his tracks."

"We won't miss him." There was a grim note in Malik's voice. "Look up in the sky. He's where the hawks are hovering."

Both Ivan and Smernoff stared into the yellowing sky. In the distance they could make out a few black dots that swooped and hovered and swooped again.

"Everything depends on how long his petrol lasts," Malik said. He was sending the Jeep over the rough ground at well over ninety kilometres an hour.

The walkie-talkie crackled into life and Smernoff hurriedly put on his headphones. He listened to the voice that came through a crackle of static, then said, "We are heading for Square seven. Send men with water after us. That's an order," and he switched off.

"What was that?" Malik asked, wrestling with the steering wheel.

"Post Five. They have found two bodies and a buick car. The bodies have been half eaten by vultures: a short and a tall man."

"Schwartz and Borg," Malik said. "Good riddance. Will they bring water to us?"

"No," Smernoff said. "Post Five is forty kilometres from us at this moment. They have no transport. Why should an Arab care what happens to us?"

"Let's have a drink now," Ivan said, wiping his cracked lips with the back of his hand. "We've got enough for a little drink, haven't we?"

Smernoff put his hand on the water skin. "Even when we have caught Girland, we still have to get out of the bush."

"We were mad to come so far without enough water," Ivan complained furiously. "Isn't there a water hole somewhere on the route?"

"Look and see," Malik said to Smernoff.

After studying the map, Smernoff said, "There is a water hole sixty kilometres from here, but to get to it we would have to cross absolute desert: no trees no shade, nothing but flat sand. Do you think Girland could be heading that way?"

"It depends on how much petrol he has left."

"Head for the water hole," Ivan urged. "We have got to have more water."

Malik hesitated. There was a chance that Girland carried spare petrol. If he did, he too would head for the water hole ... providing, of course, he knew it existed.

"Yes," he said and with his eye on the compass on the dashboard, he changed direction and headed due east.

It was in this way that they finally came to the end of the bush and saw a few kilometres ahead of them, standing in a burning plane of hard, flat sand, the stranded Deux Chevaux.

Tessa and Girland had been sitting in the little car now for over half an hour. The heat in the car was insufferable and Girland felt as if the blood in his veins was boiling. Every scrap of metal on the car was dangerous to touch. Accidentally, he had brushed against the metal window frame and now had a livid burn on his forearm.

"I'm not going to stand much more of this," he said hoarsely. "We're going to be cooked alive."

"It's much worse outside." Tessa was breathing in short, laboured gasps. "The sun is going down. In an hour the car will make shade and we can sit out."

Girland groaned.

"Another hour! I'll have burst by then!"

"It's not quite so hot as it was. Let's have a drink."

Girland didn't need any encouragement. He turned in his seat and reached for the water skin. He happened to glance through the rear window of the car and what he saw made him forget his thirst and the heat.

In the distance a cloud of sand was moving rapidly in their direction. That cloud could mean only one thing: a car was approaching at a reckless speed.

"Tessa . . . look!"

At the urgent note in his voice, Tessa jerked around.

"A car coming!" Girland snatched up one of the rifles.

"It may not be them," Tessa said. "Be careful."

"Who else could it be as far out as here?" Girland returned. Using the butt of the rifle to push open the car door, he slid out into the burning sunlight. "Stay where you are," he called to Tessa. "I'll give them a warning shot." Raising the sight of the rifle, he sent a shot over the approaching car which he could now recognise as a Jeep.

The Jeep slewed away, its four wheels skidding in the sand and stopped.

Three men climbed out. Even at a distance of half a kilometre, in the clear, brilliant light, Girland recognised Malik's giant frame and his silver blond hair.

"It's them all right," he said and adjusting the rifle sight, he fired three times, aiming carefully at the Jeep.

The three men scattered and took shelter behind the remaining shrubs.

"We have plenty of ammunition," Girland said. "We'll cripple their car. If we don't get out of this, they won't either."

Both of them, aiming at the Jeep, fired again. The bang of a bursting tyre came across the flat plain and Girland grinned.

"Nice shooting," then seeing a thickset man dodge out from behind a shrub and start across the sand, an automatic in his hand, Girland hurriedly altered the rifle sight and taking careful aim, pressed the trigger.

Moving like a bull, Ivan felt the bullet zip through his flapping shirt sleeve.

"Come back, you fool!" Malik shouted after him. "Come back!"

Ivan stopped running and looked back at Malik. Girland squeezed the trigger. A red blotch suddenly appeared on Ivan's sweat-soaked shirt and he fell forward on the sand.

"The fool!" Malik snarled.

"Never mind him," Smernoff said. He was lying by Malik's side. "What are we going to do? We'll never get near Girland without cover and look at it!"

"We'll get him when it's dark. It's just a matter of waiting.

Go and check the car and bring the water here."

Smernoff began to crawl towards the Jeep. As he was within reach of the Jeep, Girland fired again. A glancing bullet shattered the windscreen and Smernoff cursed. He cursed again when he saw a large dark stain under the car and smelt petrol fumes. He crawled around the far side of the Jeep. He saw at a glance the petrol tank had been holed three times and the last of the petrol was dribbling out of the holes. He reached into the back of the Jeep and hauled out the two full Jerry cans of petrol, dumping them in the sand. Then he grabbed hold of the water skin and a wave of panic went through him. The water skin was empty! A bullet hole in the skin told him the reason as Girland once more fired and Smernoff, flopping down, heard the bullet smash into the bonnet of the Jeep.

He crawled back to Malik.

"The water's gone," he said, his voice shaking. "And he's shooting the car to hell."

Malik's lips pulled off his white teeth in a vicious snarl.

"So the water's gone. That won't save them. They must have water with them and we can use their car. The spare petrol's all right?"

"Yes."

"Well, then ... should give you an incentive to get them." He moved further into the shade of the shrub. "Get under cover. We haven't long to wait."

"I could do with a drink," Smernoff said, a whine in his voice.

"Go and ask Girland for one," Malik sneered, "and shut up!"

Out in the blinding rays of the sun, both Tessa and Girland were suffering. He dare not get back into the car. A quick rush from the Russians would bring them within revolver shot distance. He had to keep them pinned down where they were.

"Let's have a drink, Tessa," he said, wiping the sand and sweat from his face.

She walked unsteadily to the car and returned with two glasses of water.

"The damn stuff is nearly boiling," Girland said as he sipped. "We'll have to watch out when it gets dark. That'll be their chance to get at us." He peered across the sand, screwing up his eyes against the dazzling glare. There was no sign of the Russians. "You keep watch. I'm going to fix the car."

He looked down at her.

"We have to face up to it, Tessa. We have a very slim chance of getting out of this mess. Without petrol, we're sunk. Even if we manage to kill those two, we can't hope to reach Diourbel. I'm taking damn good care, they don't use our car."

He went over to the Deux Chevaux, opened the bonnet with the barrel of his rifle, then ripped the electrical leads from their terminals. Reversing the rifle, he used the butt to smash the petrol pipe to the carburettor. Satisfied he had wrecked the engine, he returned and dropped down by Tessa's side.

"I'll take over. You get back into the car."

"I'm staying with you, Mark."

They remained silent for some moments, then Girland asked, "Just suppose we do manage to get out of here, what will you do with yourself, Tessa?"

"Go back to Paris. I can always get some kind of job, but why talk about it?"

Girland looked up at the darkening sky. The hawks still floated above them.

"As soon as it gets dark enough, we'll have to move away from the car. Malik will try to rush us. I'd like to get him if I could."

"It'll be dark in another half hour."

They lay side by side, waiting. The minutes crept by. The light slowly faded. The brilliant red of the sunset turned to orange and the stars began to appear.

Suddenly Tessa lifted her head, listened, then jumped to her feet.

"Do you hear something?" she asked excitedly. "Listen!"

"Sounds like an aircraft." Girland scrambled up.

They stood side by side, staring up at the sky.

"It is an aircraft ... a hovercraft!" Girland pointed. "There it is! Hedge-hopping ... American markings!" He began to wave his arms.

Flying low, the approaching hovercraft scattered the hawks and slowed.

They saw the pilot lean out of his open window. He waved, then gently brought the hovercraft in to land.

Girland grabbed hold of the water skin and tipped it upside down, spilling the water out onto the burning sand. Then he ran to the car and snatched up the tin box that Carey had given him. With Tessa, he ran to the hovercraft.

As the grinning pilot swung open the door, there came the

sound of a distant shot. Girland helped Tessa into the machine and looked back over his shoulder.

Followed by Smernoff, Malik was running with lurching strides, across the sand, shooting as he ran.

"Let's get out of here!" Girland said, scrambling in after Tessa and slamming the door.

The hovercraft swung away from the two running men and began to climb.

"Not waiting for your friends?"

Girland looked sharply at the man who spoke. He was sitting in the rear of the machine with a U.S. Army officer by his side.

"I'm Jack Kerman," the man said. "You may have heard of me. This is Lieutenant Ambler, Security. Just like the movies, wasn't it? You can consider yourself lucky."

Girland looked down at the two white figures far below. From this height, he now could see the hopelessness of getting out of this death trap. The flat plane extended for kilometre after kilometre to the distant horizon. The two Russians, now motionless, looked like white ants in an ocean of sand.

He drew in a deep breath before saying, "I do." Then he went on, "You wouldn't have a cold drink with you?"

Kerman grinned. He handed over a large vacuum flask.

"Gin and orange," he said. "Take it easy."

With a shaking hand, Girland poured two drinks, gave one to Tessa and saluted Kerman before he drank deep and long.

"Swell!" he said, then, "How the devil did you find us?"

"Just played it smart with a little luck," Kerman said. "After I found Janine Daulnay dead . . ."

Girland stiffened.

"She's dead?"

"Yeah. She over-played her hand and Malik got wise. She took the quick way out." Kerman shrugged. "Best way from the look of the set-up when I found her. I then went after Malik, came on your wrecked car, went on to Diourbel, phoned Ambler who came running in this fancy machine. While I was waiting for him, I nosed around the town and one of the gossipy Africans told me he had seen you go to a nearby villa. So I went there and met your pal Fantaz. I had to get a little rough with him, but he finally told me the whole story. By then Ambler had arrived. We waited until it got light enough and then took off over the bush. We've been searching for you ever since. We found your pals, Borg and Schwartz: very dead. We also found where Carey had been hiding. All the Africans there were also very dead. Then we found you and . . . I suppose Miss Carey?"

"Yes," Girland said. "You've been quite a busy bee, haven't you?"

Ambler spoke for the first time.

"You're under arrest, Girland. I have orders to fly you back to Paris tonight. Mr. Dorey wants you."

Girland shrugged.

"What about her? She can't stay in Dakar now."

"We're running a special plane back for you. V.I.P. stuff," Kerman said. "Dorey is sure to want to talk to her so she can keep us company."

Girland slumped back in his seat. Although he was weary, his mind remained busy. He wasn't worried about Dorey. The micro-film would sweeten him. He would love taking care of Radnitz, and Girland decided he would let him have all the credit. He would be happy too to hear Malik was no more. Anyway, if he did try to start trouble, Girland knew he had him where he wanted him. Dorey wouldn't want the C.I.A. to know he had been fooled by Janine.

But what about myself? Girland thought. What am I going to do now? Then he remembered he had Radnitz's five thousand dollars in his bank. Money solved most problems, he thought. I guess I'll go back to the States. I'll find something to do.

Suddenly smiling, he reached out and put his hand on Tessa's.

"We're going to celebrate after all," he said, "and you will see my Abstracts."

She smiled at him.

"Will I? We'll see. I'm making no promises, Mark."

The hovercraft droned on over the hot wasteland towards the bright lights of Dakar's airport.

All-action Fiction from Panther

*The author who 'makes Alistair Maclean look like a beginner' (*Sunday Express*)

†'The natural successor to Ian Fleming' (*Books & Bookmen*)

Bestselling Transatlantic Fiction in Panther Books

THE SOT-WEED FACTOR	John Barth	75p ☐
BEAUTIFUL LOSERS	Leonard Cohen	40p ☐
THE FAVOURITE GAME	Leonard Cohen	40p ☐
TARANTULA	Bob Dylan	35p ☐
MIDNIGHT COWBOY	James Leo Herlihy	35p ☐
LONESOME TRAVELLER	Jack Kerouac	35p ☐
DESOLATION ANGELS	Jack Kerouac	40p ☐
THE DHARMA BUMS	Jack Kerouac	40p ☐
BARBARY SHORE	Norman Mailer	40p ☐
AN AMERICAN DREAM	Norman Mailer	40p ☐
THE NAKED AND THE DEAD	Norman Mailer	60p ☐
THE BRAMBLE BUSH	Charles Mergendahl	40p ☐
TEN NORTH FREDERICK	John O'Hara	50p ☐
FROM THE TERRACE	John O'Hara	75p ☐
OURSELVES TO KNOW	John O'Hara	60p ☐
THE DICE MAN	Luke Rhinehart	60p ☐
COCKSURE	Mordecai Richler	40p ☐
ST URBAIN'S HORSEMAN	Mordecai Richler	50p ☐
MYRA BRECKINRIDGE	Gore Vidal	40p ☐
MESSIAH	Gore Vidal	40p ☐
THE CITY AND THE PILLAR	Gore Vidal	40p ☐
TWO SISTERS	Gore Vidal	35p ☐
THE JUDGEMENT OF PARIS	Gore Vidal	50p ☐
WASHINGTON D.C.	Gore Vidal	37p ☐
JULIAN	Gore Vidal	50p ☐
SLAUGHTERHOUSE 5	Kurt Vonnegut Jr	40p ☐
MOTHER NIGHT	Kurt Vonnegut Jr	35p ☐
PLAYER PIANO	Kurt Vonnegut Jr	40p ☐
GOD BLESS YOU, MR ROSEWATER		
	Kurt Vonnegut Jr	40p ☐
WELCOME TO THE MONKEY HOUSE		
	Kurt Vonnegut Jr	40p ☐

Real-life Adventure and Violence in Panther Books

All these books are available at your local bookshop or newsagent; or can be ordered direct from the publisher. Just tick the titles you want and fill in the form below.

Name...

Address ....

....

Write to Panther Cash Sales, P.O. Box 11, Falmouth, Cornwall TR10 9EN.
Please enclose remittance to the value of the cover price plus 10p postage and packing for one book, 5p for each additional copy.
Granada Publishing reserve the right to show new retail prices on covers, which may differ from those previously advertised in the text or elsewhere.